SHADOW WOLF

PROTECTOR WOLF SHIFTER SERIES
BOOK ONE

LILLIANA ROSE

Shadow Wolf

Lilliana Rose

Copyright 2023 Lilliana Rose
All Rights Reserved
ISBN (ebook): 978-0-6454402-5-6
ISBN (Print): 978-0-6454402-6-3

For my dogs,
Kimba and Sprinkles
for waiting patiently.

CHAPTER 1

amaska

Tamaska Lane scanned the growing crowd behind the roped-off doorway to the ballroom. She tapped her foot, the sound of her shoe on the polished floor a steady rhythm. Time slipped away quicker than she'd like.

Nerves knotted in her stomach, tight enough for her to want to double over, yet she remained upright, head high, abundantly confident.

The security she'd employed at the last minute hadn't arrived.

The Blood Opal was too valuable to have on display without protection, and she was beginning to think this might be the event that would break her career instead of making it.

"Where the fuck is he?" she grumbled, standing by the tall, rectangular glass cabinet positioned on the stage at the back of the ballroom.

Both the cabinet and the stage showcased her skills as a highly sought-after event manager.

Fairy lights strung between the high walls connected to the chandelier in the center, adding a touch of magic to the room. Oversized flower arrangements on pedestals along the walls, framed with white material, softened the space. It was inviting, and she hoped it would persuade potential buyers to open their wallets and spend big money. This was the event to be at on Friday night in Sydney, Australia, at the reputable Shangri-La.

She clutched her phone in one hand, trying to maintain control in a situation that was about to push her over the edge and into the mother of all meltdowns. One last thing needed to be sorted out before the event started, and time was fast running out.

The soft rainbow of colors around the opal's deep red center reassured her. The priceless Blood Opal sat proudly on a cushion of black velvet, surrounded by tiny LED lights which had been positioned to ensure the gem's beauty reflected from all angles.

And it was beautiful. Almost otherworldly. The glow of the opal drew the eye, even without the lights.

With them, it was beyond spectacular.

Just like she'd envisaged.

Of course, security actually being at the Shangri-La would help with the gem placed so front and center.

Tamaska stepped off the stage as nervous energy hummed in her veins. The evening needed to be perfect.

Through the far window, she caught sight of the Sydney Harbour Bridge that lit up as the sky darkened.

In the window's reflection, she returned a strand of wayward brown hair to the long, straight ponytail that fell down her back, perfectly aligned. She took in the rest of herself: the gym-toned body, emphasized by leather pants and a loose, see-through shirt that covered the scars on her arms and legs and gave her a chicness. A boldness. An edge. She could blend or stand out, depending on her mood and needs.

It gave her a confident edge that she fast wasn't feeling.

Tonight's reveal was the biggest in the company's history, with the exclusive Blood Opal going up for sale. As the event manager for OzOpals, responsibility for the event fell entirely on her.

Even though she had five team members to help, including her assistant Cory, she needed to push harder than usual to ensure OzOpals received the best price for this rare treasure.

So, no pressure.

She kept her face smooth and emotionless. Her boss, Carlene, would be watching.

Carlene, ready to scrutinize every detail of the night. Carlene, ready to pick every tiny move apart.

The boss from hell had given her enough motivation to start her own event management firm. Soon, her reputation would have clients lining up to book her, which was why tonight had to be perfect in every way.

At least Carlene wasn't there yet. That was a small miracle because no way Tamaska could explain why there was no security protecting the gem. Acid rose up from her stomach, and she swallowed hard.

If the security guard couldn't show up on time, how could he be qualified to guard the gem?

"You have to let me in," a male voice shouted from the entrance doors towards the front of the cavernous room.

A tall, broad-shouldered man in a suit pushed his way past the crowd, ignoring their dark stares.

What the fuck is going on now?

She was used to event management problems. She was also used to clients demanding special treatment, but there would be none of that tonight. She needed to remain impartial, especially in front of the gathering crowd.

Her heels clicked on the smooth ballroom floor as she marched over to the commotion at the entrance. This wouldn't be a good first impression for potential buyers. Everyone coming tonight had been strictly vetted before the invites went out. All their names were written on the list at the door—no exceptions, no special allowances.

"You're not on the list, sir," Cory said, standing at the entrance trying to block the muscular man from entering. Under no circumstances would he let anyone inside unless they were on the guest list. A guest list was the most basic form of security they needed to protect the Blood Opal.

"I'm the bloody security," the man snapped.

Is *he the security guard?*

Tamaska had to admit that the man, standing with a sharp suit, crisp tie, and waxed hair, was everything she'd hoped for in a guard from Shadow Protection.

He was also hot: tall, well built, with a chiseled face and dark eyes. Not to mention his mouth, wide and sensuous.

Yeah, he was definitely hot.

Her pulse increased, fluttering before she could get control of herself.

The man radiated heat and strength. Not just from the muscles; no, this came from a deeper place within. One that whispered power.

"What's going on here?" she asked.

The two men faced off much more fiercely than necessary, considering the only thing at stake was simple access to the event. They looked like they might tear each other apart. Although Cory was slight in build, a scary side radiated from him as he stood his ground.

"I'm Kodiak Day, your security for the evening." The man turned to her, and his dark eyes locked with hers, flickering with a hint of gold.

Her pulse leaped, and she tried to calm her breathing. There was something like steel in those dark depths. He looked like someone who meant business, a man who could more than take care of things.

The man, Kodiak, stepped a little closer, and that connection reached down into her. He could calm or destroy. He had the kind of power that could command anyone or anything. Sexual energy hummed around them, and she inexplicably wanted to touch him.

As he looked at her, she went still. His eyes reflected darkness, a deep well full of secrets and promises, wildness and calming seas. If she closed that gap, he could transport her—

"Or," he said softly, those low, rich tones rippling over her skin, "do you want me to go?"

That connection deepened.

He knew exactly the effect he had on her.

That made him dangerous.

Tamaska snapped out of her trance. She'd slipped into another world just by looking into his eyes. He was so damned hot, but she didn't fuck the hired help, not even for a one-night stand—especially not during an upscale market event.

She eyed him with as much animosity as she could muster, and his mouth curved so slightly she might have imagined it.

"You're late," she snapped, reconnecting sharply to her confidence.

"I'm not. I'm right on time."

She resisted the urge to check her phone. "You're not."

That almost-smile turned mocking. "I am."

He might not be late, but there wasn't time to explain why she'd expected him to be early.

She had expectations that went beyond the event that were proving hard to reign in.

"You're late to me."

She stood firm while she looked him up and down, inspecting the man she'd hired. She wouldn't relax her standards, even if the event was about to start.

Her pulse fluttered. Kodiak was well-groomed from head to toe, with a clean-shaven face, polished shoes, and even cuff links on his perfectly pressed shirt covered by his jacket. Her fingers tingled with the desire to explore the unusually toned muscles under his shirt.

The stress of the night is getting to me. I'm losing it over a security guard.

She inhaled slowly.

"Do you want me to be here or not?" he asked, smooth and cool.

"You'll have to do," she said, trying to hide her brewing thoughts. "How many came with you?"

"Six." He subtly moved his hand, and six men and women came forward, all dressed to blend in with the

7

night's clientele, as per her request to Olcan, the head of Shadow Protection.

"Good. I want security positioned around the ball-room, there and there." Tamaska pointed to the entrance, then to the table where bidders would regis-ter. She prepared to point to the glass cabinet.

He looked at her, brow slightly raised. "Don't tell me how to do my job."

"You'll do the job I'm paying you for." Heat rose inside of her as her blood pressure soared.

How *dare* he? She was running the show, not him.

"I will." He waited a beat. "The Blood Opal will be safe with us here. You'll have a successful night, but I'll run the security."

Her hands coiled together. "You'll do what I tell you."

"Then I'll walk."

He stared down at her, a dark chill overtaking the earlier warmth in his eyes.

She wanted that heat back. Between the loss of that connection and the steel and slight insolence in his tone, hot anger coursed through her blood. She couldn't afford to lose the security now, but she wasn't one to back down from an argument.

"That's not the arrangement I had with Olcan." Her breath came in a hard intake as she struggled to find her equilibrium. "I'll be informing him of your indis-cretion."

"See you later, then." Kodiak turned away, and the others followed his lead.

Fuck.

She breathed out. "Stop."

He paused and then slowly turned back to her. She almost wished she could afford to let him go. His expression hadn't changed, but the mocking stung the air.

"You're going to let us do our job, then?"

"On one condition." She wasn't about to let a man like Kodiak railroad her, especially when she was in charge.

He frowned, a stormy expression shadowing his face.

But Tamaska had enough determination to sink a battleship. "I want you standing by the Blood Opal."

Kodiak's perfect mix of danger and confidence would add to the atmosphere surrounding the gem, enticing the buyers and deterring any would-be thieves. Despite the unfortunate start, he actually seemed perfect for the job.

She squared her shoulders and kept her chin high as Kodiak stared down at her. A shiver slid down her back. This time, she didn't succumb to his allure and kept her balance.

Did he just smirk at me?

"Fine." He nodded slightly. "But I'll have you know that I like to stand where I can see everything, so I would have been in that position anyway."

"Good," she said. "Let's get this sorted, now. The guests want to see the Blood Opal."

Cory unclipped the end of the red rope and let the security team into the ballroom before rushing to stop the guests by raising his hands and calling out for them to wait.

As Kodiak strode past her, he met her gaze, and her breath stuttered. It seemed as if a part of him reached for her as she reached for him. The resulting sparks mixed with attraction and warning. Bells of all kinds rang. Inside her, a low beat of need started up, coiling with heat that could combust with a touch.

She liked a man in a suit and couldn't turn away from him. He was like a magnet just for her.

From the center of the ballroom floor, he gestured to the others. They silently moved in six different directions, leaving Kodiak alone to stand by the Blood Opal cabinet.

He turned sharply, his expression daring her to fault his actions. She couldn't deny the thrill coursing through her.

"That was stressful," Cory said from behind her, before breathing out slowly with a soft whistle.

Oddly, she wanted to know more about Kodiak, even though he'd dared to question her. Clearly, he didn't understand his position. She admired how efficiently Kodiak set up his security team, even though they had only been hired a few hours ago.

"Do you still think they were the right choice, Cory?" she asked, full of mixed emotions.

"I do. They came highly recommended."

"I hope so."

She kept her eyes fixed on Kodiak, wishing for more of that intensity. Did he bring that with him everywhere he went? Or was it aimed at her? Where exactly could that intensity lead her?

Nowhere good, that's for fucking sure.

"I'll not have anyone ruin this night, not even an overconfident security guard," she said under her breath.

Her entire being trembled with conflicting emotions.

"We've planned for success," Cory said. "It'll happen."

"Make sure you stick to the plan," she said. "I won't tolerate even the slightest deviation from our program."

He nodded, opened his iPad cover, and started to register the first guests in line.

Finally, the event was getting under way. Tamaska had spent hours planning the perfect night, and this wasn't the ideal start.

Her gut twisted with doubt, warning her that, instead of a huge success, the event could turn into her worst nightmare.

odiak

Kodiak simmered with anger as he stood by the glass cabinet, flexing his hands into fists and wishing there was something he could hit. This wasn't the time or place for him to lose his temper.

Who the fuck does she think she is?

He needed to calm down and get his control back. Tamaska had slid right under the skin in a way no one had in a long time.

The ballroom filled with people minutes after he took his position. Automatically, he switched into security mode, scanning the growing crowd for any possible thieves. All he noticed was a big whiff of human stench, reminding him how much he detested the species.

How dare she question me. No one ever questioned him. As Beta of the Shadow Pack, he was as close to Alpha as he could get for now. It would be his turn one day. But until he knew the time was right, that it was a fight he could win, he wouldn't challenge the position. There was winning, and then there was *winning*. He wanted to *win* in all the ways that mattered.

On every level.

But this woman... What gave her the audacity to make demands of him? Women didn't treat him like that.

No one treated him like that.

Even worse, he couldn't get her out of his mind. She was there, hooked in, living rent free. She drew his attention, too. He didn't give in to it, but he was as aware of her as she stood in front of him.

Occasionally, he caught her staring as he scanned the room. She was always looking at him, with little side glances; full on ones, too. The micromanager wasn't immune to him, though. Her pheromones slipped through the air and wrapped around him.

The woman probably wasn't even aware. No doubt she would love to berate him if he did one little thing wrong.

The thing was, though, he didn't do anything wrong. His wolf senses ensured a flawless performance, and he was on high alert in the crowd even though she...rattled him.

Images of her kept flaring into life inside him. He didn't need to like her to know he wanted to touch her skin. He wanted to press his mouth on hers to taste her. And—

He inhaled slowly, settling himself, smoothing those strange urges back into the place they needed to be as he stood guard. He had been in the business long enough for it to be second nature.

To earn money for his pack, Midnight Shadow, the wolf shifters had branched into the security industry. Things had calmed down with the local vampire clan, Blood Moon, as they lived in harmony with the humans, their supernatural abilities undetected. With no unrest with the vampires, they'd turned to living their lives parallel with humanity and maintaining their secret.

The wolf shifters were evolving, changing their ways to adapt to the city, far from the bushlands Kodiak's wolf craved. Not even the full moon controlled his pack anymore. They could shift on demand.

And yet all it took was one upstart female to unravel the control he had on his emotions.

His wolf side lurched to the surface. He held his breath, settling his animal side with the control of a master.

This isn't the time and place. We will run soon.

The clubhouse where the pack resided stood back-to-back with bushland, but his wolf would need more than a controlled run close to the city and humans to be consoled. He promised his wolf free rein in the acres of the Blue Mountains where the pack visited to be free to hunt. His wolf side snarled as if pushing him towards that freedom.

He continued to soothe his wolf and checked on his team members.

He'd chosen them well. They fit in perfectly with the guests as they mingled. Their telepathic-like pack connection was valuable during gigs like this one, and he easily heard that all was well with them—so far.

He had his own approach, which he'd arranged with his team, and they all knew exactly what needed to be done to protect the Blood Opal and ensure no issues arose during the evening. He didn't need Tamaska interfering on any level. That was what she'd tried to do, and it had gotten under his skin.

That was the only reason, nothing more.

Kodiak inhaled slowly. He was with humans, not the wolf shifters in his pack—aside from the best six that were here tonight. He had to keep it together, keep his dislike of humans down.

The room was getting busy. The human stench of excitement began to overwhelm his senses. That was one big reason why he tried to convince Olcan that this wasn't the job for him.

Too many humans overwhelmed them releasing so many scents with each emotion it was too easy to be bombarded. And this woman, this Tamaska, was the worst offender of the lot.

But it was their world now. Humans overran everything. And for the wellbeing of his pack, he needed money, which meant he needed to do the bidding of his Alpha in a room full of humans. That was the last place he wanted to be, but after this gig, they would have money for food and for the clubhouse repairs. The wolf shifters didn't have the same wealth the vampires had managed to build, but in time they would have enough to cover more than their basic needs. They would leave a different legacy for upcoming pups.

His skin prickled as his wolf started to rise again. Heat flared through him.

Settling his wolf was easier than settling himself.

Usually.

Right now, though, it wanted...

Kodiak turned his head. He met Tamaska's eyes once more. A thrill of electricity buzzed through him, right down to his cock.

He tried not to return her gaze, but it was like she was a drug and he was addicted. Looking at her even calmed his wolf nature, as if his wolf wanted the attraction to develop into something more.

Kodiak tore away from staring at her, confused and empty. His wolf lurched, trying to tug him back to that place, that look, that connection.

Why her? She was nothing more than human. He hated humans with a passion. Their hunters were a big reason his pack numbers were low after centuries of conflict; them and the fucking vampires. Little did humans realize that, if it wasn't for the shifters, more humans would've been bled out by the blood drinkers by now.

But that was humanity all over, wasn't it? Ignorant and arrogant, and selfish all at the same time. They would destroy everything and damn the fucking consequences if it meant a little more fun or ease of life for them.

He continued glancing through the crowd, though each person appeared the same. The emptiness didn't leave until his eyes returned to her.

His jaw clenched tight as he stared into Tamaska's eyes. Determination burned bright and fierce in their depths. He understood that feeling. Yet, the way she'd tried to tell him how to do his job still scraped along the bone, way down deep. He reached for it, held it. Much easier than the complicated tangle of emotions she set off. She was arrogant and pushy. Rude. His anger spiked, flooding through him and mixing with the desire for her he didn't want to admit existed.

Mixing. Not dampening. Not replacing.

And somehow, it made it all so much more potent.

With a sharp inhale, Kodiak forced his gaze away from her once more and continued the check he performed every few minutes. He looked around and made eye contact with the six team members, reaching out to them through their pack connection. They were

the best, handpicked, and they would have his back—
and vice versa—if he needed.

Fern stood at the far right corner of the ballroom,
perfectly placed to watch the front door. She held a
glass of champagne but hadn't sipped from it once. Her
gold dress sparkled in the lights, sitting snug around
her body. She'd be able to fight, if necessary.

Shota looked smart in his Armani suit, like
someone who attended events like this all the time. His
handsome features had attracted a few ladies, and he
was the center of their attention as they laughed at his
far-from-funny jokes. Kodiak held back a comment as
the pack connection reassured him he was doing his
job and keeping an eye on the evening's proceedings.

Skoll strolled in from the left, slipping between
groups of people as if he were a shadow himself. He
could always be counted on to find useful information
as the best eavesdropper in the pack. He nodded at
Kodiak before returning to his assigned space behind
the stage.

Onai had struck up a conversation with an older
couple near the windows. His tie was a little loose, but
the dress code tonight had strayed far from his usual
casual attire. Kodiak sensed Onai was uncomfortable,
but his discipline as a wolf along with his training
meant that it wasn't going to hinder him.

Even Channing was doing well, mingling with the
crowd without drawing attention to himself. This was
his first gig and, while his youth was a reason to hesi-

tate, Kodiak had chosen Channing because of the exceptional skill he'd shown in training during the last year. It was time he was tested, and tonight was supposed to be a straightforward gig.

Now that he'd arrived, though, Kodiak was beginning to think something more was going on than a wealthy market event. If only he could pinpoint what that might be, and get Tamaska out of his thoughts while he was at it.

Ash looked stunning and feminine in her tailored green dress, but she would fight to win at any cost. Considering the type of attention she got from the men tonight, she might well show a side Kodiak didn't want to see.

He reminded her to keep cool and wished he could take the advice himself.

Each team member did their job, and none of them had detected anything suspicious in the crowd. Time dragged on. The sooner the gig was over and they were out of there, the better.

Kodiak wasn't going to let his guard down. Then, he turned his head to the left, where Tamaska stood. Warmth flooded through him as he gazed at her, and it was as if the crowd faded away and they were the only two there.

Between them, the connection grew, wrapping tight. Her pull was beyond magnetic and as they locked eyes, it grew. He detected her increased heat and rapid pulse, knowing he was the cause of her physical reactions.

That was what the connection was: unexpected.

And it threatened to swallow the world.

He couldn't allow anything to happen. Not here, not now.

Not ever.

What the fuck was wrong with him? He looked away and it was like something wrenched inside him as he did so. Whatever fire she'd managed to light in him had to be forgotten, pronto.

Off-kilter, like he'd just been in some violent fight, he stood still by the glass cabinet, moving only his eyes to stay on guard. The human smells intensified and turned his stomach until he wanted to dry retch. He breathed in through his mouth to avoid the scents. Finally, he could deal with the smells, and he breathed in properly. He might not like them, but he needed the aromas, the stench to feel out the room on a different level.

Another smell hit him, cold and metallic. One he hadn't experienced for so many years, but one he was familiar with.

A chill shivered down his spine. His senses alert, he checked in with his team.

On it. Fern answered first, reassuring him that he hadn't imagined the smell. Then the others chimed in, confirming Kodiak's worst fears.

Is that what vampires smell like? Ick. Channing's thought was full of repulsion.

Big night for you, little pup, isn't it? Onai asked Channing. *You better get ready.*

All of you, be ready, Kodiak said. With his fear turning into reality, he switched into protective mode. Vampires were here, and truce or not with them, this was unusual.

No, wait, there was something more.

The vampires had also attempted to mask their blood scent.

Is there more than one? Channing asked.

I think so, Shota said.

Focus, Kodiak said to the team.

The vampires marked a last-minute change to the shifters' gig, and masking their scent meant only one thing. The vampires knew the shifters were here. Something was about to unfold, and it had to do with the Blood Opal.

Kodiak glanced at Tamaska and was relieved to see her talking with another woman. Tamaska looked uninterested in the conversation, but she was safe.

Why did he feel the need to protect her? She was a human, one that had provoked him like no other, so he wasn't sure where his urge to defend her was coming from. Sure, he was in the business of protecting others, but this was much deeper, more like an addiction, something he couldn't control.

She riled something in him, more than the wolf, a deep-seated need to keep her safe, to make her—

He wasn't here for her safety, only for the Blood Opal's, yet he couldn't help wanting to protect her.

While Kodiak surveyed the crowd, trying to detect where the vampires were, he began to look for Tamaska more regularly, needing to know that she was safe.

He was ready to act the moment she wasn't. But it had been so long since he'd fought with the vampires. There was a chance he could be out of form. His pulse increased, stress flooded through him.

It wouldn't take much for everything to unravel into chaos, and it was going to test Kodiak's skills to see if he could prevent this from happening.

amaska

Foreboding knotted Tamaska's stomach as she made her way from one end of the ballroom to the other, talking to as many people as possible for as little amount of time she could without seeming rude.

Everything was going according to plan, and her boss Carlene even smiled at her.

So, why the foreboding, strange sense that something, somehow was off?

Maybe because the event was so big. Or maybe it was because of that damned hot guard she was so hyper aware of.

She didn't know what was wrong with her, but she needed to get her act together.

The auction would start in thirty minutes. The tension increased with each passing second, giving Tamaska no respite. There was too much riding on this for her to relax.

If she kept her mind on those goals while sweet talking, and making sure those around her were excited and having a good time, she'd get through this.

Even with the hawk-like eyes of her boss on her. If all went well, by the end of the year, she could have her own marketing firm instead of having to answer to someone else.

Tamaska made her way through the finely dressed crowd, everyone looking cheery as they mingled sipping on champagne. And it was a large, exclusive crowd. People of all ages were there, united by their wealth and their attraction to the Blood Opal.

Whenever the knots of worry grew too strong in her belly, she found herself locking eyes with Kodiak, no matter how hard she tried not to. That jolt of electric connection elevated her, soothed her.

Each time she turned to glance at him, his eyes met hers as if he'd been already watching her. A shiver eased through her body whenever this happened, becoming a compulsion she didn't want to resist.

Kodiak stood on guard next to the glass cabinet where the Blood Opal inside shone in its glory. The guard looked solemn and hot as hell, not talking to anyone who approached him. He allowed them to look at the gem as long as they kept a meter away from the cabinet as instructed.

And he watched each and every one of those people with a singular focus.

Tamaska had taken a risk when she'd decided not to rope off the area in front of the display, but she thought it would be worth it to drive interest and, hopefully, a bidding war.

One that seemed to be paying off.

While her first encounter with Kodiak had been fiery, Tamaska had to admit he was doing his job.

Other thoughts flooded her mind too, ones she couldn't afford to indulge in right now. Maybe later she could, in the early hours of the morning when she was alone in her own bed after partying to celebrate a successful sale.

There would be partying. There would be a successful sale. And her career would be ready to take off.

"The opal might be out of my reach considering all this competition, Tamaska, but have you thought about auctioning that moody guard next to it?" asked a cheeky, slightly tipsy Essie—wife of a client, and a woman she liked.

Usually.

Tamaska laughed politely, even as the words coiled tight in her.

Kodiak would yield a strong auction, but that wasn't something she wanted to think about, let alone organize, at least not before taking him for herself. Even if in some fantasy world the man would allow such as auction to happen.

But Essie had it spot on.

The man was moody, built, and hot as the fires of hell. And she wanted his particular brand of heat to singe her in all the right places.

It was fucking hard not to keep glancing over at him, thinking how the night could end, during her client meet-and-greets. If only she could allow herself to throw caution to the wind.

Damn.

"I'm sure your husband would fork out more money for the opal than the guard," Tamaska said diplomatically as Essie's husband Jonas waved to her.

Jonas stood a nearby, in the middle of a few men talking, no doubt, all things business as they tended to do during events like this.

Tamaska had organized many of these events in the last year. Finally, she'd started to score clients with deeper pockets, which allowed her to spend money on glitz. For this event, though, the only hero in the room was the Blood Opal—even with Kodiak standing distractingly nearby.

"Have some champagne," Essie said, stopping the waitress as she walked past and picking up two glasses of bubbly.

Tamaska pursed her lips and forced herself to take the glass. She didn't drink on nights like this, ever. But she also tried to avoid saying no to clients.

"Come on, this event will be a huge success," Essie said, holding up her glass as if making a toast.

The middle-aged woman was full of life, her black sequined dress showing off her sculpted body.

"Thanks." Tamaska clinked her glass against Essie's and brought it to her lips, pretending to take a sip.

"There you go, have some fun." Essie smiled. "Enjoy your success."

Tamaska smiled back at her. Some would be intimidated by this woman who was decades her senior. She was smart, rich, and beautiful with a killer body. She had everything at her fingertips. Some people, maybe, but not Tamaska. She didn't want that life, at least, not that life when it came from a man.

No, she wanted a life of power and success she built herself.

She might be in her late twenties, but Tamaska had fast built a solid reputation for managing sophisticated events. She also wasn't about to ruin her strong reputation for the sake of social etiquette.

Not even a sip of booze would pass her lips. Tamaska had plenty of things needing her oversight to keep the event running smoothly.

She had to stay on her game.

"Excuse me, I need to make sure that there are enough canapés," she said. "I'll join you later."

"Of course. Please send some my way. The bubbly

makes me hungry." Essie leaned forward. "So does looking at that guard."

Tamaska faked a laugh and quickly slipped away from Essie before she offended the woman by not going along with her antics.

Over the years, Tamaska had learned to be a shapeshifter of sorts when dealing with people, pretending to be whoever they needed her to be. But it was getting too risky with Essie, with all that hot talk about Kodiak.

She needed to find someone else to engage in conversation.

Tamaska made her way through the crowd, wanting the reassurance of laying her eyes on the gem—or Kodiak. She placed the full glass of champagne on top of a passing waiter's silver tray and continued towards the gem.

Kodiak stood there, a calm, hot rock of a man. Just as compelling as the Blood Opal he protected and just as breathtaking.

His gaze lifted to her, and they stared at each other another timeless moment.

Tamaska ripped her attention away. She needed to concentrate.

The auction would start soon.

She needed to ensure everyone had plenty of time to enjoy the atmosphere, the lead-up. So, she made sure there was lots of bubbly flowing and plenty of nibbles.

Next, she had to—

"Are you the manager of this event?"

She spun around. A pale, slender man stood there with a hint of a smile. He had a charm about him that sent chills through her body.

"I am, and you are...?" She narrowed her eyes at him.

Who was this man, in his expensive suit, looking sharp and sophisticated? The guest list was long, but Tamaska knew everyone on it.

Had Cory cracked under the pressure and allowed someone else inside?

Her stomach tightened. Something didn't feel right.

"I know everyone on the list, and—"

"Impressive," he said, his voice smooth and sinuous.

He was trying to charm her, and her stomach twisted a little more. "So, you are...?"

"A very interested buyer," he said with an easy grin. "On behalf of someone else. Important."

Tamaska relaxed a little, despite her warning instincts. Occasionally, people would send others. Or perhaps her boss had added someone to the list at the last second. It had happened.

"Have you registered?"

"Of course," he said.

She didn't believe him. That shot through her, a bright light. She went to say so, but the words wouldn't come. And when she tried again, she was unable to voice her doubts.

Instead, she found herself saying something completely different. "Good."

His smile broadened, just a little, and her stomach lurched. "Can you tell me when the auction will start?"

Again, she went to say she didn't believe him, but the words stopped. So she went ask about who he was there representing.

"Soon."

That was not what she'd wanted to say. The floor seemed to move, and a wooziness overcame her. She put her hand to her temple.

"How long?"

"In thirty minutes," Tamaska said, even though she didn't want to.

"Thanks." He nodded politely and turned to leave.

She stood, stunned, then she stepped forward in an attempt to shake the odd feeling that had overtaken her. Her ankle rolled. Her arms flew up as she tried to right herself.

Strong arms wrapped around her, holding her tight, stopping her fall.

Everything in her short circuited as heat flared in her chest. It spread through her, flesh and bone. The arms that held her were strong, right.

She wanted to close her eyes and bask in the heat, in the touch, the warm wall of flesh behind her. And whoever it was smelled amazing. Like clean earth and moss, like trees and spice.

Who was she kidding? Tamaska knew who it was. Knew the moment he'd touched her.

She turned a little, and Kodiak looked down at her with those dark eyes, his arms still strong around her.

Her heart thudded hard and wild. She couldn't break the connection, even as small thrills raced through her veins. They were the only two people in the crowded, noisy room. Just him and her, and the beating of their hearts, the soft intakes of breaths that were slightly uneven.

Then the lights flickered, and the moment was gone. His eyes snapped up. His hands tightened and a chill went through her.

Something was wrong—she could sense it.

"Kodiak—"

"Yeah, I feel it, too."

She didn't question his meaning, and her skin prickled in alarm as something slithered through the room.

Not a tangible something. Nothing visible.

But it was there, nevertheless.

Before she could say anything, the lights flickered again.

Then they went out, plunging the room into darkness.

The guests screamed.

CHAPTER 4

odiak

She's safe.

Kodiak held Tamaska tight against his body, trying not to think about how perfectly she fit, like she'd been made for him. He breathed her in. Normally, he couldn't stand the stench of humans, but this one reminded him of wildflowers, the fresh, sweet, lemon-tinged scent of the native wax flowers.

She felt good in his arms.

The look that had passed between them still sang in his blood, like fire, like when his wolf was running free.

Then the lights went out and his wolf senses sharpened, tearing him away from the strong connection that seemed to meld him to her. A connection that had

35

caused him to leave the gem and catch her before she fell.

She might be human, but the magnetic pull went deep. It unsettled him, at the center of his bones. What the fuck was she? How could she do that to him?

He never left his post.

His team spread out to uncover what might be happening with the lights. And he...he stood there holding a woman he didn't want to let go.

It was enough to fling her from him, that thought. But he didn't. He needed to process all the information coming at him from the room, his team, his senses.

And he didn't think he liked it.

Not one bit.

Stilling, he sent his own feelers out.

His eyes adjusted to the room's darkness. There, by the small stage, something moved.

The instinct to leap into action almost over-whelmed but he held it down, searching instead with his senses, turning instinct into a finely tuned machine he could use.

Whatever it was moved again.

Tiny. Almost imperceptible.

Even to a shifter.

But it was there, and he zeroed in.

He froze.

A cold, metallic scent wound about him, familiar like the eons. And his stomach flipped.

The straightforward, easy, last-minute security job

wasn't easy at all. Everything had taken a sharp turn for the worse—in a direction Kodiak had never expected.

But perhaps one he should have done.

Things had been quiet between the wolves and the vampires in Sydney, with each group keeping to themselves and maintaining a pseudo-peace instead of fighting. Quiet for a long time.

Too long?

It was enough for some to grow complacent. Enough for others to quietly plan and wait for their move.

But what kind of move?

They would be stupid to attempt some kind of bloodbath. That would not only rock boats but rip holes in them and sink them right to the bottom of the ocean. Regardless, vampires weren't stupid. They weren't ignorant.

Kodiak stifled a growl.

He only sensed one, but the vampire had to know Kodiak was there, had to know there was more than one shifter at the event. This disturbed him to the core as he considered the brazenness of the intrusion.

It seemed the vampires had an agenda, and even the presence of wolves wasn't enough to perturb them.

Or, perhaps, stop them.

Fuck it all.

Kodiak needed to leave Tamaska, to catch the vampire before he got away. Kodiak could sense his pack members following the lead, and he needed to join them. If only he'd acted sooner.

Maybe his senses had been too infected by Tamaska.

A jolt passed through him. The man who had been talking to her.

Fuck.

That was the vampire.

It clicked into place. Shame slid into him. Sure, a vampire in a room full of so many could hide themselves, but he prided himself on being able to sniff them out, see past any ways they might have of hiding their true identity.

He'd seen the vampire but hadn't realized the man's true identity until it was too late. He'd been too caught up with Tamaska.

Kodiak shook his head, trying to clear his thoughts. Had the vampire planned this? Was Kodiak's attraction to Tamaska so obvious? He swallowed hard.

The night was getting worse by the minute, and he didn't like where it was going.

He had to turn things around, starting with getting the vampire.

Yeah, in a room brimming with humans—the vampire's favorite snack of choice.

He needed to get the bloodsucker and do it without bringing attention to who and what it was.

Not to mention him and his team.

It would take some explaining to avoid telling

Tamaska the truth. After all, the shifters, vampires, and other supernaturals lived their lives secretly alongside humans. He had to uphold his kind's secret. Otherwise, they would once again be hunted, and the pack would face extinction.

Humans loved to destroy everything they didn't understand.

They loved to simply destroy.

Fuck.

"Nobody move," Kodiak called out in a calm and commanding voice. "The power supply will be back and running shortly. Stay where you are."

He hoped that would do the trick. Just like he hoped against all odds that his worst nightmare hadn't come true.

He dared a glance at the cabinet. The gem was no longer there.

What the fuck do vampires want with the Blood Opal?

There was no way Kodiak was going to let the vampires get away with this. Because that was who'd taken it. He knew that.

He started to let Tamaska go, but she wobbled, and he steadied her, her flesh warm and inviting beneath his hands.

"Are you all right?" he asked.

"I'm...I don't know." Her words slurred, an effect from the vampire trying to reach into her mind and control her.

He'd seen it before, but it was usually a lot worse. She must be strong. His heart beat a little faster.

"I need to let you go," he said against her hair. "Can you stand?"

She lifted her hands and closed them over his. A bolt of electricity shocked him at the touch.

"I…"

He counted slowly in the back of his mind.

I don't sense the vampire, Fern said.

Okay, hold your position, he said, and then added, *Channing is fast, and he might do better searching outside for the blood drinker. Shota, you and Channing search outside—*

Where are you, boss? That came from Channing, who was clearly nearby. *The human? You're with the human?*

The vampire got to her. Just do what I say. He didn't need a wet behind the ears pup questioning him. Not when he could do that shit himself. And she was the boss in this situation. One who had been compromised. *Skoll, Fern, stay on exits. The crowd isn't going to hold much longer.*

They weren't. He knew that from the rise in the voices and energy and the stench of them.

Ash, Onai, search the crowd. Now.

He shifted a little more of his attention back to the woman in his arms.

"Tamaska?"

"I…" She stopped, then started again. "I…I'm all right …"

He carefully let her go, her hands touching his.

She tried to take a step, but she wobbled. He stayed by her side, his arm around her.

Why can't I leave her?

He should get her to a chair and put another human in charge of her. Yet the urge to stay with her was strong. It would be easy to write it off as him needing to protect her as part of his job. And it was; she'd hired him, so she was as important as the gem. But it was a lie. It was more than him doing his job.

Whatever it was ran deep, beyond bone, like it could slide into his soul. It was as if an invisible tether held him to her—which was impossible, because he fucking hated humans.

I don't see anyone here. Channing's thought was full of the thrill of the chase, as well as frustration. *Or sense a blood drinker.*

No one here, Fern said.

What if— Skoll began.

We can't deal in what if bullshit. Get the vampire. He has the opal. Kodiak sent the thought out to his team through their pack connection with an urgency that would spur them to chase the vampire and bring it down.

Inside, he still had people on the doors, but now wasn't the time for them to hold positions. Not with the opal gone. While he would normally take off and join the search, he couldn't.

41

Leaving Tamaska in this state was out of the question.

But he was still the leader here.

If you need to leave the door or take off outside after someone, make sure you have the right lead. The Blood Opal must be returned. Find it. That's your priority. Kodiak sent the instructions through the telepathic-like bond to his team.

His team responded and he felt them go, on the hunt for the vampire. He didn't want to stand here but how could he not?

Tamaska had been manipulated by the vampire and someone had to take control and explain the unexplainable. Someone had to make sure she was okay.

"My team is on it," he said. "Let's sit you down and—"

"I can't move." The words were soft and as wobbly as she was. "I don't understand..."

"We're on it."

Fuck everything. He didn't want to consider how his life or his team would change if the gem was lost.

How or why it was so important to the vampires, he didn't know. But if it was, then it was important on a different level for him and his pack, too.

Even if it wasn't, the job paid out big, and there was too much at stake. Besides, Kodiak wasn't used to being on the losing side. He'd been made to fight and to win. Are vampires stealing a valuable gem? Not on his watch.

That damn cabinet drew his attention in the dark. He could see it clear as if the lights shone down on it.

He could see the emptiness inside, where the gem had sat.

Taken.

He closed his eyes, no longer wanting to see the empty cabinet.

His team was out there, and he heard them as they moved and sent back messages. They also knew what was at stake.

There was a vampire on the run, and Kodiak would make him pay big time for crossing his pack. If only he could leave Tamaska's side.

He wasn't there to keep her safe from hitting the ground.

He was there because she had hold of him.

She was in his blood.

Somehow.

Some way.

He knew what she was. And what she would do.

She would be his downfall.

A human would destroy him.

And he couldn't stop it from happening.

CHAPTER 5

amaska

The cold sensation that had hit Tamaska in the belly still permeated her, yet heat kept her standing. It gave her a strange strength.

She needed to move, but that would mean Kodiak's strong arms would no long be wrapped around her. And she wanted to sink into the hard wall of living muscle behind her.

No.

She was in charge and had to keep it together.

Why were the lights off?

"Tamaska? Can you stand on your own? Sit?"

Of course she could. She pushed away the hands

even though she craved them. She took a step, almost stumbling over as her knees wobbled. Strong arms wrapped around her and she was no longer falling. Her mind whirled, trying to get back into the clear space it had been before...before... Fuck.

What was wrong with her?

It felt like someone had reached in her head, put everything out of order, and then dumped a veil over it all.

She didn't have time for any of this. The night's auction was too important to fumble. She had to be on the ball.

As she stayed in the warm cocoon of sweet safety, she could feel her head start to clear a little. It wasn't fast enough. Coiling her hands, she forced her brain to process the recent events muddling in her head.

What had happened?

She'd been speaking to a man whose face she could no longer describe, just that he was pale. He had tried to charm her, but he'd only left her cold. She hadn't seen him before. She knew that, no matter what the sudden whispers in her brain said. He'd mentioned the opal and then she'd stumbled, her limbs unable to move properly.

Kodiak had caught her, and then the lights had gone off and she'd plummeted into darkness.

But something just before... She'd looked into the man's eyes the moment before everything went dark.

She'd looked, and she'd seen something. What had she seen? She couldn't pin it down—.

The stranger had spoken to her and reached into her.

That was what it had felt like. He'd reached in and stopped her saying what she'd wanted to say. He'd mesmerized her in a way that made her want to scrub her skin. Then, he'd gone, and she'd fallen and Kodiak was there. Even now, Kodiak was there, holding her.

The lights flickered back on.

Everything assaulted her senses at her at once. The buzz from Kodiak's touch. The panic filling the room. Chatter that built. People milling, looking about.

With the sudden flare of light came a burst of clarity, hard and sharp.

And the opal.

Tamaska stared at the glass cabinet and gasped.

The Blood Opal was gone.

Ripping free of Kodiak's disturbing, soothing, electrifying touch, she stumbled forward but righted herself, narrowly keeping out of his touch.

"Where is it?" She almost screamed the words but stopped herself.

Blind panic threatened to eat her then and there.

"Are you okay?" Kodiak asked.

She pushed his hands away as he spoke.

She didn't want Kodiak next to her. Didn't want him touching her.

This was his fault. He was there to protect the Blood Opal, and now it was gone. She didn't care about her safety or his help. The gem was more important.

"The opal," she said, glaring around the room, trying to get herself under her iron control.

"Don't panic—"

"I'm not panicking." She clenched her hands as strength came back to her, along with a fury she didn't quite understand. "Where is the fucking opal?"

"Gone."

Gone.

The word was like jagged ice as it slashed through her.

Gone.

How the fuck was it gone?

That damned box shouldn't be empty.

"I'll get it back," Kodiak said. "My team's looking now."

She turned on him. "This is your fault. You shouldn't have left your post."

"And let you faceplant?"

Kodiak's expression clearly showed he was furious. That somehow radiated from his entire being, and it coiled and writhed and whipped about her.

"Yes. I'm not important."

She got out her phone from the small handbag she'd slung over her shoulder, hands shaking, mind whirling.

The opal was gone. Her future.

Gone.

What the fuck was she going to do now? She dialed the police. Quickly going through to them why she needed them. She hung up only slightly relieved the police were on their way.

"Like it or not, you're important. You're running this thing," said Kodiak.

"And you're meant to be protecting the Blood Opal." She flashed him a hard look. "Do you know how much that thing is worth and you, what? Let it slip through your fingers?"

A muscle worked in his jaw, the only break in the rock of his emotionless expression. That, and the vibrations of his fury in the air.

"I didn't. There's a team of us, and you were about to hit the ground hard. I stepped away a moment and the lights went dark," he said. "It's not my fault."

She didn't need excuses. She needed the fucking opal back.

For all she knew, he'd done something to her.

Even as she thought it, it didn't make sense. How? She hadn't eaten or drunk anything. He really hadn't touched her until she'd started to fall.

As she waited for the call to go through, she looked about. "Where's your team?"

"I told you. Going after the v...the ...whoever it was." He stumbled over his words.

Tamaska took that as an admission of guilt. "Your fault."

"It's not." He sucked in a breath. "And it's not theirs,

49

either. The lights went out. Mayhem happened and we're on it. I sent them out. Whoever took the gem knew exactly what they were doing."

"You sound guilty."

"Damn it—"

Tamaska ignored him as the police answered her call. "I need to report a robbery. The Blood Opal, at the Shangri-La building."

She didn't need to say more than that. The number she called wasn't triple zero, and it wasn't a call to the station.

The opal was expensive enough, and this event big enough she had a number to call if things went south.

Cops were on standby, but it had been decided not to have an official law enforcement presence here. That always made the rich jumpy, and it gave off the wrong sort of vibe to potential buyers.

It drove prices down.

She glared at Kodiak while giving the details to the police. Why the hell was he still standing there? Then again, what else could she expect? He'd lost focus and failed.

She finished the call. "The police are on their way."

"Okay." He had his hand raised to his head as he spoke, his dark gaze on her. "Search again, inside and out."

"Now you're doing your job?"

His eyes narrowed into dangerous slits, and he took

a step closer. His presence wrapped tight about her, making all her nerve endings tingle. "I've been doing my fucking job since before I walked into this place. You chose to put a priceless rock on display. You chose a place with very little on door security measures. Believe me, a velvet rope and checklist don't usually sit above metal detectors and background checks."

There was something else, hidden in his words, she couldn't grasp.

Or maybe he was simply trying to cover his fine ass.

"That's what I hired you for, Kodiak."

"The lights went out. My people are on it. Calm the fuck down."

"Speak to me like that again, and I'll be serving you your balls on a silver platter."

A small smile crossed his mouth. "I'd like to see you try."

She took a breath and shut down the conversation as she looked out around the huge room. Lots of the clients were pale with shock, many on their phones. The owners of OzOpals stood with a horrific mix of anger and surprise on their faces as they stared at the empty box, now lit bright for all to see her failure.

She shivered, her knees weakening.

Carlene stood on the other side of the room, face pale, eyes angry.

Tamaska's life was over.

"Please," she said, raising her voice. "Please stay put.

I don't think any of you are responsible for the theft, but the police are coming, and I need your help."

Inside Tamaska, butterflies flared into life and warred with each other.

She squared her shoulders and took a step, right as her legs began to give way on her.

Once more that weird veil settled over her, but she fought against it. She couldn't afford not to have all her wits about her.

Her head spun, and a strong arm wrapped around her waist. It took her a few seconds to realize Kodiak's arms were around her. "W-what are you doing?"

"Helping you."

"I don't...don't need help. You have to catch the thief, not stand here next to me."

"Tamaska, listen to me. I'm not doing this for my health or a quick thrill. Trust me, you're not that enticing."

She wanted to laugh, but really, there was nothing funny at all. This was the worst night of her entire life. No one would employ her as an event manager anymore. She could kiss her business plans for the end of the year goodbye. Her career was ruined, just as it was starting to take off. She felt like screaming and crying at the same time.

As her adrenaline faded, an ache radiated in her arm. She rubbed her hand over it, as if that would make the pain dissipate.

"Are you all right?" There was genuine concern in Kodiak's voice, but it didn't soften her anger.

The weirdness that had made her almost fall swept over her again and she clung to that anger like it was a lifeline.

"It's nothing—"

A new pain shot up her arm.

She doubled over, clutching her arm. What was happening? How could she be okay one minute and then falling back into the murky darkness that wanted her mind?

"This is bad," Kodiak said.

Her head went fuzzy, and her vision blurred. She tried to speak, but her words tumbled out in a slurred mess. "Wha.. you…"

What the fuck is wrong with me?

The sensation went as quickly as it came, just like earlier. Her vision slowly sharpened, and the dizziness left her.

"Who knows what he gave you," Kodiak said, and she thought he'd been talking for a little while. "You need to come with me."

Those words were more than clear.

"Gave…me?"

"There you are," he said. "Yes. I think you were drugged. You need to come with me."

"Like hell I do. I'm not going anywhere, least of all with you."

Tamaska's words made sense again, much to her

relief. No matter what happened, she had to put on a brave face and an air of confidence.

A sharp bolt of agony coursed down her arm, stealing her breath. But the pain didn't matter, not when the Blood Opal had been stolen under her fucking nose.

She didn't care if she might've been drugged. There was a job to do, a mess to clean up. Besides, Kodiak had probably just held onto her arm too tight. Compounded by her panic over the theft, her body was simply overreacting.

Her stomach roiled as the realization of the robbery settled in. There was no way she was going to take the fall for this.

"This is all your fault," Tamaska said, glaring at Kodiak and ignoring the warning throb in her arm.

She swayed, not sure she could stay on her feet but unwilling to fall apart. She'd fought hard to get the job, and she would keep fighting until she got what she wanted.

Pointing with her good hand, she aimed her finger right at the air in front of his face. "And you are going to pay for it."

There was no way she was going to lose her job or pick up the pieces of her career because of one incompetent man.

Anger blazed through her as she glared at Kodiak.

Her dreams were going up in smoke, leaving nothing for her to salvage.

Tamaska wasn't going to let that happen. But pinning this on Kodiak wasn't going to be enough to save her ass.

How was she going to get herself out of this mess and still keep her job?

 odiak

Kodiak locked eyes with Tamaska. She was weak, drugged by that fucking vampire. But there she was, trying to blame him, still spitting fire.

In another world, another circumstance, he might just admire her for it.

But not here and now.

He let his gaze move over her. Apart from the waves of whatever kept hitting her, she seemed in one piece. She rubbed her arm, and he got the feeling that the vampire had more than one tactic up its sleeve, both supernatural and mundane.

Supernatural he could deal with—she hadn't been

bitten, wasn't tainted with vampire blood that he could tell. But supernatural wore off.

Drugs, on the other hand...

It depended on what the fuck they used. It sure as shit seemed like the blood drinker hadn't been able to control her by normal means and had slipped something to her instead.

It was easy enough to use a coated needle.

Tamaska's eyes glittered and she rubbed her arm. "You had the gem stolen on your watch."

"There is no way this is my fault," Kodiak said, holding back a growl.

He wasn't going to take blame for the stolen opal. How could he have known there would be vampires? If he'd known the bloodsuckers were going to be there, he would've brought more pack members to protect the opal. Or, better yet, he would have sought out the Blood Moon clan and stopped the theft from happening in the first place.

Silently, he called Channing back to keep the crowds away from the empty opal box.

The others would know what to do, but he'd rather have the young pup here, close to him.

If the vampire hadn't yet been caught, they'd have to go deeper and that wasn't for Channing. That kind of work was on a different level.

Kodiak drew in a breath, but all that hit him was panic and excitement and fear. And anger.

Not all of it from Tamaska.

He was betting her boss was the woman standing, watching. She had that air about her. But he shifted his attention back to Tamaska.

"You need to come with me. We need to get the room locked down and all the information on everyone." That sounded like the best approach.

He would need that information, too.

If the vampire was here, maybe someone had invited them.

The list and the clipboard mafia she had didn't seem the type to wave someone in without their name on the list, though, and it wasn't a plus one kind of event.

Still, blood drinkers had their skills. He really did need to get her out of here, take somewhere to keep an eye on her.

If she stopped trying to pin the blame on him, he would be much happier.

She didn't seem inclined to stop.

"I'm not going anywhere."

"You are," he said. "We need to find out who's behind this."

"Yes," she said. "You."

He closed the gap between them and without touching her, brought his face in close. "Stop trying to say it's my fault."

"Why? It is *fully* your fault."

Tamaska's eyes reflected a fiery anger that burned his soul. He wasn't used to human women glaring at him like that. If there hadn't been so much riding on the night's gig, it would be oddly refreshing.

Right now, it was a pain in his fucking ass.

Well, if she wasn't going to go or sit, she could damn well stay with him.

He looked about as he silently made sure his team had the entire place locked down.

The answering affirmatives should have soothed him.

They didn't.

But there wasn't much he could do about that.

People rushed around them, panicking. In his peripheral vision, he noticed a few people approaching the cabinet. Fortunately, Channing used his charm and gentle strength to push back the disbelieving clients. Even though it was only his first event, and an unusually stressful one, he was stepping up and proving himself worthy of Kodiak's team.

He was proud of Channing; he simply didn't have time to show that.

The rest of the team worked like a well-oiled machine. He just wished the circumstances were different.

It wasn't as if vampires were going about breaking treaties and overstepping bounds these days. They hadn't in a long time.

Maybe this blood drinker was nothing more than a renegade—they happened, just like the old cliché of the lone wolf. But those were very few and far between.

And people, supernaturals included, were creatures of habit.

So, if he could work out what the importance of the opal had to the vampires, and where the vampire would take it, then his upcoming work would be a little easier.

At least in terms of finding a path.

"Your team better stop everyone from leaving before the police get here," Tamaska said. She stumbled forward as someone pushed past her.

Kodiak reached to help Tamaska get her balance, but she pushed his arms away.

"We're on it," he said.

"Just like you were with the opal?"

Kodiak glared at her. A growl rumbled in his throat. His wolf side wanted to surface, to rush after the vampires and rip them apart for ruining his reputation.

Settle down. Not yet.

Allowing his wolf to surface wouldn't help him find the vampire, and it wasn't about to help him, no matter how much the wolf side pushed.

Kodiak wasn't going to let his restless wolf take over. He fully controlled if and when he would transform, and he prided himself on that.

None of his pack members were forced to turn at the full moon, to run and hunt. They had tamed their inner wolves over many hours of training. That was necessary when living in a big city with humans.

But that didn't mean their wolf sides were always quiet.

Kodiak wasn't about to lose control in a room full of humans. That would require too much explanation —though trickery could explain a lot.

Trickery.

His mind locked onto the thought. Could that be what the vampires had done? They were good at tricks.

Maybe the Opal is still there?

He shifted uneasily, not wanting to leave Tamaska who still wasn't exactly steady on her feet. But the desire to investigate the glass cabinet overwhelmed him.

His eyes locked on hers again. The frisson of electricity buzzed his flesh. He enjoyed the fire in her eyes, even as it fuelled his anger. How could he be so conflicted? Over a human? If she were a wolf, they would have been well on their way to be mated by now.

He wasn't about to act on the primal instincts firing through his body.

They way he was feeling was all because of the thrill of the chase, the fire in her, the events happening around them. Nothing more and nothing less.

He took a step away, and she caught his forearm.

A wildness lit the anger in her gaze. "I'm not finished yet."

"Yeah, you are."

She snatched her hand away, her glare intensifying.

Kodiak breathed out. It was his nature to protect her, even if she was human— a hot human. Her outfit, the leather pants that painted her long legs and the opaque, long-sleeved top revealed obvious curves and toned muscles his hands longed to touch.

He wanted to slide his hands over her, peel back the clothes, and reveal the warm and naked flesh within. Fuck, he wanted to taste her skin and mouth, breathe that wax flower scent down deep into him. He wanted to thrust into her, on top, beneath, behind. He wanted her mouth on his cock.

What the actual fuck was he thinking?

Those kinds of thoughts were dangerous. He couldn't afford to have feelings for a human, not even lust. He couldn't afford to think only about himself—he had to consider his pack.

It was his duty as Beta to set an example for the pups. It had taken generations, but their pack had finally cultivated a discipline that no other wolf shifters had managed by controlling their wolf sides and living among humans.

He wouldn't upset that balance by failing to control his primal urges towards a human woman.

He'd come too close to that already by leaving his post to assist Tamaska, and now the Blood Opal was gone.

It wasn't fair, placing that blame squarely on his shoulders. He hadn't factored in vampires.

No one in his pack had done that.

No whispers about them planning anything had made the rounds. His pack kept well-pricked ears to the ground for the untoward, the unusual from those realms, even if something as valuable as the opal wasn't floating about.

The vampires had money, didn't they? Stealing wasn't their thing.

So the vampires turning up like this was completely unexpected.

The entire nightmare wouldn't have happened if it weren't for the vampires. His pack members would've caught a human, but vampires took more effort. The pack had been caught off guard.

Kodiak suppressed a growl. They weren't on their game tonight, which was unacceptable.

A shiver of caution and delight coursed through him as he stood here with Tamaska.

"I need to find the Blood Opal."

He couldn't have let that happen. His duty was to protect—technically the opal, but also her. It was almost like he cared.

He swallowed hard at the realization. He didn't like the conflicting thoughts rattling through his mind. If only he could shake them out.

Whoever had bumped into Tamaska in the first place, when she'd spoken to the vampire, had been part of a deliberate plan. It had been a distraction.

A distraction he'd fallen for. His nature was to always protect.

To anyone else, his teammates might have seemed slow to act, but he knew they hadn't. The theft must have been planned in minute detail. It never would have worked unless the vampires had known the wolf shifters would be there.

Unease slid through his veins.

Had someone on his team...?

No, that wasn't even a thing. A member of his pack working with the hated vampires? He knew them, all of them, and they wouldn't. But he couldn't shake the idea the vampires had known the shifters would be there.

Hurt the girl and get him out of the way, and then cause chaos with the lights.

He ran a hand through his hair, trying to grasp the fleeting possibilities whirling through his head.

"Did you hear me?" Tamaska snapped her fingers in front of his face.

Kodiak resisted the urge to grab her fingers and put them in his mouth, bite down on them with just enough force to turn the anger into lust, then show her just who and what he was and that he was her Alpha.

But he didn't. He wasn't. He needed to concentrate.

The more he thought about it, the more he circled back to the conclusion the vampires must have had a well-executed strategy and perhaps inside information. Maybe a human sympathizer who knew of the supernaturals? Maybe the one who had recommended his pack.

His gaze slid back to her.

Only Tamaska's last-minute hire of Shadow Protection had caused the pack to fail.

Was she doing this herself? To pin the blame on him and his pack?

"I'm your boss tonight, remember?" she said. "And you're failing in so many ways."

Kodiak inhaled slowly. He couldn't tell her what he was thinking. She was human and couldn't learn about the supernatural beings that lived with her kind, not without dire consequences—like possibly getting killed. There was too much she didn't understand, the level of ignorance she had would be like a death sentence. Although she'd gotten under his skin, he didn't want Tamaska to lose her life because she'd learned that he spent part of his time running around on all fours.

She didn't need to know.

"I work for you, and part of my job is to keep you safe. You also hired us last minute without any actual security measures in place."

She frowned. "You're the security measure."

"You know exactly what I'm talking about. A rope and a guy with a list isn't what I call state of the art alarm systems. And I'm very much aware of how those work, *boss*." He almost snarled the word but kept himself in check. "And how long they take to put in place."

"You're security so—"

"What?" He dropped his voice to a murmur.

She involuntarily leaned in, rewarding him with that fresh-sweet scent, even through the fear and anger that stung the air around her.

"You going to try and tell me I'm meant to do that, too? Magic it all out of thin air? I protect bodies and things and we do it all low key. You wanted us tech free. That's what you have. So don't complain about me not doing my job when you don't do yours."

Kodiak glanced over his shoulder. Two pack members were talking near the cabinet with serious expressions. They hadn't caught the vampires.

A knot formed in Kodiak's stomach. He needed to oversee the search, to get to his team and talk to them, not stand here wasting time arguing with this irritating woman.

"You were all told what I needed," she said, her eyes flashing and setting desire tumbling through his blood. "It was one reason why I wanted you on time."

"We were on time."

"My time." Her words were a snap. "That's before the event starts. Before a guest even thinks of showing."

Great, no one had told him that. But he couldn't say that. Instead, he deliberately looked over at his crew. He threw out questions to them and got nothing but questions back. Shit. He counted slowly, then turned his attention back to Tamaska.

She looked at him expectantly. What the hell had

she been saying? It had been too easy to tune her out just then.

"I'm going to let Olcan know about your incompetence." As if to prove her point, Tamaska took out her cell and began dialing.

Olcan would blame Kodiak for this. He was the leader tonight and anything going wrong would rest on his own shoulders.

Kodiak wanted to rip the cell from her and talk to his boss himself. Why hadn't he thought to call him first?

Because he'd been too caught up in all of this. Too caught up in her.

He hoped against all odds that one of his pack members might have called Olcan already without letting him know, but he doubted it.

Olcan would naturally be furious when he found out the Blood Opal was stolen, especially by bloodsuckers. And it brought him back around to the big question.

Why the hell were the vamps back on shifter territory?

Kodiak shivered.

A war was brewing.

He felt that right down in his marrow. A war. And he was going to end up in the thick of the fighting.

"Olcan," Tamaska said, "your fucking team failed. The Blood Opal has been stolen."

Kodiak clenched his fists to stop himself from

ripping the cell out of her hand. He silently cursed at her.

She thought him incompetent? He would prove her wrong.

He was going to find the opal.

 *odiak*

Kodiak turned on his heel, not wanting to hear any more of Tamaska's cell conversation with Olcan. His wolf ears had picked up enough of the exchange to understand Olcan was furious.

Just like Kodiak knew he'd be.

He should be back in the clubhouse having a beer with his team by now, or better yet, back in his apartment cheering the weekend football match, congratulating his pack on an easy job and toasting many more gigs to come.

This job had, of course, been about the money, which they weren't likely to get now.

That would be pinned squarely on him and like it or

not, fair or not, that was the way of things. Being in charge meant both accolades and blame.

But that wasn't the biggest problem he and his clan now faced.

Yes, they'd likely lose the money.

But this was a high-profile job.

People would hear of it. Come to their own conclusions and blame Shadow Protection.

Their reputation in the security business would take a huge dent, and future clients might taper off. He had to find out what had gone wrong, and quickly.

Kodiak went to check the cabinet, pushing past the people crowded around. They shook their heads and took photos with cells in hand.

At least none of them stood right up at it; they had to stand at a distance. Channing had done a good job of keeping people from getting too close to the cabinet.

Kodiak nodded as Channing stepped out of the way, still maintaining his diligence as more people tried to approach.

"Please, keep back," Channing said, even as he cast a worried glance at Kodiak.

The seriousness of what had happened wasn't lost on any of them.

The fact that Kodiak had stayed not to protect the empty box, would make it difficult to explain to Olcan. Dread of facing his Alpha weighed heavier on Kodiak's shoulders every moment.

He wasn't afraid of reprimand but of something else

he wasn't sure he could explain, something that went deeper.

Right now, he couldn't think about that. He needed to concentrate on the job at hand.

The opal.

He stepped up to the cabinet and used his sharp wolf vision to inspect the glass casing. There were no signs it had been moved, let alone any cracks. This wasn't a smash-and-grab. This was a well-planned theft. The vampire must have known exactly what the set-up would be.

The metallic smell of blood hung weakly on the air, increasing Kodiak's frustration. Olcan wouldn't like hearing that the vampires were up to something, especially after the few years of calm between their kinds. Now Kodiak's pack would have to deal with the blood-feeders again.

Kodiak and the other wolves would need to get on the streets and find the vampires before they killed any humans if it came down to that.

And every instinct told him it would.

After all, why the fuck had they suddenly appeared? Here? Where shifters were?

If there had been one vamp, there would be more.

That meant they were stepping outside the boundaries that had been set up.

Not only that, this area teemed with humans.

Vampire bloodlust couldn't be trusted, especially

when they were around humans. The temptation was too much.

The vampires had rules and held with treaties—because there were wolf shifters around to keep them in check.

It could be they were dealing with not one but a group of renegade vampires. But from what he understood, they held their own kind to certain rules to follow.

Or it wasn't that at all. Perhaps the bloodsuckers had seen an opportunity and taken it.

Maybe the robbery wouldn't have happened if Shadow Protection had been properly briefed instead of getting hired at the last minute. Then Kodiak wouldn't be there, trying to get out of a mess and restore his and Shadow Protection's reputations.

There was no point in going through what-ifs. He had to focus on moving forward.

There were no noticeable changes to the cabinet. Kodiak put his hand on it to peer inside, standing so close his breath fogged the glass. Earlier, the gem sat on a custom cushion with an indent and a clear plastic stand for the opal to nest inside. The stand was gone now, too.

He looked about, in case it had been knocked over, but it wasn't there.

Why take a plastic stand?

That simply added more bulk to the theft, and it held no value.

Kodiak's pulse quickened. Maybe this was a lead.

He kept searching.

The cushion lay on the bottom of the cabinet, positioned on a wooden plinth. A thread in the middle of the pillow caught his eye. He frowned as a possibility formed in his mind. It would've been a simple plan in execution, difficult in its setting up, but plausible since vampires moved fast.

Kodiak squatted down to take a closer look at the base of the cabinet. He put his hands on the carved wood, following the flowing pattern of vines and leaves. He would take time to admire the fine craftsmanship if he wasn't in the position he was in.

Instead, he kept moving his hands over the vines and leaves, searching…

A metallic click rang out.

Kodiak's breath caught in his throat.

He moved around to the back of the base, where he'd heard the sound, and his heart lurched. He tugged carefully on a piece of protruding wood. A wooden creak sounded as a secret door opened.

Shuffling forward, he peered inside the darkness, his wolf eyes shifting quickly so he could see. Nothing caught his attention until he looked up.

There was a hole in the wood. He reached for it, his fingers touching the soft cushion before exploring the hole.

It was a simple plan, all right, once all the pieces had been fitted together. Brazen, too. They had relied on their fast speed, the dark room, and a great deal of foreplanning.

It worried Kodiak how much they already knew.

Inside job. That was what this said to him.

But how? He and his team hadn't detected the stench of vampire until that one had appeared.

Could Tamaska have been involved? He didn't think so. She appeared completely innocent, and no scent of bloodsucker clung to her. Besides, why would they have tried mind tricks and then drugged her if she was in on it?

But someone on her team had to be involved. Kodiak didn't like that one bit, because that meant she was in danger. To indulge his illogical need to protect her, he was going to find the traitor, even if she didn't want his help.

The night's events played over in his mind as he withdrew his hand from inside the cabinet. It deeply annoyed Kodiak that he'd had the chance to upset the vampires' plan. If only he'd been more alert.

Why hadn't he seen them?

Kodiak closed his eyes as the events unfolded in his mind. Was it her? Was she his weakness? Maybe he shouldn't have gone to her side, to stop her from falling.

She was right. He'd failed because he went to her.

No, that was the weird, unwanted attraction talking. He would have done the same for anyone else he worked for.

But he wouldn't have been so drawn to them. Never had been before. And...

Kodiak stood.

He would right this wrong, no matter what.

He needed to check in with his team. He scanned the room. Shit. The cops were at the ballroom entrance, notebooks out, taking to staff and guests. There were more officers than would usually be at a theft like this. Then again, there weren't really thefts like this, not something so priceless. When he thought about it, it was a wonder the whole place didn't teem with officers.

They would want to talk to him—and his team. *That was* another conversation he didn't look forward to. There would be suspicion thrown his way, accusations, and the whole damn Shadow Protection organization dissected and looked at under a magnifying glass— not to mention explaining how he'd failed to stop the theft.

But it wasn't just that.

The last thing the pack needed was the police looking in closely to what they were and discovering their secret.

He needed to keep his wolf tied down and under tight control. He needed to play it cool, calm, and professional, no matter how much the pretty and disturbing Tamaska breathed fire down his neck.

The cops pushed past Fern, who'd been standing at

the door to stop people from leaving before they could be interviewed.

No one in the room was responsible for this, but he needed to follow the process and satisfy the humans. Otherwise, he would definitely end up with more problems.

Dealing with vampires was more than enough for now.

Before the police could catch up with him, Kodiak turned away, trying to follow the weak scent of the vampire who'd taken the Blood Opal. He made his way to a side door. It opened, and Shota came through, slightly out of breath.

Kodiak raised an eyebrow at him, hoping Shota had a lead—or even better, was returning with the gem.

Shota shook his head and shrugged. *I chased a vampire, but he was too fast.*

Fuck. Kodiak suppressed a growl and clenched his hands into fists. Anger threatened to consume him, the kind that would release his wolf.

Kodiak's hands clenched tighter, even though he'd expected that response from Shota.

Otherwise, Shota would have let him know telepathically. Still, it pissed him off. He wanted—needed—a lead.

Shota didn't seem bothered by Kodiak's reaction. He knew him too well. "They were quick and didn't leave much of a scent. Once they got outside, they split up. I had to pick one to follow."

Kodiak went suddenly still.

"There was more than one?"

"At least three."

"Fuck."

They were outwitted by fucking vampires. Kodiak ran his hand through his hair, messing it up.

"The others?" Shota asked, hope in his voice. "I haven't had time or space to check in. Maybe—"

"Nothing since the last time you all checked in. Fern's at the door to keep the guests here, and I haven't seen anyone else, apart from Channing."

Something green flashed to Kodiak's right, and he turned as Ash approached. Her dress helped her fit into the event, but it was hardly the attire for chasing thieves. At least its cut wouldn't inhibit her fighting.

Kodiak inhaled slowly, hoping she'd have good news, anything to set him on the right path and get the gem back.

"I was in the kitchen. I thought one of them went that way, but there were too many people. I couldn't follow the vampire," Ash said.

Kodiak narrowed his eyes. "They were organized. We've got three—"

"Shit, maybe there were more of them. It would explain how they got away from us so easily," Shota said.

"We need to get our shit together here." Kodiak glared from one to the other. "How many were there? I need to understand exactly what we're dealing with."

Shota met his gaze. "One, maybe two inside."

"I didn't pick up a stronger scent than two inside," Kodiak said. "And out there?"

"Their scent gets caught up with humans in such a small space inside. But outside? Definitely one or two more. They were organized and quick," Ash said, standing next to Shota with a worried expression on her face. "It's been, well, years since we've had an encounter with their kind. I wasn't expecting them to be here. I really wasn't expecting anything like this to happen. Who steals like that these days?"

"What do vampires need to steal for?" asked Shota.

Kodiak shook his head. Fucked if he knew why. Just that they did. And they were brazen as hell. The vampires certainly had no problem stealing the Blood Opal in public.

He looked around the room. People crowded around the police, hoping to get out of there before midnight.

Skoll strode up to them with a frown. Kodiak didn't bother asking if he'd found any leads.

"We need to get out there and find them, quickly, or we won't be getting any income," Kodiak said.

"Oh. The one I chased had a blood spot tattoo on his upper arm," Shota said. "Like those from the Blood Moon clan."

Kodiak swung his gaze back to Shota. That was indeed something. Not much, but it confirmed they were dealing with Sydney's dominant clan.

It might make things easier or harder. Right then, he didn't know, but there was one way to find out, and that was to take action.

"The Blood Moon clan, then," Kodiak muttered.

The design signified a twisted commitment to bleed all wolves, and the clan members all had it tattooed on their arms.

The theft seemed like something Blood Moon would do. Perhaps they needed money? Vampires were good with money, but maybe they were up to something that would cost a hell of a lot more than they had. They could sell the gem.

Of course, it could just be to fund their underground bloodlust.

The clan had their own nightclub, Blood Moon Nightclub, with a reputation dark enough that even the police didn't bother to go there. The only humans there were those who allowed their blood to be drunk, the vampire poisoning becoming their addiction until they were bled to death.

Kodiak's gut roiled at the thought that was where they needed to go in order to get answers.

"I want you all to take a good look around the ballroom, the kitchen, the entrance, the outside of the building, and the toilets," he said. "They must have left something behind that can help us get the gem back."

His team members nodded and moved off to see what else they could find.

Kodiak stood in the main room, desperately

listening to police interviews for information that would help him get the Blood Opal back.

After nearly twenty minutes of finding out nothing at all, he joined in the search.

He made his way through one of the back rooms to the ballroom and found nothing. He went still as the hairs on the back of his neck raised and his wolf shifted inside him. Awareness licked his skin. He turned and came face-to-face with Tamaska.

Why did he seem to have an extra sense whenever she was around?

Her sweet-clean feminine scent hit him and imprinted on his olfactory receptors, deeper than it had before. This might be because they were alone and all the other human stenches faded back while her scent seemed to grow and twine around him. Even though he didn't want to, he surely could track her through the city and beyond.

"I want you all the fuck out of here now," Tamaska said, her eyes fiery.

Kodiak understood her anger.

Her job was also on the line.

She needed someone to take it out on. Still, it spiked his temperature, even though she had no idea about the life-threatening danger out there, or that Kodiak was her best chance of survival.

"Tamaska, look, I get it—"

"Maybe other women you work for forgive you for your shortcomings because you're good looking. Not me. I don't care what you look like. All I care about is what you let happen on your watch. So get out."

Kodiak's anger increased, his wolf side lurking in the background, desperate to get out and sink its teeth into the vampires who had been inside the Shangrila. If Kodiak knew his wolf would go unnoticed in the city, he would give it freedom to hunt. But that was too risky.

There was only one thing he could do—reassure Tamaska that he would get the Blood Opal back and fix their mess.

But would she listen?

He had a bad feeling she was going to make things harder than they needed to be.

Starting with him.

amaska

Tamaska wanted to believe that Kodiak would get the precious gem back, but it was his fucking fault it was stolen in the first place.

If she held on to that anger, she had strength.

If she held on to that anger, she would stay grounded.

And if she held on, maybe she wouldn't feel herself slipping under the magnetic spell the man seemed to weave about her.

"I'm not going anywhere. Someone planned this. I can show you—"

"I doubt you'll get it back before the police do," she said.

How the hell could he, anyway? He was only security, not a detective. He didn't have the skills to find something valuable like the Blood Opal. Considering it was his fault the prize had been stolen, Kodiak could hardly have the aptitude to retrieve it before the police, with all their resources.

"You'd better believe I will."

The fiery determination in his eyes sent a delightful shiver down her back.

"Show me, and then I'll believe you." She glared at him. "But I won't ever forgive you."

She turned away, walking back into the main space. Her arm throbbed and she rubbed it again.

She hadn't fallen but...what had he said? She'd been drugged? Her sore arm gave credence to that idea. She probably should get herself checked out by a medic but honestly there were bigger things she needed to attend to.

How she wished one of the waiters would walk past with a tray of champagne glasses. She'd down one right now, maybe two. She didn't give a damn about her no-drinking policy at work anymore. The night had turned into a disaster she wanted to forget, and she needed something to make that happen.

Then again, a couple of glasses of champagne weren't going to do that. And they certainly weren't going to get the opal back, either.

She didn't have time to get drunk.

What she needed was to work out her next move.

"I'm Officer Jammu. Miss…?" a female officer said, stepping in front of Tamaska.

"Lane. Tamaska Lane. I'm coordinating the event."

No emotion passed over the face of the officer. "Can you please tell me what happened, Miss Lane?"

She clutched pen and paper in her hands.

"Of course."

Tamaska told the officer how the night's events had unfolded.

The officer nodded and jotted down notes as she spoke and Tamaska tried to keep the anger down. It wasn't going to help, not when she needed to think.

"The security was a last-minute change, you said?" Office Jammu raised a dark eyebrow.

Tamaska sighed. "Yes, they were recommended by my assistant, Cory. The last group couldn't pull their weight, so I sacked them. Maybe that wasn't the best idea."

"Shadow Protection does have a good reputation," the officer said, making a note.

"So I've heard."

"You don't sound impressed."

"Shadow Protection allowed the Blood Opal to be stolen under their noses," Tamaska said fighting the anger. "You tell me if I should be impressed. It was left to sit there, unprotected."

"I've spoken to Kodiak, the one in charge of security tonight. He mentioned he'd stopped you from falling, which is why he wasn't beside the gem. But he also wasn't far from it at all. Is that right?"

She closed her eyes and rubbed her temples, her head starting to ache.

"I was close enough and I did almost fall, but I didn't hire a personal protection service. So he should have stayed at his post." She opened her eyes and met the unreadable gaze of the officer. "The Blood Opal would still be here if he'd stayed on guard."

"Perhaps." The officer's tone remained neutral. "Perhaps not. It looks like this was well planned from the box. Did you notice anything strange about it?"

"No. OzOpals installed it themselves." She hadn't even thought maybe they'd taken it.

But the moment the idea of insurance fraud came to her mind, she dismissed it. They stood to earn far more on the sale than from insurance, not to mention their premiums would rise.

"Do you have any leads?" Tamaska asked.

"It's too early to tell, but we'll find the thieves." The officer snapped the notepad shut. "You're free to go."

Tamaska turned away, glad to have that conversation over with. But her to-do list wasn't getting any shorter as she made her way through the crowd, looking for Cory.

A policeman dusted the glass cabinet, looking for fingerprints. Kodiak stood nearby to point out where he'd touched it. Tamaska glared at him, and he looked up.

Heart lurching, she turned away. No man had ever managed to affect her so intensely before. What was it with Kodiak, with the way he looked at her, that brought her anger and newfound animalistic desire to the surface?

"Oh, my God! There you are!" Cory rushed up to her, frowning, his shirt hanging out of his pants. He looked flustered, which wasn't at all like him. "*Carlene* wants to talk to you!"

Tamaska bit down on the groan. "Of course."

She should have sought Carlene out immediately, but the chaos and the aftermath had left almost no time to do that. Now she had to face the music for her failures.

Tamaska might blame Kodiak—and she did—but she also wasn't an idiot. She was in charge; she was responsible. It was as simple and as devastating as that. If only she hadn't changed security at the last minute. She hadn't liked the previous group's slack work ethic. Cory had suggested she change staff since she wasn't happy. So she'd employed Shadow Protection on his recommendation as well as from of her friend, Tahla, who had used them recently and thought they were reliable.

They probably were. Mostly.

Tamaska strode over to Carlene, who typed busily on her cell. Tamaska took a deep breath, hoping she wasn't about to lose her job.

"I don't know how this happened, Carlene. I'm so

sorry the event was ruined. I hired Shadow Protection on good recommendation," she said.

Carlene had an edge that could cut even the toughest steel and she stared stormily at Tamaska. "This shouldn't have happened."

Tamaska braced herself for a censure. "I agree."

And she did. It shouldn't have happened.

"I will do everything I can to ensure the Blood Opal is found and returned to you," Tamaska added.

"Might be best to leave that to the authorities," Carlene said as she finished typing.

Tamaska definitely wasn't going to do that. This was her mess, and she would fix it. She didn't care if that was the best thing to do or not. It was her responsibility to right the night's disastrous events. "Regardless of my employment status, I'll do what I can to see the Blood Opal found."

"Which brings us to your job," Carlene said, with a frown.

Tamaska waited. Working for this woman wasn't fun, which would now be a hundred times worse after the theft.

Her eyes burned hot and her vision blurred, but she blinked fast, willing herself not to give in to something as unexpected and useless as tears.

She didn't want Carlene to hate her. Connections meant everything in this business as did parting on good terms. But if that wasn't going to happen, then crying in front of this woman would be the worst thing she could do.

"I didn't steal the Blood Opal or give information to anyone, I swear it." The words rushed from her mouth.

Some might love a job like this for the rich and famous who abounded these events, or perhaps some hoped to meet a rich husband.

Tamaska loved it for the challenge and the thrill, the doors that opened on different worlds, and the art of creating an atmosphere that invited people to part with their money for amazing, one-of-a-kind items.

"That's hardly reassuring, Tamaska." Carlene put her hands on her hips and looked at her.

Tamaska's face started to heat as she tried not to give her emotions away. Carlene viewed them as weak and unneeded.

"I'll make it up to the business," Tamaska said.

"It's worth fucking millions. How are you going to make that up in one lifetime?" Carlene tapped her finger on her arm, waiting for an answer.

"I'm aware," Tamaska said carefully, "that might be an impossible thing, but I'll do all I can to get it back."

"You're adding detective to your list of so-called skills?"

Tamaska clenched a hand at her side. "I'll do anything and everything I can. And that Kodiak—"

"What about him? Please don't tell me you're going to try and pass the blame along. This is your gig, your problem, Tamaska."

"I know," she said.

"You're lucky the police seem to think his team did a good job, and whatever this was, it wasn't something any of us could have foreseen. Otherwise, I'd sack you here and now."

"The police?" Shock raced through Tamaska and her mind whirled.

"Yes, and I've spoken to Kodiak. I've dealt with enough security over the years to tell if they're up to scratch or not."

Tamaska closed her eyes. Of course, Carlene had been checking up on her before they spoke.

"Kodiak is up to scratch?" That didn't sound right. Kodiak was Tamaska's number-one suspect.

"He is. That's lucky for you, because it meant you were at least doing part of your job tonight."

"You're not going to sack me?" Tamaska asked, her voice soft.

"Not *yet*. The police might think we couldn't have foreseen someone taking the gem the way it was, but I expect you to think of all options." Carlene's cold gaze skimmed her. "It is what it is. But you *will* work your fucking arse off. Consider yourself on probation."

"Th...thanks. I'll make sure the rest of the diamond mining account is seamless."

Tamaska's unexpected flutter of elation was quickly squashed by Carlene.

"No. You won't."

She breathed out. "Excuse me?"

"You've lost this account, along with the diamond mining account."

"You can't…" Tamaska let her voice fade away as Carlene's stare darkened.

"I have. *You* can take over the cupcake lady and help her get started with marketing."

"I'm overqualified for that."

"Not right now, you're not," Carlene spat, stepping forward and looking like she could explode with rage at any second. "This wasn't entirely your fault, but someone has to take the fall. That's you."

Tamaska held her breath as she kept her eyes locked on Carlene's.

"You'll show up on Monday and do your best to prove you should keep your job, no matter what I tell you to do. Is that clear?"

"Yes." Tamaska kept her head high.

"Now, get the fuck out of my sight." Carlene's phone buzzed, and she answered the call, turning her back on Tamaska.

She didn't need to be told twice. She hurried away, finding herself heading towards the stage, wanting answers. She scanned the room.

Her eyes met Kodiak's as he talked with his security team. Her breath caught. Out of them all, he stood out. He shone with a dark and compelling magnetism. But she looked away before her emotions betrayed her. She wouldn't give in to them.

Her stomach rumbled. She hadn't eaten today, and

the hunger clawed at her. Both hungers: one for food and the other for...

No, she shifted her mind from Kodiak to everything else.

She should be celebrating a successful auction, and instead she was stuck wondering who the hell could have stolen the precious gem.

She went to the glass cabinet to see for herself. Perhaps she could pick up a clue the others had missed. Like Kodiak. Her vision wavered. She rubbed her temple again. If it wasn't Kodiak, she needed to find out more about the thief so she could start her own investigation.

A plainclothes detective, his badge on his hip, was going over the cabinet.

"I'm Tamaska. I organised the whole event. Do you have anything?"

"The security guard worked out how they took the gem," the detective said, standing as Tamaska approached. He showed her a secret panel and a hole that led to the gem. It took her breath and made her head spin.

"That's saved us a bit of time," the detective said.

Bloody hell, had the whole roomful of people formed a Kodiak appreciation society when she hadn't been looking?

"That's good," she forced herself to say.

Her personal opinions on the man in question

didn't matter, not unless Kodiak turned out to be the thief.

The detective dusted for fingerprints. Tamaska turned, not wanting to see the empty cabinet. It only reminded her of the theft.

The damned cabinet was meant to be state of the art, and OzOpals didn't cut corners. They were a respected company. So she was back at square one.

Normally, this would be the part of the night where she could relax and enjoy her success after organizing an event. Not tonight. She'd failed to protect the opal, failed to sell it and just...failed. Fury stormed inside.

She didn't know quite what to do. Standing around was useless and with the police everywhere, she couldn't exactly push them aside and do their job. Better to wait until they were done and she had the reports. But she could ask around, see if maybe one of her clients had seen something.

Her skin prickled with awareness, and she glanced up. Kodiak was still talking with his team on the other side of the cabinet, but his gaze burned against her flesh. She wanted nothing more than to go to him for reasons she didn't even begin to understand. That draw to him was strong, but she wasn't giving in. Besides, she had nothing more to say to him.

With a sigh of frustration, she headed towards the kitchen. Staff always saw things, so asking them questions wouldn't hurt.

Something on the ground caught her eye. A business card. She stooped to pick it up. The title's artistic lettering stood out.

Blood Moon Nightclub.

She'd heard of it but had never been. It was one of Sydney's underground nightclubs.

Blood Moon...

The reference to blood wasn't lost on Tamaska. Tonight had revolved around the Blood Opal. The nightclub's name had to be more than a coincidence.

Tamaska flipped the card over in her fingers.

Celebrate our 10th birthday.

Her senses tingled and there was something just out of reach. Every time she tried to latch onto it, the thought slipped away like wisps of smoke. Instead, she stared down at the card, at the date for the club's birthday. It was the following night, Saturday.

Tamaska pressed her lips together and shivered. Had the thieves dropped this card? It was a long shot, to be sure. An edgy, clandestine kind of place like the Blood Moon Nightclub wouldn't suit the clientele present at the Blood Opal auction. It was too downscale, too steeped in the culture of hard dance beats and cheap drinks. Or, more likely, cheap drinks with a hefty price tag, but that kind of club like she'd heard Blood Moon to be was worlds from her rich clientele from suburbs like Vaucluse, Tamarama, Centennial Park, and even Woolwich.

The people who came to these things were old and established money, new rich, the famous...Those with the kind of jobs who wouldn't know of places like Blood Moon, and if they did, wouldn't ever think of going.

Maybe one of the waiters had dropped the card? It could easily mean nothing, but from the way Tamaska's body tingled with a mix of excitement and fear, she knew she'd found something significant.

Her boss and the police had warned her not to hunt for the gem, but she wasn't about to listen to them.

If it meant she'd have a chance of finding the gem, then she would go to the Blood Moon Nightclub on Saturday.

CHAPTER 9

odiak

Back at the club house, Kodiak stood in front of Olcan, every muscle taut and ready for action as he held his Alpha's dark stare. He was aware of all the pack members witnessing the exchange. The assembly in the meeting room had been called before Kodiak had returned.

He needed to tread carefully, remain calm, and keep his wolf from surfacing. Being the Beta poised to be Alpha when the time came wasn't just hard won. Nor was it by birth. He might be strong in body, but he had to be strong in mind, showing he was of leader stock.

It was how he'd reached Beta, and one thing could send that tumbling.

Not the loss of the opal, though that didn't help.

Tamaska.

She had that power.

Whether she knew it or not.

"Why did you leave your position?" Olcan asked, his dark hair thinning ever so slightly. He'd been the Alpha for decades.

The time was coming; when Olcan would have to step down. They both knew that.

Another reason to step carefully. He was next in line for the top position.

"Instinct."

Kodiak's reply was short and sharp. It was the truth.

"You shouldn't have."

The double-edged meaning wasn't lost on Kodiak, but he let it slide and pushed on. "The human woman hired us, and the vampire tried to hurt her."

Olcan waited.

"We don't have to like them to protect them. And she showed all signs of mind manipulation." That she'd thrown off. He kept that and the strange, resentful admiration to himself. "And drugged. He drugged her. The opal was secure, the team the best."

"I'm not asking about the merits of your team. Yet."

"The vampires always plan ahead. So this would have been set before we entered the place. And no doubt they had a back-up plan, too."

"Oh? So you thought why bother protecting it? I'm shocked you didn't hand it to them yourself."

Kodiak's wolf shifted, wanting to be free, to kill vampires. "I didn't say that. I made an educated guess. I made a decision."

"To rush to a human female, very pretty so I hear. You rushed to her and stayed and didn't go after the vampire?" Olcan stepped closer to Kodiak, as if challenging him. "You might say *you* let him get away."

Kodiak narrowed his eyes, the tension in him growing. "There was an entire team. I was near the opal, yes. But eyes of the team were also on it."

"The team is to blame?"

Kodiak silently cursed. Laying blame at anyone's feet other than the bloodsuckers wasn't his intention. And Olcan was definitely pushing.

"You were the one who left the Blood Opal unattended." Olcan edged closer.

Angry heat radiated from Olcan, but it only spurred Kodiak to stand his ground. "And I take full responsibility. There's no blame being laid down. The team acted flawlessly. The moment the vampires were detected we went into positions."

"Yes, because she was compromised by a vampire." He let his gaze run over Oclan, stopping shy of insolence. "Or should I have left her to be drained?"

Was this the time to challenge Olcan for leadership and take control once and for all? Kodiak moved forward, closing the gap between them.

"Do you think he wanted to drain her?"

"I don't know." Kodiak met Oclan's gaze dead on.

"The Blood Opal was the only thing of value in that room."

Kodiak swallowed hard. If it was just inanimate things they cared about, the job and not the life that always came with it—human life—then how were they different to the vampires? The lack of bloodlust?

Yes, he'd left his post because of a human woman, but he suspected what this was really about centered around the fact Kodiak's strength and standing grew by the day. That threatened Olcan.

This might be the perfect opportunity to push him back down into safer territory if the narrative was tweaked for Olcan's benefit.

Kodiak felt as if his entire being was under scrutiny, like Olcan was trying to paint him foolish and weak— and using not only the stolen gem, but the fact he'd chosen to protect a human.

"You can't mate with a human woman," Olcan said. "It's against the pack's laws."

"I don't intend to."

"Could've fooled me," Olcan said, pushing his muscled chest forward. Kodiak mirrored the gesture; his strength matched the Alpha's. "Running off to help."

"She's nothing more than a stupid human who had no idea about the danger she's in," Kodiak said.

Only an inch remained between their noses as they squared off in the meeting room of the clubhouse with the rest of the pack watching. "We protect, and she hired us. Why don't you blame those fucking vampires?"

"Because your sorry ass is here, and you were in charge. The blame rests with you, and you alone." Olcan narrowed his eyes.

Kodiak clenched his jaw, every muscle in his body ready to defeat his Alpha if necessary. But this was manipulation, a ploy to make him strike first.

He wasn't going to do it. Not until he had to. Not until the time was right.

"Fine, blame me." The words tasted bitter on his tongue. "I'm man enough to shoulder that. And I'm smart enough to know I did the right thing. I protected life."

"You should have done both." Olcan swung and landed a square punch on Kodiak's jaw, sending him stumbling backwards.

Kodiak recovered quickly, allowing his wolf to take over. He launched back at Olcan, deliberately landing a punch on his shoulder.

It was a warning.

He knew how these things played. And now wasn't the time to make his move for Alpha position.

None of the pack members came to stop the fight.

They watched.

Kodiak felt the frustration of the night, of the entire fucking situation, push at him. But he harnessed it, hard as that was, and focused. He used it to fight Oclan with just enough power to give him a glimpse of what he was capable of, stopping short of releasing all the anger and energy that had built up.

The Alpha put up a good defense, but Kodiak could feel the strain in the other man. Kodiak feigned dropping his guard as Olcan stepped back, nose bleeding. Olcan lunged forward and took Kodiak with a punch.

Kodiak flew backwards and landed on his back on the floor. Pain shot through him. He looked up as Olcan stood over him.

A grin of triumph lit the Alpha's face. "Not this time."

He wiped away blood with his shirt sleeve.

Next time, Kodiak thought, trying to gauge whether the pack leader understood what had happened, that he'd let the Alpha win. If Olcan did, then he kept that knowledge close.

The time was definitely coming for the challenge, and when it did, the job was his. Just not right then.

"This is my punishment, then?"

"Fuck, no," Olcan said, then spat a mix of blood and saliva onto the floor. He stepped back and looked at the pack. "Those who were there tonight, step forward."

Kodiak got up from the ground, brushing off his suit and trying to regain his composure. This was only a set-back, one of his own design.

Right now, he needed to find out the truth. He would make the vampires pay for everything.

Kodiak's teammates stood by him, and their support permeated him as they waited to hear what

Olcan had to say. Whatever it was, he got the feeling it wouldn't be good.

Olcan was a fine leader, if a little past his prime.

Kodiak was meant to be Alpha; it beat hard in his blood. But that didn't mean the road would be easy. Right now, with the theft of the opal, things were a little precarious.

He glanced at Moki, his only serious challenge to the position of Beta, because Moki wanted to be Alpha, too.

Moki might be strong, but he was too rash, too ready with his fists and claws and teeth. So he gave him a long, steady look, as if to say *don't even think about challenging me.*

Moki stared back, then lowered his eyes. Kodiak folded his arms across his chest. He wasn't about to get into a real fight for his Beta position over one disastrous incident.

He would win, but he didn't want to expend energy on something so useless, not when the vampires were in the picture once again.

Olcan rubbed his fingers over his chin. He shook his head, then sighed heavily. "The vampires were well-organized, which doesn't bode well for us. We need to find out what they're planning and why the fuck they want the Blood Opal."

"Do you think it might have some supernatural properties?" Channing asked from behind Kodiak.

He turned, staring down Channing for speaking out

of turn. The young pup had potential, but was still untamed in so many ways, and right now, the kid was on a high from his first big gig. He needed to learn. Channing lowered his eyes.

"We need to find out quickly what the Blood Opal has to offer the vampires. Could it simply be the name? A publicity stunt?" The questions rolled through Kodiak's mind.

"I feel the vampires were sending us a message. They could have stolen it for the money, but we need to be sure. Their club does very well—they're never short of money—so I would wager there's another motivation," Olcan said.

Kodiak nodded. "It's priceless, and they're not into selling items on the black market."

Olcan closed his eyes. When his eyelids opened, his dark eyes were focused and determined. "The only way you can redeem yourself after tonight's fuck-up is to find the Blood Opal and tell me what the vampires plan to do with it."

Kodiak narrowed his eyes, but he said nothing.

"I want a daily report on the blood-feeders, and if I think you haven't made enough progress, you can kiss your sorry asses out of the pack." Olcan looked at each and every one of the team who had been on duty tonight.

Kodiak nodded once more, ready for the biggest challenge of his life—had been since the moment the vampires set foot in that room and stole the gem. "Consider it done."

"Only when you show me the Blood Opal."

"You'll have it," Kodiak said, keeping his voice even.

"I will make it clear. That opal will not be returned to the humans."

Why? What did Olcan know? Or was this about simple greed and the fact the gem was worth so much? Kodiak's chest tightened. Apart from those pressing questions, he'd promised Tamaska he would return the Blood Opal to her. But there was no way he could go against his Alpha.

At least not until he knew exactly what was going on.

He was right not to challenge for Alpha tonight.

"Understood, Kodiak?" Olcan's gaze settled on him with an intensity he hadn't seen before.

"Crystal clear," Kodiak said tightly, trying to untangle his new dilemma.

Olcan nodded and left. The other pack members followed him, leaving Kodiak alone with his team.

They would all have to work fast and hard. Kodiak couldn't waste any more time.

"Ash, I want you to research the Blood Opal," he said.

She was the best at getting information, both on the internet and from books. If there was something written about the Blood Opal, Ash would find it.

"It won't be easy to find anything on the Blood

Opal. You know the records here in Australia only go back a few hundred years, so it's not likely this gem has ever been mentioned before," Ash said.

"Then maybe something else convinced the vampires that the Blood Opal has supernatural abilities," Kodiak said.

"I'll widen my search," she said with a sigh.

Her green dress looked out of place in the clubhouse.

"Good." Kodiak paused, looking at her until she realized he expected her to start immediately.

"I'll be in the dungeon on the computer, then, if anyone needs me or wants to help me." Ash turned and headed to the basement, where the computers were kept along with training gear and a cage—just in case someone couldn't control their full-moon hunting urges.

Fortunately, though, the cage hadn't been used in years. The well-disciplined pack had risen above their weaknesses. But that could all fall apart, thanks to the Blood Moon vampire clan, setting them up tonight, and with whatever they had planned against the wolves.

"This isn't going to be good for business. Now we know the vampires need to be put back in their place since they're causing trouble again. They're going to keep us busy, and we won't have time for anything else for a while." Kodiak ran his hand through his hair.

The rest of his team nodded.

"We have to find the Blood Moon clan."

Their lair. The heart of them.

This was going to be dangerous. It had been a long time since he'd faced a challenge like this, and he was keen to sink his teeth into some vampire flesh.

But the only place to find vampire flesh right now was the Blood Moon Nightclub.

That should be safe enough, but if they did their job right and found the information they needed, then Kodiak would then be taking his team into the heart of the vampire lair, and there they could all end up dead.

They had no options.

"I've heard their club is ramping up for a special celebration tomorrow night. I want us there. And it should be safe…as safe as stepping inside a vampire-run nightclub can be. There's even the slightest chance that's where they're hiding the gem." Kodiak looked at them all.

He didn't really think that's where they would hide it, but…

"We'll go. I'll make sure the gem is returned," Shota said.

Skoll nodded.

"Can't wait," Channing said, punching a fist into his other hand.

"And after that," Kodiak said, "we'll find their lair."

He would take the week to get them ready for that, to train the pup for what lay ahead.

"Tonight, tomorrow, and the week following, I want

you all in pairs, walking the streets, checking out the vampires' usual haunts." He pointed to the rest of the team. "Skoll, take Channing with you. Make sure he knows which spots."

"I will." Skoll patted Channing's back.

"Then we'll meet here. You better find something." They needed just a sliver of a lead. That was all.

"We will," Skoll said.

"Then, we'll plan how to get into the nightclub."

Kodiak hoped that would be possible. Infiltrating the nightclub felt like a fool's errand. They were shifters and the vampires would know that.

Still... the nightclub was public enough. Humans went. And the wolves did have their uneasy pact with the blood suckers.

Kodiak guessed they'd find out soon enough.

He was also going to track Tamaska and make sure she was safe, but he didn't tell them that.

The gem doesn't get returned to the humans. Olcan's command echoed in Kodiak's mind, eating at him. Why would Olcan want a priceless piece they would have to sell and compromise their whole protection services and reputation they'd built? But right now, Kodiak had a bigger dilemma.

He'd promised Tamaska he'd return the Blood Opal to her. He wasn't one to break promises, but he also wasn't one to go against his Alpha, and his pack.

Soon, Kodiak would have to choose.

amaska

Tamaska couldn't believe she hadn't been fired on the spot the night before. That thought rolled around her head as she jogged through Western Parklands of Sydney on Saturday morning, sweat beading on her forehead.

The fresh morning air brought a lightness to her steps as she ran, filling her lungs with the sweetness of the day. The canopy of shade from the surrounding tree cover protected her from the harsh Australian sun.

And maybe something else. That warmth and peace the tree's shade brought her went deeper than just skin protection. It was like she had a guardian angel watching over her, which was stupid.

If she had one, then where the hell was it last night?

Carlene, at least, hadn't called to say she'd changed her mind and was going to fire her, anyway, so she had that.

Tamaska still had a job to go to on Monday morning—except she would be performing activities reserved for the apprentices' assistants. That would be embarrassing.

Better to be embarrassed than to be fired. At least now she could work on building up her reputation again.

Her plans for her own business might be set back a little, but they weren't destroyed—yet. And if she played everything right, and found the opal, then she'd be right back on her track.

But it still hurt. And not just for herself.

She could only assume the people on her team would also be put on notice, and it made her sick that she was the reason they might lose their jobs. She had to make amends, and the only way to do that was to get the Blood Opal back. There was no way she could wait for the police to find it. She had to take a risk.

She turned her music up extra loud as she ran through the park. Pounding against the footpath in her sneakers was the best way for her to forget about last night's nightmare auction. The exercise gave her a physical outlet to release the frustration, anger, and stress before it consumed her.

It gave her space to try and formulate a plan. A starting point.

Hopefully, it would also make her forget about Kodiak.

When she wasn't consumed by memories of the theft, she was ruminating on the sexy security guy who'd gotten under her skin. Was it really only a few hours ago? It felt like a lifetime. Now he was buried deep into her bones.

She desperately wanted to cling to her hate for him because that seemed to offset the weird, wild attraction that went beyond just the physical attributes that would draw any eye. And she desperately wanted to continue to lay the blame for the theft at his feet.

Perhaps he shouldn't have left his post to help her, but he'd also been on point the rest of the night, as had his team. Then again, was that how they did it? Pretended to be upstanding and helpful while they robbed a place blind?

But how?

She just needed something.

A glance at the morning's paper had turned her stomach to acid. Seeing the theft on the front page along with her name disturbed her deeply. It made it sound it was her fault, simply by being the organizer.

Her cell had been buzzing all morning with messages and calls from acquaintances, but Tamaska hadn't answered a single call or responded to any messages. Most of them probably just wanted to gossip about the theft. Others wanted to indulge in Schaden-freude—that was, enjoy her misfortune as firsthand as they could get.

Her friends were messaging her repeatedly, demanding to know if she was really all right. They knew how much the job meant to her, how much pride she took in making her events into huge successes.

She couldn't face any of it—at least, not until after she'd gone for her morning jog, showered, and had a coffee. Then she would get started countering the damage to her reputation even though it was tempting to hide under her covers. She wouldn't do that.

She followed the path around a bend. There hadn't been anyone else around for a while. That wasn't so unusual, considering how early it was on a Saturday morning.

Her mind kept turning to the Blood Moon Night-club and their anniversary event tonight.

She was going; there was no doubt about that. If any chance stood with there being a link between the club and the opal, she would take it.

She would prefer not to go on her own. Not that she was worried about trouble, but a single woman out at a club would always draw attention. But that wasn't a big deal. Some of her friends would probably offer to go with her for safety. She reckoned Tahla would be up for the adventure, but Tamaska would need a cover story to explain to her why she wanted to go to a club like that. Maybe a new potential client?

And, since the theft, she couldn't be choosy about her clients.

That might convince Tahla to come along without making her worry that she was doing something dangerous that should be left to the police.

Her skin prickled as she ran, and the shadows somehow seemed darker, which was silly. An icy shiver trailed down along her spine and even though no one was round, an uncomfortableness, like she was being watched or followed, settled in her stomach.

But as she glanced about, no one was there.

It was in her mind. After last night, who could blame her for jumping at the slightest shadow or expecting trouble?

Even so, she slowed down. This was her usual morning jogging route. She knew every inch by heart, and never had felt anything spooky like this before.

As she ran farther along, the sensations grew instead of receding.

She hit pause on the music app on her watch and the loud beat in her ear pods stopped.

Where were the voices? The rumbling of traffic beyond the Western Sydney Parklands?

Why did it feel like she'd suddenly plunged deep into the bush at night?

Fuck, the opal thing really had gotten to her.

She turned around, slowing her run to just above a brisk walk, but no one was behind her. Then, she squinted at the trees to make sure no one was lurking there. Above, the birds sang as if they were happy about the new day. But that was all she heard. If anyone was around, Tamaska couldn't see them. Worse, she couldn't hear them.

And she should be able to in the park.

She sucked in a hard, deep breath.

All in my mind. Stop acting crazy.

She quickened her pace, driven by the need to purge herself of the strange feeling of being watched, or being followed. Purge herself of everything that had happened last night. Purge herself of the lingering disturbing effect of Kodiak.

She wanted to fling herself past the breaking point. Only then could last night's events be replaced by physical pain and exhaustion.

Her body began to ache, and her breath became labored as she pushed herself. Her leg muscles felt like dead weights and she struggled to keep moving, but there was no way she was stopping before the creepy feeling had passed.

She stumbled, lost her balance, and tumbled to the ground. She skidded across the concrete path and winced at the discomfort as it shot through her.

Fuck.

She closed her eyes as lancing streaks of pain filled her body. Then, that agony focused to a point. Finally, it eased, leaving her heavy with exhaustion and nothing else.

Tamaska had reached her breaking point, just like

she wanted. But she hadn't intended to find it lying injured on the ground, wondering if the damage was worse than grazed skin.

Ouch.

Her upper left arm spasmed in a sharp cramp, in the same spot she'd been somehow hurt last night. She sat up and placed a hand over the tender spot and rubbed it.

Not hurt, drugged. That was what Kodiak had said. It still didn't sit well in her.

She froze. There was a flash of darkness, as if someone stood to her left, and she turned her head. For a second, there was nothing. Then a huge, sleek dog came bounding out of the bushes.

She screamed, her fear of dogs taking over her entire being.

It was a giant of a beast, so much bigger than any dog she'd ever seen before, with clean patches of ochre fur. And it was beautiful. It didn't seem like a feral dog.

She froze, staring at it.

She couldn't move as it bounded onto the path coming right at her. Then it paused, stopping short, standing in front of her as its yellow and golden-flecked eyes stared straight into hers, sending heat spiraling through her.

The dog panted. The sight of the rapid flutter of its ribs that came with the breaths it took, almost like it was in total control, chilled her. Its mouth opened and the lips drew back, exposing long, sharp teeth. But in those eyes, intelligence glittered. The dog looked like it was on the hunt.

Tamaska waited for it to come and sink its white teeth into her flesh. Terror ricocheted through her, along with the horrible memories. Bracing herself at the thought of more pain, she couldn't move as fear gripped her.

A dog had attacked her when she'd been a small child, a savage thing with hate and bloodlust in its eyes, the jaws strong and hungry for meat.

She'd fought and screamed and cried. She'd been too young to fight it off, and it had left scars on her arms and legs. She'd been lucky it hadn't sunk its teeth into her face. Fortunately, neighbors came to help her, saving her life.

Ever since, she'd had a huge fear of dogs of any size.

Now, here she was, face to face with one that wasn't on any leash. It looked down into her, almost like it knew her.

She swallowed over the hot, hard lump in her throat. The dog didn't know her. It was just a huge dog, one that was too close, too big. She was scared shitless. She'd recognized the glint in its eye, the need to attack, the same look she'd seen in the dog who'd attacked her when she was a child.

The dog turned and ran off into the bushes, back towards the place where she'd first felt like someone had watched her.

Tamaska exhaled in relief and confusion. The dog could have bitten her, even attacked her, but it hadn't.

The thing had looked at her almost like it had been checking up on her.

She raised a shaking hand, the heel of her palm scraped raw but, ignoring the bite of pain, she pushed her hand over her hair.

How had her life suddenly become so strange and complicated?

As she looked about, she realized she could hear voices and traffic once again, all the sounds of Sydney bubbling back in. They hadn't been there before, had they?

She couldn't sit on the concrete path all day.

Gritting her teeth, she put her scraped hands down and attempted to push up. Her legs, still leaden, trembled, and she collapsed back down.

"Are you all right?" A couple rushed up to her before she could try again. Both dressed in active wear and looking like they were outside for fitness.

The fear started to disappear, along with the shock of everything, and she took a breath.

"Yes."

She was, surprisingly. Her ankle hurt a little, and there was that odd stinging in her arm. But she felt better than she had earlier. Her legs weren't as leaden as moments ago.

She tried to stand once more, but her legs wouldn't hold her weight.

Tears of frustration stung her eyes.

"Sit a bit longer," the woman said.

The adrenaline generated during the encounter eased, and her body shook as she tried and failed to stand once more. She hated feeling so weak.

"I'll call an ambulance," the woman said.

"No, it's not that bad. I pushed myself a little too hard running and I just had a fright when I fell. You're right, though. I need a few minutes sitting here."

Facing a dog like that up close and somehow escaping unscathed had left her more rattled than her fall.

Why didn't it attack me?

She couldn't shake that question, or the feeling that her life was getting crazy.

And somehow, someway, Kodiak was involved.

 odiak

Kodiak's paws hit the ground hard, his claws digging into the damp soil and pushing off as he chased Tamaska's voyeur.

In his wolf form, he jumped easily over a fallen branch in the small area of bushland that marked the perimeter of the park.

He'd been right to go and keep watch over her. Now, he had his reward—a lead. At least he hoped that was what it was. Every instinct he possessed said it was.

The Western Sydney Parklands were popular among city dwellers during the day, and among supernaturals during the night including pack members and other shifters. The park boasted over five thousand hectares with walking and cycling paths, as well as picnic areas and of course plenty of trees and native wildlife. A type of Australian oasis in the outer suburbs of Sydney, providing a chance to escape the busy city life.

While the cul-de-sac where the pack lived bordered the bush that was heavily populated with the native plants and trees, it wasn't enough. The bush gave them a place to run when needed, like here.

They couldn't hunt so much in the bushland close to the city, since there weren't many kangaroos.

Humans ate them as did the pack, and on occasion, the pack would go out to the country to roam and hunt properly.

They kept away from protected native animals and endangered species. Just as they kept from the livestock in the country humans bred for food.

The park, though, was Kodiak's usual stomping ground, a place where he could run in both human and wolf form and keep an eye on the goings on. He knew it well.

As wolf, he was faster, stronger, and able to cover more ground.

Tamaska's scent had caught him by surprise. He didn't have the strength to resist following her sweetness in the air for the chance to see her once more.

Close to her but hidden, he followed her easily, enjoying the sight of her tight ass as she jogged.

Out of nowhere came a flash of a shadow moving fast toward Tamaska. Straight away, he knew it was a vampire.

He rushed to give chase. The lust to rip apart flesh and destroy evil taking over, but he'd paused after seeing her hurt on the ground.

The fear in her eyes had locked him there, and he had only been able to watch, making sure she was fine. He'd wanted to soothe her with his nose or paws or tongue, but the terror stopped him.

Instead, he'd leaped after the attacker. He'd managed to hit them with his paws, forcing them to flee instead of attack.

Tongue lolling to one side, he ran after the shadow. Trees flashed past him as he sprinted. He hoped to sink his sharp teeth into the attacker, to taste their blood and rip their flesh apart.

How dare they threaten someone under his protection? He could no longer deny his need to protect Tamaska, beyond the job they were hired to do, beyond the pack's stance to protect those weaker than them.

There was something about her that attracted him, and he couldn't control those feelings. Ordinarily, he would complete a job, protect people, and then move on. That hadn't been the case with Tamaska.

It wasn't just about getting the Blood Opal back. His protectiveness stemmed from a need to claim her as his own.

But he wasn't about to do that. Instead, he would

take revenge on whomever he was chasing. Plus, maybe his target could give him a lead on the Blood Opal's location.

He wanted to find the opal. It was a matter of pride, completing the job he'd been hired to do. But it went beyond that. He needed to stake his claim as Alpha sooner rather than later. Why did Olcan want the gem?

And he wanted to know why the vampires did, too.

Magic? Or just money?

For now, though, he wanted whoever had stalked Tamaska.

The entire incident had happened so quickly. He'd detected her would-be attacker a second before they'd rushed towards her.

The vampire was solid, strong, and incredibly fast. Kodiak hated to think what would have happened if he hadn't been there.

What is she thinking, going out here so early by herself?

Then again, she had no idea what types of supernatural beings, including him, shared the earth with humankind.

Anger burned inside Kodiak's veins, directed not at Tamaska but at the vampire who had tried to hurt her.

This wasn't the usual time for vampires to be out and about. The sun would soon be peeking over the horizon and the sky was already becoming blue, pushing away the night and the nightmares that lurked in the dark. Right now, it wasn't safe for a vampire to be out.

He tracked the scent, detecting the musky, metallic blood odor that convinced him he was chasing a vampire. The contradicting information was confusing. It was too light for a creature who would burn to ash beneath the sun to be outside.

What the fuck was going on?

That motivated him to speed up. If he was right, then soon there would be nowhere for the vampire to go. The vampire would have to find a hiding spot for the day.

This could be Kodiak's chance to catch the attacker and rip him apart. Bloodlust stirred inside him, saliva thickening in his mouth at the thought of fighting. He was made for this. He had missed that vital excitement of taking down a vampire. That thrill of the chase, knowing his quarry was within reach.

Letting his wolf take full control of the chase. The feel of the air in his pelt, with its earthy hues which matched Australia's typical ochre, was freeing. Kodiak pushed forward, his senses fully engaged as he closed in on his fleeing target.

Although they were originally from America, a few of his kind had emigrated to escape the Dust Bowl and the Depression. After finding their way to Australia, they'd claimed the continent as their new home. They'd thrived in their new land, adapting easily, and now they were once more changing to thrive in an increasingly urban landscape.

To really run, to completely release his wolf, was like nothing else. A special gift.

He rarely went into the city in wolf form. If seen, he would draw too much attention. He didn't need to be hunted by humans.

He wouldn't allow himself to be killed, and he might not like them, but he didn't want to kill humans, either. Besides, the humans would hunt him down out of revenge if he ever had to hurt one of them.

To defend himself, he could change a human into a wolf, but no one in his pack had ever done that for as long as he could remember. He descended from a long line of purebred wolf shifters that weren't permitted to breed with humans.

His pack kept to themselves, occasionally associating with other Australian packs, but never converting humans. They'd agreed on that to protect themselves since it had taken so long for them to build up the numbers after first coming to Australia. That had been over a century ago.

One thing hadn't changed—the need to keep the vampires from creating total chaos and killing people.

Shifters served as protectors in the shadows, quietly working, unbeknownst to humans. They had been excellent protectors for generations, and it annoyed Kodiak that the vampires were up to something again and had to be stopped.

Whatever the vampires were planning caused Kodiak's stomach to tighten. First, they'd brazenly stolen the Blood Opal for reasons he didn't quite understand. Now, they were roaming around outside when they should have been indoors, cowering at the light.

Well, one roamed.

Perhaps this vampire had discovered a type of magic that allowed him to stay outside? If so, where, and how?

Or could it have something to do with the Blood Opal?

Thoughts crowded Kodiak's mind like a pack around a kill, tearing apart the details as though they were flesh. If he found the vampire, there was a chance of finding answers.

It didn't make sense if he looked at it objectively, but instinct told him time was most definitely running out.

Kodiak knew the layout of the thinning bushes that signaled the end of the park. He had to use the terrain to his advantage. Using his smell and his sight, he predicted where the vampire would go next.

Kodiak cut around the path, hoping to reach the vampire before the stretch of grass in front of the buildings. The grass marked the beginning of the suburbs of western Sydney where it would be harder to stay unnoticed by the humans.

As Kodiak calculated where he would attack and launched himself from the ground.

He felt as if he were flying. He reached out for the body he wanted to assault, but he met only air.

Fuck.

Had he missed?

Kodiak looked down. Everything was happening in slow motion. He could see the dead leaves on the ground, a few crawling ants, some red flowers, and small animal tracks in the rich soil between the bushes.

It was as if he were suspended in the air and time had stopped. Then, a shadow passed under him as he began to fall. His front paws landed on the back of whoever it was.

They yelled out in surprise and pain as his claws ripped into their flesh. The sound of their agony spurred him on, along with the hot wetness of the blood in his claws. With it came that particular metallic stench.

It was a vampire. He knew that for certain now.

Kodiak snapped at its neck, hoping to find flesh. The vampire turned hard and fast, rolling onto the ground. Kodiak attempted to push his claws deeper into the vampire's muscle, but he was too late. The motion tipped him off the vampire's back.

Kodiak growled as he rolled through the undergrowth to get back on his paws. Determination to bring this monster down surged through him. He launched himself towards the vampire, his teeth bared, claws extended.

This time, the creature was ready, holding out a knife.

Kodiak saw it too late. He twisted in an attempt to

get out of the blade's way. A sharp burning sensation cut into his flesh, and he crashed to the ground with a whimper.

He turned to attack once more, but the vampire was already running across the grass.

Kodiak could have followed him—the wound wasn't too bad—but a bleeding animal out in the open was much too risky in such a popular space.

He glared at the vampire, which was running over the open space towards the closest building. Height, build, hair color. He burned those details in deep. It wasn't any blood sucker that Kodiak was familiar with. Perhaps he'd been turned recently or was one that didn't matter if they burned to ash in the sun.

But he didn't think so.

The vampire had revealed a tattoo on his arm as he'd wielded the knife.

A tattoo Kodiak knew: a moon.

This wasn't a freak accident.

Tamaska was in trouble. That was more than obvious after the attempted attack on her earlier. And Kodiak was going to have his hands full trying to find the Blood Opal, let alone protect her.

He didn't even want to think why the Blood Moon clan wanted Tamaska.

With a chilling, loud growl designed to warn off the fleeing vampire, Kodiak turned back to the bushes' cover. Pain from the bleeding wound gripped tight around his chest, but he forced himself to run back to where he'd left Tamaska.

Is she all right?

It had been difficult to leave, but his focus had needed to be on the attacker. Now he had to return to her, check she was okay. Zigzagging back the way he'd come, he leaped onto the path. Her sweet, fresh wax flower scent was thick in the air, but she wasn't there.

Kodiak took his time smelling the ground where she'd fallen. Worry weaved through him as he detected the distinct odor of her blood. The scent wasn't strong, so she hadn't been badly injured when she'd hit the ground.

He rushed down the path for a few meters, following her footsteps. The need to see her and to make sure she was all right was strong and urgent.

The path went further into the bush, then veered back towards grassy ovals for human sports. Trees beyond that stretched far away from where he'd chased the vampire. He sensed he was getting close to her and hurried on, ignoring the faintness from his blood loss, and the sharp pull of his wound.

Up ahead, she limped across the grass towards the street where he couldn't follow her.

Kodiak watched her, not wanting to take his wolf eyes off her, protecting her from a distance. If needed, he was ready to leap out and risk his own safety and secrecy.

Tamaska glanced back over her shoulder, and their

eyes connected. It was as if she was seeing him for what he was, a wolf, and she wasn't at all scared. Not in that small, breathless moment.

She paused. Their eyes remained locked as if a trance stretched between them. How he wished he could go to her, walk with her, and stay by her side.

But it could never be. He had to stay in the shadows, out of sight, despite the strong connection between them. She was human, after all.

He blinked, stepped backwards, then turned and slipped back under the cover of the bushes and leaves.

Kodiak didn't like the change in behavior of the vampires. This wasn't going to end well.

CHAPTER 12

odiak

Kodiak limped back to the clubhouse, weakened from the attack. He slipped back into human form, naked and bloodied, and opened the back door. His team-mates were there waiting for him. Skota and Ash were playing chess, Channing and Skoll were making good use of the pool table, Onai played games on his phone and sat drinking coffee while flicking through a maga-zine about cooking desserts.

"We've been waiting for you," Channing muttered.

Kodiak growled a warning, and the young pup looked at the floor.

"What the fuck happened?" Skoll asked, his gaze zeroing in on the wound.

Kodiak grunted, grabbing clothes from the cupboard in the back room. The cupboard stayed stocked with spare clothes for those frequent times the packmates returned after shifting into wolf forms.

Kodiak only wished he'd changed out of his suit before shifting. He'd liked that one. But he'd been too restless to stay indoors, and the need to go and check on Tamaska had been too strong, and it turned out, for good reason.

"Vampire," Kodiak said as he slipped on a pair of jeans, wincing in pain from the laceration on his side.

"Didn't come off too well, did you?" Skoll tried to take a closer look at the wound, but Kodiak brushed him away.

"Who are you, my mother? It will heal quickly enough."

Skoll snorted. "In these very recent times, who the fuck knows. Was it a vampire?"

Already the wound had started healing. "You know it was."

He was glad to be a wolf today. By the time he'd finished getting dressed, the skin around the wound had almost sealed, leaving only a bloody mess on his skin and the urge to eat a pound of steak.

There was little point denying who had wounded him. The vampire stench was in the air from his close contact, and all he wanted was to wash it off. But Olcan was there already so a shower would have to wait.

"Out now?" Skoll asked. "Risky."

"Just like last night."

"You're letting the vampires get the best of you," Olcan said, leaning against the doorway to the meeting area where the team had assembled after a night of patrolling.

Kodiak clenched his jaw, stopping himself from snarling at his leader. Olcan was either deliberately needling him or not, but it didn't matter. Giving in to those base instincts wouldn't do anything to help, so Kodiak kept calm on the surface. "Minor hurdle."

"Looks like more than that." Olcan pushed off the doorframe and stepped into the room. "What happened?"

"Nothing I can't handle," Kodiak said softly as Oclan stepped farther into the room.

"So, what do you have for me?" Olcan asked, crossing his arms. "Anything? Or should I send you all packing now?"

Kodiak couldn't believe how serious Olcan was about kicking them out of the pack. His entire life had turned to shambles the moment they'd taken that damn job. He couldn't even blame Tamaska. But he knew one thing; he didn't like not being in control, and he hated not having answers, almost as much as he hated the ridiculous push from the Alpha.

Were they meant to have answers a handful of hours later?

Stay calm.

"I didn't find anything online," Ash said, looking at the floor, her shoulders rising and falling.

If he didn't know better, he would say she was upset. But he knew her. She was furious at being asked to do things to fit some weird time frame that seemed to be thrown at them.

It wasn't reassuring for her not to find anything at all, not even a crumb. Ash was great at finding information.

His gaze shifted to the Alpha. What was his agenda? The question was one he kept coming back to, like something he needed to pick at.

"Not promising," Olcan grumbled, looking angrier than Kodiak had ever seen him before.

Again, why? Because he knew his time was up, or something darker?

Onai looked at the Alpha. "We were sent on a normal job that turned into anything but normal."

The Alpha didn't even acknowledge Onai. "I need something. The pack's reputation is always in your hands the moment you step out. Not one job is to be treated like you all treated it. Not one job is run of the mill. And now we have a vampire."

Kodiak met the Alpha's gaze. "More than one."

"I counted about a dozen vampires out on the street," Skoll said.

He looked relaxed in his track pants and loose t-shirt, hair damp from the shower.

The hair on the back of Kodiak's neck rose, and his

skin prickled. That wasn't a good sign. That wasn't what he'd been told last night. They'd all said around four, so either they were lying now, or lying then. Or had kept that back.

His money was on a lie.

One that could now cost them—big time.

"I only counted six," Shota said.

"Me too," Onai added.

Dressed in all black, Onai didn't seem bothered as he now sat in the lounge chair with his legs dangling over the arm.

"That's too many," Olcan said, straightening up as he shook his head. "After being quiet for years. That's just way too many vampires to be out and about and stealing things. Being seen." His gaze flickered to Kodiak. "And, as you say, this morning. A risky and dangerous thing to do. But why the fuck are they out now, making a splash?"

"It makes no sense," Skoll said.

"It has to be the Blood Opal that drew them out," Kodiak said, rubbing his temples and keeping his tone even, weighing out what he needed to say next.

There was no way around it. He had to just say it and let Olcan judge him. Apart from that attraction for the woman that beat hard in his blood, protecting her was what they did, and it was the right thing.

"One of them attacked Tamaska, the woman who organized the event. They're overly interested in her."

Olcan sighed heavily, even as he gave Kodiak a long,

cool look. "They've always had been interested in feeding on humans. That's not enough."

A rumble sounded from Kodiak's throat. "Skoll said he counted about a dozen of them on the streets last night, and the others I sent out saw a few, too. Vamps don't usually do that. They don't go around in a pack, and they don't make it obvious. Combine that with attacking the human who hired us at the event—and yes, I know the signs of someone drugged by a vampire —not to mention attacking her in the early morning, I'm going to venture out and say it just might be enough."

He kept his gaze steady on the Alpha and his voice calm. "More than enough, I would think. This, with the stealing of a priceless gem, is more than vampires showing their natural instinct of feeding on humans."

"You have something to say?"

"Yes, Olcan, and you know this like I do. You're mad it went south, I get it, but you're smart. It's why you're Alpha." He waited a beat. "This is more than a coincidence. They're ramping up their activities. They have their club, too. They don't need to feed out in the open."

"A weak start. To keep your place in the pack, I need results." Olcan glared at each member of the team.

The tension in the room rose.

"You need to do better," he said. "This pack has to be strong if we're going to survive, especially now that the vampires are showing their fucking fangs."

"We are strong," Kodiak said. "And we've only just started looking into this all. We're not giving up until we find out what the blood suckers are up to and we get the opal. But threats? You're better than that, aren't you?"

Olcan narrowed his eyes at Kodiak, ignoring those final words. Kodiak didn't expect any less from the Alpha.

"You better have more for me tomorrow morning." The Alpha turned and stalked out. "I'll be waiting here for your report."

Kodiak breathed out slowly.

"What are we going to do?" Channing asked, looking rather pale at the prospect of losing his pack.

"The only thing we can do," Kodiak said.

"Keep trying?" Channing didn't sound confident.

"Go to the Blood Moon Nightclub as we planned."

"I'm ready."

Kodiak lifted a corner of his mouth as he looked at the pup. "There'll be vampires there."

"And plenty of humans for them to feed on," Onai added.

"We need to work out how to get in without them noticing us." Kodiak crossed his arms and glanced at Ash. "Rest up for an hour or so, and then try to find information on the Blood Opal in more unusual places. Start with its history—who found it, and who has owned it."

"I will," Ash said. "There'll be some history on

OzOpal's site. I was saving that as I didn't think it would be useful to us, but if we're going to go that route…"

"I think we leave no stone unturned," Kodiak said. "There has to be something that can tell us why it's so valuable to the vampires. Even the tiniest thing, no matter how seemingly unimportant…"

Ash nodded. "I'll find it."

"I know you will. But we need this as soon as possible, not later. Not with Olcan breathing down our necks like he is." Kodiak's strength started to return to full power as he talked with his team. "The rest of you, head out and see what you can find. Old known haunts, humans who know of the supernaturals, or even those who didn't realize they knew vamps."

"You think we'll find something?" Fern poured herself a glass of water from the jug on the side table.

He shrugged. "Maybe, maybe not."

"But," Shota said, "we won't know if we don't try."

"After you come back this afternoon, you can all rest, then we're all going to the club. You know the drill." Kodiak instructed his team. "Wear clothes that will fit in. Get the scent-masking spray from Martha and use it. We have to get in and stay in there long enough to find information. Otherwise…"

He swallowed down a sigh. It wouldn't be wise to dismiss Oclan's threat of ousting them from the pack. But that wasn't what bothered him. He would take the

Alpha down if he had to, before he'd plan to, if it came to that.

A slim chance existed he would lose, and they would be out, but they could form their own small pack. He didn't want that. He loved his pack, as did the others. They were all life blood, even Oclan.

Which was why he had to make his move properly and with respect.

But Kodiak's fear was perhaps there was something else going on.

It wasn't like Oclan to be so hardline.

Then again, it wasn't like Kodiak to be obsessed with a human. And he was. There was something about her that got to him. He feared perhaps he'd stayed a little too long with her. Not to protect her, but because he wanted to be that close to her, to take in that wild buzz of erotic energy he'd been hit with the moment their gazes had met for the first time.

Tonight, he and his team were heading to the vampire's club. He needed to find everything he could on the opal and why they'd taken it. That club held answers. He felt that in his bones.

But if he was there, who would watch Tamaska? He couldn't ask anyone else, and he couldn't skip this. He thought of asking her to stay in, but she was stubborn and would deliberately head out if he did that. Much better to leave her be and check after the club.

He would have to do something he hated: rely on hope that she would be okay.

No matter what that hungry part of him whispered and urged, the opal and the club and the cohesiveness of the pack all took priority.

"We'll meet here at six tonight to formulate the plan. Be ready." He made sure he looked at each of his team members. Their strong gazes made his confidence rise. They were up to the challenge, even Channing.

They had to be. Otherwise, they might not come back alive.

CHAPTER 13

*amaska*

The huge dog's eyes appeared in Tamaska's mind as she poured a glass of wine back safe in her apartment. Something was amiss since then encounter, but she couldn't work out what. The week at work with her boss harassing her had been long and tiresome.

Tonight was the night of the Blood Moon Night Club celebrations. It was late afternoon, and she still needed to decide what to wear tonight to the club, as well as get someone to come along.

Not just someone: her friend, Tahla. But Tahla didn't surface on a Saturday until after two p.m. It was her own personal rule. So, Tamaska had gotten home, showered, pulled on sweats, and eaten lunch. Now it was time for another ice pack for her ankle and a drink, and then on into the night and hopefully finding what happened to the opal.

That was the plan.

It wasn't much, but it was all she had, so it would have to do.

She walked to the lounge room. A dog barked in the distance outside, bringing that other one into her head once again. She shivered. Those eyes reminded her of a person she'd met, but she didn't know whom.

She could imagine those wolf eyes in perfect detail, their earthy orange color speckled with yellow and gold.

How was that even possible? She'd been a good hundred feet from the dog. Her skin prickled as she sat on the couch and put on the ice pack. She sipped her chardonnay.

Why was she calling them wolf eyes? There were no wolves in Australia, and certainly not in the city of Sydney.

Her fear of dogs surfaced with memories she'd spent a lifetime trying to repress.

The scars on her arms and legs had faded with time, but she usually covered up her limbs anyway. The biggest scar from the dog bite remained on her thigh, and she always knew it was there.

Everything had happened so fast earlier that morning. Then, after the couple had helped her, all Tamaska had wanted to do was to get home.

Why had the dog been watching her? It had been acting like a human, which was weird.

Unsettled by the feeling of being watched when she limped across the grass after getting up, she'd glanced backward and seen the dog again. Something about its eyes caused her to stop and stare back.

In that moment, she wasn't scared of the dog.

That fact perplexed her now, hours after the event since she'd had time to mull it over. It was much better to think about the dog than to torment herself over her job. She was on probation and would have to work her ass off on the next project, promoting cupcakes to prove she deserved her position.

Now, she needed to put her mind to the nightclub.

She'd only heard stories and rumors about it and the goings on in the lower levels where the real kink and weird things happened.

People loved it.

Certain people.

Give her a bar and a good wine to drink and she was happy chatting with friends and checking out the potential male prospects.

She couldn't stop thinking about going to the Blood Moon Nightclub, especially with its reputation of drugs use and prostitution. She just hoped that would help her find the Blood Opal.

The few hours home since the incident in the parklands, she'd been searching online to see what she could find about the Blood Opal. It had been a waste of time. Not even the OzOpals site had much about it, only the information they had for the event.

There was shrouded in mystery, and then there was just seemingly appearing out of thin air with a scant and generic sales pitch.

As for the robbery, if the police did have any leads, they weren't letting on, and Tamaska got the feeling they were stumped. That only reinforced her resolve to go to the night club and conduct her own investigation.

She adjusted the ice pack wrapped in a tea towel on her ankle. She'd checked her arm that still hurt but there wasn't any mark. So damn strange.

With a sigh, she picked up her phone and pressed call on Tahla's number.

Tahla picked up almost immediately.

"Tam, give me all the hot tea."

Tamaska half laughed. "You want bickies with that?"

She could almost hear Tahla roll her eyes.

"Hot tea, as in gossip? Come on, you have to stay up with the lingo if you wanna be cool."

"No tea," Tamaska said. "None at all."

"It sucks." Tahla sighed. "Did you get fired?"

"No. I'm still trying to work out how I dodged that bullet."

"Well, it wasn't your fault. I bet Shadow Protection is furious this happened on their watch. Whoever took it must have been master criminals."

Yeah, or else the security wasn't as good as Tahla made out.

Tamaska closed her eyes. Some of that anger from last night still beat hot and hard in her veins, but with a little space, she could see they hadn't messed up, as much as she wanted to believe that they had.

Kodiak still annoyed her—and made her think the kind of thoughts she shouldn't about him. She hadn't wanted him to leave her side, not way down deep, not where it mattered.

But she hadn't been important. The gem had been, and he'd let it slip through…and there she went again, blaming him.

"They didn't make it sound that way in the papers. With my name in there, it looks like I had something to do with it."

"Only idiots would think that!" Tahla said.

Tamaska smiled. "Actually, I called for a reason."

"If you want me to kick some butt, point me in a direction."

"I was thinking maybe I want to take a break, get my mind off all this. Go out?"

"There's this really sweet new bar that opened on King's Street. Old school cocktails, live jazz band, hot men…?"

Tamaska cleared her throat. "Actually, I was thinking of something more."

"Like what?"

Tamaska turned the ice pack and took a healthy swallow of her drink. "Something new. Edgy. I really need to go clubbing."

"You?" Tahla laughed. "We went like years ago, twice. You didn't like it."

"Well, I've heard things about the Blood Moon Club."

"No way."

"Why not? They have their tenth birthday tonight. It sounds wild."

"That's the problem."

"And it sounds like just the thing I need." Tamaska took another swallow of her drink. "Please?"

Tahla blew out a noisy breath. "There's Pieta's. That's meant to be good, safe."

"I want to go to the Blood Moon."

"That place isn't safe. I'm not going."

Shit. "Well, I'll go on my own. I have a hot dress, and—"

"You can't go by yourself."

"Then come with."

"Fine." The worry was heavy in Tahla's voice. "Only to stop you being sold into slavery or something."

Tamaska forced a laugh. "They don't do that."

"Some people go missing from there. What am I meant to think, Tamaska?"

She'd heard that, too. "People do dumb things, Tahla. And it's really popular."

"Among certain people."

"Lots of people. All types."

"I said fine, but we keep an eye on each other and don't accept drinks from strangers, okay?"

"Okay. You're the best. Look at it like an adventure. I'll meet you at yours around ten."

After she hung up, she sat a little longer and finished her wine, the alcohol warming the cold inside her from going to the Blood Moon Nightclub.

It was popular, though. And they had business cards. Just because some people got up to all sorts of things in there, she wasn't going to. And Tahla would be there.

Surely nothing bad would happen to them, not if they stayed together. They'd already agreed not to leave one another's side. The club had a reputation for only allowing a certain type of customer, though—hot and sexy, showing a bit of skin.

The club was also the place to go if you wanted *any* sort of recreational drugs. Apparently, even the music itself was addictive, with its mesmerizing beats. Then, there were the rumors of nights that ended in orgies, along with other serious kink activities on the lower level. None of that sounded appealing.

Tamaska had no idea what she was going to do once she got into the club, but she was sure it would become obvious. Then she would act. It wasn't the best plan, but she was going with it, regardless.

Perhaps the strange guy who had talked to her at the event before she'd fallen would be there so she could follow if he had possible leads. She was certain he hadn't been on the guest list. It was all too convenient that the pain in her arm, the fall, and then the theft had all happened immediately after she'd spoken with him.

After another glass of wine and dinner, she tried on different outfits and finally settled on a black dress, the hem just covering the old bite mark on her leg. Then she showered, pulled back her hair, dressed, and put on makeup. She slipped on a pair of heels and checked out her handiwork

She turned from side to side in the full-length, wood-framed mirror leaning against the wall in the corner of her bedroom. She had to check out her dress from all angles to ensure it was in sitting in place. The nightclub had a dark reputation, and while the dress was simple, it made her look smoking hot—just the look she was going for.

Security wouldn't say no to her, not with how much skin she was showing and with her gym-toned curves, which were amplified by the dress. The low-cut front displayed her cleavage in a tempting manner.

Tamaska flicked her rich, long brown hair behind her shoulders with two hands, the strands tickling the exposed skin on her back. She was glad she'd persisted in clocking up the weekly hours at the gym.

She put her hands on her hips, admiring her reflection. She released her hair from its band and fluffed it out. It curled loosely around her finished makeup. She'd used lots of black eyeliner and smoky eyeshadow to highlight her eyes.

The low heels she'd put on to help with the ankle

didn't fit the vibe of the dress though. There was only one pair of shoes she could wear with this outfit, her high, strappy heels.

Holding her breath, she put one black shoe on her good foot, then the other on her injured foot.

Her ankle complained sharply about the high heels. Tamaska forced herself to stand still while the discomfort subsided before taking a few practice steps in her bedroom.

The pain could be ignored, especially if she took some more over-the-counter pain relievers like paracetamol. She wasn't going to allow a bad ankle to hold her back from what might be her only chance to find the Blood Opal.

The intercom buzzed in her apartment. Tamaska walked cautiously to the small box on the wall near her kitchen. It was a roomy apartment, one that had hosted many parties in the years she'd lived there.

"I'm here." Tahla's voice sounded through the speaker.

"Coming."

Thank goodness Tahla hadn't bailed.

Tamaska grabbed her black clutch, the one with a long strap, then opened it to ensure her cell, money, and keys were inside. She dropped in a rich red lipstick, then snapped the clasp shut.

A ripple of excitement flowed through her as she locked her door and hurried to the elevator, which, fortunately, was on its way down from the fifth floor.

Stepping inside, she briefly smiled to the few people there and waited as the doors closed.

Finally, the time had arrived where she could take some real action to find the Blood Opal. She would put everything right, keep her job, stop her team from being fired, and show up that stupid security guard, Kodiak. The thought of him made unexpected heat rise to her cheeks. In a different time and place, maybe something could've happened between them.

The elevator jerked to a stop and the doors glided open. Tamaska hurried out, spying Tahla through the glass doors.

Tahla wore a figure-hugging silver sequined dress, her blonde hair that almost reached her waist styled straight. She waited with her arms crossed over her chest, a small handbag hanging off her shoulder.

"About time," Tahla grumbled. "I was thinking about going back home."

Tamaska rolled her eyes at Tahla's dramatic comments. "Like hell you were. Dressing up like this is too much effort to waste."

"True, but I'd rather go down to the Angel Wings Club. Or Pieta's. Why don't we start there?"

"No, we can go to one of those after," Tamaska said, raising her hand to hail a taxi.

One stopped, and she and Tahla slid into the back. Tamaska told the driver where to go and leaned back against the seat, an uncomfortable feeling growing in her belly. It was too late to doubt herself.

She looked out the window at the dark streets to distract herself. It was pretty early to be going to the Blood Moon Nightclub, but already there were drunk partygoers out on the footpath. They stumbled along, clutching at each other, laughing at something that was probably only funny to intoxicated people.

That wasn't going to be her tonight. She was going to stay stone-cold sober. This was about finding information, not partying.

"It's only because of what happened last night, isn't it?" Tahla asked, sitting close to Tamaska as if she needed the reassurance of close proximity.

"What?" Tamaska had been lost in her thoughts, imagining what she might do after arriving at the club.

"This? It's your way of blowing off steam, because you're worried about losing your job. That's all, right?"

Tamaska sighed. She could always trust Tahla to dig deeper, to find her real motivations, except in this instance. The entire situation was too unsettling, plus she didn't want her friend to be trying to put her off from her own investigation to find the gem.

"That's all. I just want to try a new place. Who knows? Maybe I could host an event there someday."

Tahla scoffed. "Yeah, right. I don't believe you."

Tamaska rolled her eyes and sighed. She took Tahla's hand and squeezed it. "Thanks for coming tonight. I owe you."

"Big time." Tahla's expression was filled with anxiety. "Trust me, I'm going to cash in on it, too."

Tamaska smiled. "You might just enjoy yourself tonight, you know."

"Doubt it. Blood Moon isn't my scene, from what I've heard, or yours—even if you think it might be good for potential clients."

Tamaska closed her mouth, stopping herself from correcting her friend. Tahla would go straight home if she knew her real motive. There was no way Tahla would support her in looking for the gem.

"Make sure you stay close to me at all times," she said, pointing at Tamaska in a warning gesture.

"I will." Tamaska meant what she had promised.

"We're here," the taxi driver said as he pulled up behind the line of vehicles dropping patrons off at the club.

Tamaska glanced between the front seats through the windscreen to see a Lamborghini in front.

"You ladies sure you want to be here?" the driver asked. "I can take you somewhere else. I won't even charge you."

"No, this is the right place for us tonight," she said quickly before Tahla could take the driver up on his offer. While Tamaska's stomach twisted and turned, there was no way she was backing out.

She handed over the fare.

"Your choice," the driver said.

"My choice, yes." She opened the door and stepped out on to the footpath. "Fuck."

The line to the front entrance extended through the darkness along the length of the building.

Everyone waiting to go inside was dressed in the skimpiest clothing possible, just short of public indecency. They made her and Tahla's dresses seem modest.

"What?" Tahla asked, slamming the taxi door before moving to stand next to Tamaska.

"There's a bit of a wait to get inside." She pointed to the line.

"We might not make it in." There was distinct hope in Tahla's voice.

Tamaska had come this far already and wasn't about to let a long line steal her big chance to get inside. This could be her only chance to find out who stole the Blood Opal.

"Come on, let's join the queue."

If they were lucky, they might only have to wait an hour. If they were unlucky, though, they might wait all night and still not get in.

A string of swear words echoed onto the street as the security guard turned away a young couple.

"What do you mean we don't fucking cut it?" the woman yelled as she stumbled away.

"Get out of here before you regret it," the security guard said. He was tall, thick-set, and had biceps so wide Tamaska didn't think her hands could fit around them.

She swallowed hard as she walked past the entrance,

past the people who were waiting—mostly tapping on their cellphones—to the back of the line. Getting inside the nightclub might be a bit trickier than she'd thought. Simply showing up might not be enough, not for her and Tahla. They were nobodies in the club's dark scene.

"We can go home. The taxi is just down the road. I can run and get it," Tahla said.

"No, we're waiting."

If that was what it took to get inside and learn about the Blood Opal's theft, then that was what she was going to do—no matter what.

CHAPTER 14

 *odiak*

Kodiak stood in the territory of the vampires, hating being so close to vampires and not being able to do anything about it—like take the damn blood suckers out.

Kodiak's pack hadn't gone looking for them. The shifters knew the club existed, but they left the vampires to their revelries.

They had their own form of treaty. The vamps didn't cause issues too big to ignore in the human world, and didn't bother shifters, and the shifters let them be.

It worked.

Except now they'd made a move of sorts.

Perhaps their pack should've gone after the vampires more aggressively and sought to eliminate them. Then he would've been living a peaceful life instead of standing there in the sharp, cool night, investigating what the hell had brought the vampires to the surface. Whatever the reason, Kodiak didn't want to be kept in the dark. He hoped he would find out more tonight.

He had to. Simple as that.

Kodiak waited across the road from the nightclub, hands in the pockets of his designer jeans, senses on high alert. There was a line to get inside, full of hopeful women in revealing dresses and men in shirts that showed smooth, toned chests. Most of the men wore sharp dress pants and sunglasses, even though it was nighttime. He should have been wearing the suit he'd torn apart when he'd shifted into his wolf form to protect Tamaska.

"Want us to check out back?" Ash asked, dressed in her usual black jeans and tight top. It wasn't at all club attire, but she looked hot, and Kodiak reckoned the guards would let her in.

Kodiak shook his head. "We need a way in."

"The front door?" Shota's sarcasm wasn't lost on him.

Kodiak sighed. "That meathead security guy won't let us in. Too many dicks, not enough chicks as they say. At least in our group. And...look at that line."

"It's long and they're really being hardline." Skoll

whistled low. "I guess birthday bashes come with extra security."

"I'm not spending my night wasting time in a line that wraps around the block." Kodiak folded his arms.

"Around the side, then?" Shota asked, wearing suit pants and a white shirt that opened in the front. They'd all dressed to blend in at the club; well, they would blend in if they ever managed to find a way inside.

Then, hopefully with all the people, Martha's clever sweat-masking spray, sweat, drugs, alcohol, and smoke, they wouldn't be outed as wolves. They only needed enough time to gain some intel, if not to steal back the gem.

That was, if the vampires kept the damn thing there.

First priority was getting in sooner rather than later or not at all.

Kodiak sighed. If he knew vampires as well as he thought he did, then the club probably had multiple entrances.

The nightclub was an old, converted warehouse, a huge wrought-iron building with gridded glass skylights on the roof to stop anyone unauthorized from entering. A series of windows along the building's side had thick black bars. The whole club was painted black and had no signs in front, as if arrogantly assuming everyone already knew it was the coolest place to be.

Coolest, edgiest, most underground of the underground clubs. That was the vibe.

Lights from the party inside flashed staccato through the windows, brilliant white with occasional reds and blues. Sometimes, the flashing would stop, and instead a spotlight would swing around, flashing through the windows in time with the music blasting so loud Kodiak could hear it from the other side of the street.

His ears hurt from the sound and the heavy beat due to his sharp wolf hearing that partly stayed with him in his human form.

The industrial district was a smart choice for clandestine activities, like the club, and there were no neighbors to complain about the noise. The location also added to the sense of danger for the club's human visitors.

He'd bet anything a high percentage of the humans were repeat attendees. They would barely even understand why they were going there. Most of them were probably hooked on vampire poison without even realizing it.

A haze of scented smoke from the front door puffed into the night, lingering in the freezing air whenever anyone was allowed inside. The thick metal door opened briefly, then shut.

There were two lines—one very long roped-off area, and the other for priority guests who simply walked up to the security guards and got it immediately. The priority guests were the vampires. He didn't have to see or smell them to know that.

Only the humans had to wait.

Kodiak inspected the long line of people. Remaining in line was part of the experience. The vampires made their customers wait to heighten their thirst for the activities inside, to make them more willing to fulfill the vampires' blood needs. It disgusted Kodiak, his stomach turning at the mere thought of the vampires' behavior.

If only the shifters had annihilated the vampires instead of allowing a fake truce. Olcan had said it was about balance, all those years ago, part of the supernatural pecking order. If they eliminated the vampires, a bigger enemy would rise up, one that might be harder for them to fight. Nature, as they said, hated a vacuum.

But Kodiak didn't care about Olcan's beliefs as they were just theories, not necessarily based on reality.

Humans, though, had been the wolves' biggest foe even as the wolves protected them from the vampires. Kodiak supposed things could change, just not in a way he could control. After all, no one could control human nature.

He looked at the front of the warehouse.

"We're going to have to split up earlier than I wanted," he said, with a grumbling edge to his deep voice.

They'd gone over their basic plan. All clubs had a secret room which looked out over the floor. Since vampires enjoyed watching the guests to pick out their nightly victims, a secret room had to exist within the walls of Blood Moon. Ash's research suggested as much.

The scheme was a bit risky, because the secret room would likely have the best security. It would also be a good place to hide the Blood Opal, if the vampires kept it here and not in another place, like their lair. Perhaps this was their lair. He didn't know, and that was what he wanted to find out.

The original strategy had been to enter through the front, interspersed through the line. With it so long, it made sense to go together—if they weren't shifters. But there were six of them, too many to go in at once with their wolf scents, even if their scents were masked.

While they all wore the special concoction Martha made for the pack to hide their supernatural scents, there was still a risk a vampire with an excellent sense of smell could detect them. Especially if they tried to enter all at once.

He needed a different plan.

"You think you can all find your own way in?" Kodiak turned around to look at his team.

"Sure," Ash said with a shrug.

"Why not? I love a challenge." Skoll smirked.

The other four nodded.

Kodiak knew he could trust them. That was why he'd chosen these members of the pack for this mission. They were more than capable of handling themselves and followed instructions without question. Kodiak might only be the pack Beta, but he got just as annoyed as Olcan when faced with disobedience.

"Text me when you're inside and start mingling. We need to find the secret room as quickly as possible."

"What are you going to do?" Shota asked.

Channing grinned. "In through the roof?"

Skoll smacked the back of his head. "Fool."

"I'm going in through the front door."

"With that line?" Ash tilted her head. "You're hot, but they prefer the babes. Maybe I should—"

"You worry about yourselves, not me," Skoll said. "I'll be in before you."

Onai laughed. "You think so? She's right. With that line?"

"If I had to line up with you bozos, we'd be in line til dawn, so I'm betting without you weighing me down, I'll be in first."

"A wager?" Skoll looked interested.

"Definitely."

"The usual?" Shota asked.

Channing looked back and forth between them. "What's the usual?"

"You'll find out, little pup." Fern hooked an arm around his waist. "Either way."

"I'll beat you all," Kodiak said.

Turning the mission into a competition the whole team could enjoy, including himself, was always fun

163

and it had that bonus of taking stress off them. Stress that could lead to the wrong sort of attention.

"Reward for the first in, huh?" Onai said. "What if I spot a lone vamp?"

Kodiak laughed. "Fine. You can have extra hunting time, but you still miss out on any reward."

"What's the reward?" Channing asked. "Money?"

"It's always extra freedom and wolf hunting time," Skoll said.

"That sounds great to me," Ash said.

"It's all mine," Shota said. "I'm gonna win this."

"You need to get in before me, otherwise no one will win any freedom," Kodiak added, enjoying the friendly competition. "Or maybe I'll put you losers on extra cleaning duty."

"I'd like to see you try," Skoll said.

Kodiak gave a sharp nod, indicating that they should move out. "See you all soon."

The team members crossed the road, Shota and Ash linking arms as if they were a couple. They played their part well as they stepped out from the shadows.

Kodiak raised an eyebrow, thinking their affection might be more than an act. If that were true, he would need to readjust his team members. Claiming a love interest from within the team was never a good idea. Then again, he might have been wrong about them as he'd never seen anything else to make him think that way.

The other members headed in different directions,

some hanging back to ensure they weren't be seen as a group. To the untrained eye, they didn't look like a team. Thanks to their sleazy attire, they looked like hopeful club patrons.

Kodiak was pleased to see his team taking up the challenge. Not for one moment did he think any of them would fail. That meant he better hurry up and devise a plan to get inside before one of his team members beat him to it.

He looked back at the growing line of hopefuls, all of whom were impatient to get inside the club. Excitement on social media had grown around the nightclub, which advertised the anniversary bash as Sydney's underground party of the year.

The vampires were getting too confident, not hiding as much anymore, he realized. This was a huge warning to Kodiak and the rest of the pack. They were all on high alert, ready for whatever might come.

Kodiak watched from across the street, hidden in the darkness of the night as he took in the scene, looking for anything that might cause a distraction that could give him the chance to slip through the front door.

The security guard at the front of the line was currently sizing up two women. The guard, while a vampire, did look like he had more muscles than brains. Kodiak believed he was the weakest link at the entrance. The other two guards, dressed in suits, looked ready for action, eyes alert as they double-checked the accepted patrons.

Kodiak figured he could get past the big guard, but not the other two. He ran a hand through his hair while he considered his options, his pulse increasing as he felt his chance to get in before the others slipping away.

A movement at the front of the queue caught his attention. This was his chance. Without a plan, he squared his shoulders and strode across the road.

With a rapid sinking sensation in his gut, Kodiak realized why he'd been fixated on the two women at the front of the queue.

What the fuck is she thinking?

Irritation rippled inside of him. The club was not at all safe for a sexy woman like Tamaska, especially since she'd already caught the vampires' interest last night. The vampires inside would suck her dry without any regard for her life. This was the most stupid place she could be. It was too dangerous.

Of course, she had no bloody idea the place was run by vampires. At best, she might have heard the rumors of it being a dangerous place, and where to go to get the 'best' drugs.

He couldn't let her and her friend enter alone.

Without another thought, he crossed the road to join her, to keep her safe.

The guard nodded, then unclipped the red rope sectioning off the front of the queue, letting Tamaska and her friend move towards the front door.

Fuck.

He'd hesitated too long. He quickened his pace, risking getting run over as he rushed to the footpath.

Bang!

Kodiak flinched at the sound, his wolf begging to take charge. He refused to allow that. This wasn't a situation his wolf could improve. He glanced in the direction of the explosion. One of his team members rushed away after creating the perfect distraction by kicking over a garbage bin.

Kodiak could take advantage of that timing.

The commotion intensified as garbage lids rattled on the concrete. Screams came from two men in pain on the ground. The two guards in suits rushed over to investigate. As Tamaska grabbed her friend's hand and dragged her through the door the third guard held open, Kodiak took his chance.

In a flash, he was by their sides, pushing them inside so he would be out of sight.

"Hurry up," he said, hoping he'd moved quickly enough in his human form to fool the dumb-ass guard.

"Hey!" the guard yelled.

"What the hell?" Tamaska said, trying to twist around to look at Kodiak as he maneuvered both women forward along a narrow, dingy corridor towards the party inside.

"Come back here!" the guard yelled, but he couldn't follow since he was now the only one watching the entrance.

Kodiak didn't look back, not wanting the guard to notice his face, not after the commotion. With his hand on Tamaska's arm, her skin making his buzz with desire, Kodiak moved the women along and into where the partying really began.

Her being here was a problem, but one he could handle. He had to stay close to her. She needed his protection, even if she didn't want it. Or realize it.

"Who the hell do you think you are?" Tamaska said as she darted forward and spun around. "Fuck! What are you doing here?"

Her fiery eyes connected with his. Everything in him burst into flames of need and desire. The effect she'd had on him from last night hadn't diminished. No, it had heightened. He sucked in a breath, forcing himself calm down.

Then he took in her outfit properly. Smoking and hot didn't even begin to describe her.

"I could ask you the same question." He stepped closer to her. "This isn't the type of nightclub for you two."

Tamaska narrowed her eyes. "You're not on the books now, Kodiak. And the fifties passed us decades ago, so unhand me and find some other woman to force your old-fashioned ways on. I can take care of myself."

"I'm all for going home," said the blonde woman next to Tamaska. Then she ran her gaze over him. "Or he can get all old-fashioned on me."

"Go home. I'm staying," Tamaska said, glaring at her friend. "And hands off."

"Fine, then, but first tell me who this hottie is." The blonde smiled. "Since I have to keep my hands to myself."

"I just meant…" Tamaska rolled her eyes and huffed angrily. "He's trouble."

"I like trouble."

"Not from him. He's the guy who got the Blood Opal stolen, Tahla, so stay away from him."

"Shh," hissed Kodiak. "Don't mention the gem here. You don't know what you're getting yourself into."

"What do you know? Is it here? Is the person who stole it here?" Tamaska asked, her eyes flaring with anger.

"Didn't you just say he took it?" Tahla frowned.

"I didn't take it. I'm looking for it, like I promised. You still haven't answered my question." The longer he talked to Tamaska, the thinner his patience wore and the worse his desire to take her became.

"I'm here blowing off steam. It's been a stressful time."

Kodiak knew she was lying. Then, it dawned on him that she was looking for the gem as well. How did she even know to come here? What information had she found?

He grabbed her arm and yanked her towards him. She pushed back, fighting his vise-like hold on her.

"What do you know? Tell me now," he said, drawing her in and up against him.

He tried not to think of how good she felt, all that softness and heat, that sweet, fresh scent of hers cutting through the stench of the place.

He wanted to bury his face in her throat and breathe her in, maybe taste her skin while he was there.

"Let me go." She squirmed, but all she did was push up closer to him. Her breath came unevenly.

Those sparks between them were threatening to turn into raging flames. Everything in his body tightened as he held her against him.

"Not until you give me answers." His gaze dropped her mouth; it was luscious and appealing with the red lipstick. Not that it hadn't been before. The lipstick just added an extra jolt of exaggerated sexual pull to her. "You have no idea what really goes on here." "You're just being dramatic. It's a sleazy nightclub, like any other."

"Like fucking hell it is. You could lose your life here."

"The only person threatening me here is you." She gave a small tug on her arm, but it was weak and she stayed pressed against him, like she wanted that as much as him.

Wanted and didn't all at the same time.

She was pure desire, and every second was harder to deny that fact.

She looked at his mouth and licked her lips, then

she raised her eyes to his. The bolt of need raced to his cock, making him hard.

They were surrounded by people, but as far as he was concerned, they were alone. He loosened his hold and she stayed where she was.

Damn, it was the hottest thing.

She fought like a she-wolf.

He bet she fucked better.

"I am not. I'm protecting you," Kodiak said softly.

"And if I don't want you to?" She put her hand on his chest and it burned like a brand.

"That's too bad. It's my job."

"I didn't hire you to protect me." She swayed a little closer and those fine breasts brushed against them, her hand and their clothes the only thing keeping them from touching skin on skin.

He bet she tasted like fine whiskey.

"No, you didn't," he said, dipping his head to her ear, "but here I am, and we both know this is something deeper than that."

"No, we don't," she said, but her voice wobbled.

Shit, he couldn't stand here like this, getting hotter and more turned on by the second.

"Fine, then." He abruptly let her go. "You'll regret being here."

He stepped back, needing the distance, needing to let the crowd flow into his senses once more. She was dangerous, the way she could make him forget everything but her.

"Doubt it."

Kodiak hoped against all odds she'd step around him, head for the door, and leave this place. His gut roiled as she turned and slipped into the crowd.

She was staying, then. If only he could tell her the truth. Then she would go.

As he reflected on the confidence and determination she'd shown while standing up to him, he reconsidered. She was the sort of woman who didn't mind a bit of danger.

Is that why I'm drawn to her?

His cell buzzed once, then again, refocusing his attention. He looked at his phone.

His team members were finally inside the club. Inside, his wolf surged but he kept it down. He wanted to yell at them how they needed to tighten their training. He wanted someone to take his rising temper out on, but there wasn't anyone. And he didn't know why he was so fucking angry.

Yes, he did.

It was Tamaska. What really fueled his temper was seeing hot, sexy Tamaska heading away from him and knowing he had no way to stop her. He was going to have to watch her while looking for the secret room, and that wasn't going to be easy.

He just hoped nothing inappropriate would happen to her. Otherwise, he'd never forgive himself.

CHAPTER 15

amaska

Tamaska pushed through the crowd of dancing people, getting as far away from Kodiak as she could. How dare he tell her to go home? Who did he think he was? It wasn't like he was her boyfriend, and even if he was, he had no right to tell her what to do. She wasn't the sort of woman who blindly obeyed a man. Especially one she didn't know. Or like.

She was attracted to him, that was a different story, and one she didn't want to read.

Did she?

The way he'd looked at her, like he wanted to devour her, had lit a fire in her. She'd pressed up against him, even when he'd loosened his hold and she could have easily got away.

"Wait up, Tamaska," Tahla called from behind her, over the beat of the music.

Tamaska slowed down and turned around, glancing back she couldn't see Kodiak. A shiver coursed down her spine, and a sense of loss pooled in her gut now that she couldn't see his deep eyes and strong body. How could she have turned him down?

Wonder darted along her veins.

How on earth had she come up with the strength to do that when she'd wanted to rise up and place her mouth on his and see—

She drew a sharp breath.

Her anger cooled, but not enough to forgive him for his brutish behavior.

How could he demand to know why she was there, when he clearly knew something about the Blood Opal's location?

He must, because why else was he here?

Try as she might, she couldn't fit him into someone who frequented a club like this one.

A small smile twisted on her mouth.

Not unless that girl was her.

Her heart thudded hard and wild at that thought.

They might not like each other but the tension and attraction couldn't be denied. When they got near, it seemed like they could create enough electricity to light up the city.

"What's gotten into you?" Tahla asked as she pushed past two dancing guys. She stumbled, and one of them caught her.

"Hey, beautiful, stay with us," he said.

Tamaska flicked a glance at them, irritated. She wanted to get to the bar and get a drink, so she had something to hold and then look around. She kept walking.

"Ugh, these guys are the worst. I'll buy us some drinks and we can relax."

When Tahla didn't answer, Tamaska stopped and turned.

Tahla was swaying woozily. The guy had an arm around her and grinned down at her, leaning in. Tahla said something. His friend smiled and came up behind Tahla, closing her in between them.

"Not tonight, boys," Tamaska said, taking her friend's hand. Tahla resisted, and Tamaska pulled harder. "Come on, Tahla. He isn't your type."

"I'll be back," she said, slurring, as Tamaska dragged her away.

Tamaska shook her head. "What's gotten into you?"

"Nothing." Tahla looked back over her shoulder and smiled.

Tamaska pushed her forward. "So, you want to stay, then?"

"Of course." Tahla blinked blankly at her. "Why wouldn't I? Have you seen the talent here?"

"You took something, didn't you?" Tamaska asked,

continuing to drag Tahla through the crowd, determined to get away from the guys that had trapped her friend in some sort of psychological web.

"No, I haven't." Tahla's face pinched, like she was trying not to cry. "Why would you say that? I just...I don't know. I told you I didn't want to come here."

Tamaska pursed her lips, not wanting to upset her friend. *I'm just going to have to keep a closer eye on her.* That wasn't what she wanted out of the night.

"I know," Tamaska said, "but we're here now, and I didn't like the look of those guys."

"But you could plaster yourself on that hottie earlier?" Tahla took a step towards the dance floor. "I felt good dancing with them. I want to go again."

"No, you don't. We just got here."

Tamaska looked around, overwhelmed. How the fuck was she meant to find anything in this nightclub to help her get the Blood Opal back? Or at least find out what had happened to it. What if she was completely wrong? Doubt crept into the corners of her mind.

"But I do!"

"We'll get a drink." Tamaska kept moving through the people, holding Tahla, towards the bar.

"I reckon we should relax a bit, and dancing would get us to do just that."

Tahla pulled free and ran back to the dance floor, leaving Tamaska no option but to follow.

She tried to grab Tahla. "What are you doing now?"

"Dancing! Can't you feel the beat? Fuck, it's…it's…" Tahla spun around, laughing. "It's intoxicatingly good. The best thing I've ever experienced."

Tamaska sighed. Maybe a dance would help her unwind. She would let the beat carry away all her worries, and fuck, she had plenty of those. She inched closer to Tahla and let her body move in time with the heavy bass beats coming from the lit-up stage to her right.

A DJ was busy flicking switches, controlling the music with a serious expression on his face. Tahla was right. The music and the atmosphere were really indescribable, compared to what she'd experienced in nightclubs before.

"See?" Tahla said. "It's the best way to get our legs moving, after standing for over an hour outside."

Tamaska laughed, feeling her spirit lighten. She allowed her mind and body to be further swept up with the beat of the music. She felt sexy, confident, and free. It was as if she'd become weightless, simply from dancing.

She spun around, finding it easy to move with the music. Even her ankle no longer hurt. It was as if time had faded away and they were all caught in some sort of warp. All that mattered was the rhythm of the music, the sense of being alive, and the arousal from all the dancing patrons' pheromones released as they gave themselves over to the music.

She smiled at Tahla, glad her friend was having a good time even though she hadn't wanted to come.

Sweat beaded on Tamaska's skin, but she ignored it, continuing to dance, flowing with the notes as if she was an extension of the music, an instrument being played in a way that brought her close to an organismic sensation. She'd never experienced this outside of a bed, or with strangers. Fuck, it was good, and she wanted more.

She closed her eyes, dancing. Then, it was as if a small voice in her head reminded her why she was here.

What was wrong with her? She was wasting time dancing when she needed to be searching for information. Her eyes flicked open, and she stopped moving.

She was dancing alone in that sea of people.

Where the fuck had Tahla gone? Panic rose in Tamaska's chest, and her stomach clenched tight with fear.

Hadn't I only closed my eyes for a moment? Or was it longer? She couldn't be sure.

Tamaska stumbled. Someone caught her by the arm, stopping her from falling to the floor and being trampled.

"Careful." A man younger than Tamaska smiled at her.

His eyes were fully black, and she felt herself getting lost in an enticing darkness. She'd felt similarly when that strange man had talked to her at the Shangrila, before the theft.

Her skin prickled with a mix of fear and delight.

"Thanks," she stammered, righting her footing so she stood facing the man.

"Want to dance?" he asked, moving in closer, his body nearly touching hers.

She could feel the heat radiating from him as he lowered his chin, letting her look deeper into his eyes.

"I… I…no." Tamaska wasn't sure why her mind felt so blurred.

She hadn't drunk anything since arriving or swallowed any pills. She ran her hands up her arms. Had someone pricked her with something? She had been so lost in the music, she couldn't be sure.

Maybe I'm tired?

It had been the biggest two days of her life since the gem had been stolen.

Or was that one day? Last night it went missing. Last night. She clung to that, even as it slipped away again.

It had been such an emotional rollercoaster ride and maybe she was starting to fall apart. Then, there had been the weird incident in the park and the dog watching her. Her fear of dogs had surfaced all day as she'd worked out how to search for the Blood Opal.

Finally, there had been the encounter with Kodiak, who she'd never wanted to see again. No wonder her mind was clouding up.

Kodiak.

His name in her head gave her strength.

Kodiak.

I have to get out of here.

Tamaska tried to move, but the man inched closer to her, looking her up and down, soaking her up with his eyes. Like he could get inside her, like he could control her.

She went to step away, but he slid an arm about her and locked eyes with her. This wasn't like with Kodiak. It was different, like a blanket coming down on her.

She shivered with delight, unable to move away, weirdly warming to the idea of whatever fun she might have with the guy.

He was fucking hot, with dark hair shiny from styling wax, a clean-shaven face, and a dark shirt unbuttoned to show off his chest. Her fingers tingled with the urge to touch him.

She sighed, losing her resolve and the ability to say no.

"You've got great ankles," he said.

What did he just say?

Her...ankles?

A spark in her mind suggested that comment was weird, but the spark quickly went out as he pointed to her injured foot. "Especially that one."

Tamaska shivered, thinking that somehow in the low light he'd managed to see her scratches. She had to get away, but it was as if he had some sort of hold on her.

"You look pale. You've been dancing for so long. Here, have a sip of my drink." He held up a plastic cup with a clear liquid and ice inside.

Tamaska went to shake her head. Instead, she found herself opening her mouth, wanting to taste the drink. It was as if he could manipulate her mind as he moved the cup closer to her mouth.

Her lips parted, eager for the coolness of the ice on her tongue. The plastic pressed ever so gently down on her bottom lip as he tipped the cup.

She trembled, not knowing what she was going to taste. She smelled a hint of alcohol.

Her eyes locked with his, and the darkness seemed to embrace her in a coldness that was pleasant and invigorating after all that dancing. She entered a different sort of trance as the liquid hit her tongue. A small part of her mind remained lucid, and thoughts rushed to the surface, battling for her attention.

What the fuck am I doing? And where the fuck is Tahla?

How could she have forgotten about her friend so easily? Tamaska was ashamed of herself.

She had no idea how she'd gotten so lost since arriving at the nightclub. Then, she swallowed a small mouthful of the liquid flowing into her mouth.

A soothing heat eased down her throat and into her stomach, extending into every part of her body.

She wanted more.

CHAPTER 16

odiak

Kodiak couldn't hold back anymore.

Whatever was in the liquid the vampire was giving her was going to fuck with her, and he had to put a stop to it. Now. After being here for what seemed like hours, he'd made no progress in finding the secret room.

Tamaska was more important.

Kodiak rushed through the crowd, pushing others out of the way without a care. A few people cursed at him, but he ignored them. He needed to get to Tamaska before she consumed too much of the vampires' drug and was lost to him forever.

It pained his heart to see her throat move as she

swallowed. Without thinking, he crashed forward and pushed the cup out of the way. He was glad most of the liquid splashed onto the floor instead of into Tamaska's mouth. She screamed in surprise, her eyes glassy and unfocused until he looked into them. He sighed with relief as they cleared and she zeroed in on him, desire sparking high. He grabbed her hand and drew her behind him.

"Fuck off," the guy said. "She's mine."

"She's not," Kodiak said, squaring off with the man.

"She is, and there are rules here. You look new, so maybe I can excuse you this once if you fuck off now." The guy narrowed his eyes at Kodiak.

Kodiak stood still, his mind scrambling to remember the rules that Ash had gone over with the team. It didn't help that he expected to be identified as a wolf any moment now.

"You asked for it, then." The guy shook his arm, and a small knife dropped down from inside his shirt.

Shit. Kodiak needed to end this here and now without too much attention. So, he did something he didn't want to do.

"Amdis has laid claim on her," Kodiak spat, hating the words.

The man froze, staring at him, mouth slightly agape.

Amdis was the vampire leader, and the only one who could lay a claim like this on a human. A vampire would only use the name with seriousness and power, but it was better than bloodshed right now.

If that happened, no amount of masking would hide who and what he was from a vampire.

"Why the fuck is he sending you?" The vampire glared. "I don't even know you."

"Last-minute change," Kodiak said, standing confident. "He can't keep his eyes off this one."

"I can see why. Fuck that, I'm not touching her again. Amdis can see everything down here." The vampire glanced up to an area that looked like part of a closed-in platform jutting out from the second level.

There had been a similar structure on the other side of the club, but now Kodiak knew which side was more important.

Looking closer, Kodiak noticed the dark glass. It would be the perfect spot for the leader of the vampires to look out and keep an eye on things.

Maybe tonight will end up just fine.

Kodiak tightened his hold on Tamaska and turned, pulling her behind him as he headed towards the dark glass. He ignored her protests as she tried to tug him backwards and kept moving as far away from the vampire as possible.

Once out of sight, he dragged her over to a less crowded area in the left corner of the room.

"I told you coming here wasn't a good idea, yet you were so bloody determined to stay. You have no idea what was in that liquid." He turned on her, ready to give her one hell of a lecture. He was angry that she'd put her precious life in danger.

But holy fuck did she look good.

"It was just a drink, Kodiak."

"No, it wasn't. And you, as usual, got yourself tangled up in trouble."

"I wasn't in any trouble," she said with a huff as she swayed, poking him in the chest, her finger a brand on him.

"Like hell you weren't."

What did those lips of hers taste like? Maybe he could kiss some sense into her, or at least get her out of his system. But he doubted a simple kiss would be enough. Just like he doubted a kiss with her would be simple. "I thought you were smart, but your stubborn-ness could land you in deep water."

"The only thing that's trouble and getting me in deep water is you."

He sucked in a breath as her words zinged through his blood, sending a great deal of it to his cock.

Was she...flirting?

Was he?

Shit.

And where the hell was her damn friend?

He hated to think about where the blonde might be or what trouble she might be in. It had been too hard to keep an eye on them both. Additionally, there were reports from his team, and he had to keep an eye on them. He needed to message them that he'd found the secret room. But first, he needed to deal with Tamaska.

"Fuck. I should tie you up," he said.

"Kinky."

"Then at least you won't be able to land yourself in trouble."

"Kinky," she said again, the remnants of whatever the vampire had been doing to her still lingering.

He could imagine tying her up in some kink role play game with her and exploring her body, learning all the things that made her tick, made her hot, made her pant and moan and come.

He could have her at his mercy like that, a willing captive, one he could tease with his mouth and lips and tongue. He could drive her to the edge of ecstasy over and over but never quite letting her reach that sweet nirvana.

And then he could do it all again, this time thrusting into her, using her mouth, her pussy, her—

Fuck.

He growled, moving his free hand through his hair as he pushed his mind from those thoughts and tried to think of a way to look after her and get his team to the secret room. He took a moment, breathing deep, getting himself back under control.

Then he met her gaze.

Her eyes were full of desire.

It pushed the fires and those X-rated images right back into his head.

She blinked, her eyes clearing, and now she looked back at him with innocence, along with a heat he was finding hard to ignore.

No wonder a vampire had tried to coerce her.

The conflicting emotions generated a primal desire in his body that he'd been trying to overlook ever since he'd met her.

"I can look after myself," she said. "Just stop fucking thinking you're saving me, or protecting me, or whatever the fuck it is you think you're doing."

Her lack of gratitude didn't surprise him. She was human.

What the fuck did she know? Despite her humanity, he wanted her. She was fire and sin and sweetness hidden in all that bluster.

She was like nothing he'd ever met or known before.

"I think," he said, trailing a finger over those lush lips, "I'm saving you from yourself."

"Who's going to save me from you?"

He laughed and it was like a sigh as the awareness between them burned bright and compelling. "Or me from you."

"I don't need you." She whispered so only heard because of his wolf hearing and his special connection to this woman.

Her words were soaked in a longing he more than understood.

"You do," he said. "And more than that, you want me. You hate it, but you do. Deny it."

Her lashes lowered and her cheeks turned pink. "I'm going."

"Maybe," he said when she didn't move, "you do want me to tie you up. Like that woman behind us?"

She turned, going still as she took in the sight of a woman, clad only in panties, tied to a pole. Her head was thrown back in ecstasy as three men—vampires—circled her. One licked her throat, another took a breast to roll and pinch her nipple, and the third slid his hand into her underwear.

The woman's thighs parted, and his hand moved as he fingered her.

Tamaska let out a small moan. That sound, full of a lust that slipped along Kodiak's veins, turned the heat up in him.

He came up behind her, sliding a hand around her middle, splaying it out in a way that claimed her to anyone who glanced their way.

"Of course, Tamaska, when I tie you up, there's just going to be you and me. I don't share."

She leaned her head back against his chest, and he let the fantasy she was take him. It was as wild and thrilling a trip as any drug could be.

"We will never do that," she said.

"You want that. Or maybe you just want it skin on skin and nothing at all stopping us. Is that it? No rope?

No kink? Just you, begging me to take you in every way you can think of."

"Yes…" She moaned, clasping her hands on him. One ran along his thigh, the other on his ass as she ground hers against his cock. "Yes…no. No."

"Lying isn't your forte, Tamaska." He couldn't fuck her. Could he? "It's a fact."

"You want to own a woman, is that it?"

"I already own you." The words were out before he could stop them. He said them low, but she heard, because she went still.

"What do you want from me? Isn't it enough you ruined my career? Do you want to keep hurting me, is that it?"

He bent his head, moving his mouth on her ear, and he breathed that wax flower scent of hers in deep, even as he tightened his hold on her.

"I'd never hurt you, Tamaska."

"You say that, but there are more ways to hurt than the physical."

"I wouldn't hurt you," he said, but that was a lie because they couldn't be together, no matter what this thing was that beat and breathed between them.

"Let me go." Her words were a plea.

Kodiak did something he never thought he could: he let her go and nudged her from him.

She snapped a glance at him, and resentment shone in those depths, but then she nodded. "Thank you."

"Tamaska—"

"I'm not leaving," she said. "So don't even start again."

"I'm protecting you, that's it. I might want you, and you might want me, but we're not going to do anything about that."

She licked her lips and took a step towards him. "And if I do want to do something about it…?"

"You're a smart woman. You'll do the right thing."

"And what's that, Kodiak?"

Was the poison of the vampire still stirring up the lust in her? No, that lust had been there since the moment their eyes had met last night. But perhaps it was making her say the things on her mind when she preferred to hide behind insults and hate.

She took another step towards him and splayed her hand on his chest. He could barely think. Releasing her had taken most of his self-restraint and he wasn't a man built for such things.

When he wanted, he took.

But she was human and…

Hell. She looked at him like she wanted to rip off his clothes and fuck him here and now.

Her eyes glittered with carnal lust, like she wanted to strip back all humanity's constructs and get down to the bare boned honest business of sex.

As the music's beat built, thrumming with the desire in his veins, the last of his control snapped.

He caught her hand and lifted it, without breaking eye contact. He took two of her fingers into his mouth and sucked on them, letting his tongue slide over them, before biting down. She moaned, that low-throated sound that set him ablaze and made the desire within him combust.

This was inevitable. It was fate.

He released her fingers and drew her in. She sighed and wrapped her arms around his neck, rising on her toes so her mouth was a whisper from him.

His breath caught and he lowered his lips, catching hers. It was a taste, a nibble. She was hot and soft.

A groan broke free from his lips before he kissed her again. This time, she met him, her mouth as needy as his, as savage.

It was like an eternity of lust burst from them. The kiss was a carnal, dark exploration and he couldn't get enough.

He wanted it all.

Now.

He didn't give a fuck they were in the vampire club. He didn't give a damn about the opal.

Right then, the only dangerous thing was not to continue.

He pulled her in hard against him and kissed her once more.

This could cost him his life, and hers.

And he didn't give a damn.

CHAPTER 17

*amaska*

Tamaska melted into Kodiak. His strength and heat enveloped her, sparking her desire. His hardness pressed against her low belly, which drove her to want him even more.

He tasted like nothing she'd ever experienced before. He was pure erotic darkness, like running free, naked and pagan. His mouth was both hard and soft; his tongue demanded and cajoled. His hard body she plastered against was pure artistry.

The beat of the music echoed in her soul, intensifying her desires. A hungry lust burst from her as her lips crushed against Kodiak's.

Fuck, he tastes good. She wanted more. She pushed him to deepen the kiss, loving how he allowed her to.

He wrapped his arms around her, drawing her closer. One hand tangled in her hair, the other sliding down her back to cup her ass, to bring her in so his hardness pressed into her. Oh, he did feel big. She wanted it all. She wanted him.

He tightened his fingers in her hair, the tug riding straight through her nervous system to her clit as he angled her head to go deeper with the kiss.

The heat spiked, burning away thought and inhibition. All she wanted was in her arms.

Sensations swirled as he left her mouth, biting and kissing down her throat. He sucked at her pulse point, and she gasped in burning need. She took his hair in her hand and pulled his head up. Those dark eyes sparked with savage lust and desire, a feral grin on his face as their gazes clashed.

Tamaska shoved him back and he went, dragging her up on him. He took her mouth, the kiss a wild mating of heat and naked desire.

Her entire being throbbed.

Darkness came about them as they moved under the stairs and against a heavy softness. A curtain.

They both scrabbled at the velvet, pulling it back, as their mouths kept coming together in hotter and hotter kisses.

She pushed the curtain free. He picked her up in his

arms and shuffled back into the space as she wrapped her legs around his hips.

Tamaska threw back her head, offering her throat to his hot and hungry mouth as the heat and steel of his erection thrust against her panties.

It was better than any sex she'd had, and they were clothed. Christ. She dug her fingers into him as she ground against him. If it was like this when they just touched, what would it be like with him thrusting into her?

She needed to know. She needed him.

They tumbled down onto a couch and she was splayed over him.

Their eyes met, and he gave her a wolfish grin, one that sent an arrow of excitement straight to her core.

She dipped in and brushed her mouth with his. He caught her bottom lip between sharp teeth and drew his tongue over it, making her moan low.

He released her but his hand was back in her hair, the other at her waist, holding her against him.

"Where are we?" She slurred the words, not really that interested as she glanced up. They must be in a private room, hidden under the upstairs balcony, which extended out into the revamped warehouse.

"Wrong question."

The growl of his voice raced along her senses, and she deliberately squirmed down against him. "What's the right one?"

"Why are we talking and not doing?"

"You think you're in control?"

His hand on her waist slid down then up along her thigh. He slipped his fingers between them, his gaze locked on her, a kind of triumph in those eyes that was pure and unadulterated sex.

Then he ran a finger along the gusset of her panties, sending shockwaves of need through her.

"I know so." His fingers moved to the beat of the music, up and down along her slit until she almost lost her mind.

Then he took his fingers away.

"I don't think so," she said. "I am."

"Show me."

Music, playing in the main area, heavy with bass beats, filtered into the small room. A long red couch sat against the wall and two small armchairs were arranged on either side. The rooms were set up for patrons to use as they pleased. A hint of privacy along with the fast beat of the music provided an atmosphere of pure sex with just that right hint of naughtiness. That they could be caught added to the thrill.

Tamaska undulated on his lap, the hardness of his erection pushing at the apex of her thighs. She was hot and wet as she teased him. He growled, as she reached down to take hold of him through the jeans. Damn, he was big. She continued her game with her hand and with her pussy, feeling him grow harder and larger as she did so.

Her head dropped backwards, and she closed her eyes, enjoying the intense ripple of white edged desire that coursed through her. She let go of his cock and held him tight around his neck, leaning backwards, wanting to feel him move between her legs, using just her pussy as stimulation.

His hand came down on her hips and he moved her hard over him. She groaned with delight as waves of pleasure coursed through her, moisture pooling between her legs in anticipation of what was to come. She held back, not giving in to what she really wanted, which was to have him inside of her. She wanted to see how much pleasure they could build between them before it was too much, and the tension exploded. She could endure a good tease and sensed that he could, too.

He adjusted his hold on her, to allow one hand to dip into the low neckline of her dress to cup her breast. He tweaked her nipple, sending a thunderbolt of pleasure through her. She nearly begged him to fuck her. Sounds of pleasure came from her lips as she pushed her breasts upwards, wanting him to feel her more.

He laughed low and kissed her throat, then pulled down the front of the dress to expose her breasts for his full access. He pinched her nipple playfully, and she gasped as a burst of desire spiked in her, arrowing down to right between her legs. She pushed into his hard cock, still trapped in the confine of his jeans, arching her body with pleasure as he played her nipple into a tight, hard nub.

Her mind whirled, the tension high enough to make her want to beg for more. Instead, she allowed herself to rise, stretching her torso towards him. His hand moved to her back to hold her, and his mouth latched onto her breast, biting down on the soft tissue. His tongue flicked her hard nipple, stimulating her to a level she'd never reached before.

Oh God, she could come from this alone...

To keep herself steady, she tightened her thighs either side of his while his mouth explored her breast. She ground her hips into him, trying to get him to lose control first as the lustful heat built around them. Instead, she fast felt herself coming.

She slid her hands down his chest, enjoying the toned feel of his muscles through his shirt. He released her nipple, then found her lips and his musky heat burst into her mouth.

Inside the tight space between their bodies, she moved her hands down to find the top of his jeans and began to unbutton them. The heat snapped at her skin as she brushed against his hardness, trying to push the clothing away. He held her tight and leaned back a little to give her room. She finally managed to undo the last buttons, releasing his hardened cock for her to wrap her fingers around.

He moaned into the kiss as she tightened her grip. Then, she started to move her hand up and down his cock, right to the tip, running her thumb over the silken, broad head.

Kodiak growled into her mouth and his cock swelled even more as she pushed down with her fingers, then up.

He broke the kiss. "Fuck, Tamaska, you keep doing that and it's going to be over before it begins."

She laughed, feeling wild and free, a sexual goddess, one who could command this man with a touch. "I thought you were stronger than that."

"I didn't know you were a witch."

"Goddess to you."

"Then that makes me your God."

Words kept tumbling and they just stoked the fires, nonsensical as they were.

He kissed her again, and she met him, their tongues tangling as the heat built. She had to hand it to him. He had kept her safe during their fall to the couch earlier, balancing the thrill and spice of that danger with a level of ease and control that surprised her. It turned her on, knowing he could keep her safe, lead the way, and keep it all going, upping the ante every step.

Her heart squeezed, wild and elated feelings whirling inside of her. Feelings of heat and need and unstoppable desire she should have pushed away. That wasn't happening, she reminded herself as she eased her legs farther apart to shove herself against his hardness.

His lips met hers once more, this time with more

urgency than before. She matched his movements, showing him she was just as eager as he was.

Music from the DJ filtered to them, the beats quickening with their desire, finding a fast pace. The heavy beats of the bass drove her to let go of any sense of propriety, of control, of anything that told her what she was doing with Kodiak was something to avoid.

She didn't care. This needed to be brought to completion, and she knew he was the man to bring her to the heights of an orgasm like no other.

She pressed down into him, loving the sounds of pleasure escaping from lips that matched her own. She kept moving on him, a charged dance or eroticism that melded with the music.

They might have been in their own space, far away from here. Right then, she didn't care about anything but him. She needed him inside her, to ease the ache that throbbed through her body.

He slid his hands up her thighs and under the skirt of her dress, pushing it up around her waist. There, he danced his fingers over her inner thighs and along the line of lace on her panties.

Tamaska drew in a sharp breath as he slipped his fingers under the edge of her panties and touched her bare, wet flesh.

Pleasure exploded through her, and she cried out, almost coming there and then. He laughed against her mouth as he pushed his fingers into her fleshy folds.

"Oh, God."

The invasion of him inside her was unexpected but needed. It was everything she could ever want and never imagined.

He groaned, starting a rhythm, moving down and kissing her breast as she kept that motion going on his cock.

"Holy fuck." He lifted his head and kissed her hard. He shifted the now wet material of her panties to the side. "I need to be in you."

"Yes…"

He adjusted their position, and using his hand on hers, aligned himself against her naked flesh, then thrust his cock inside her. A sharp scream of pleasure echoed from her as the burst of sexual delight coursed through her.

Kodiak stretched and filled her as he pushed all the way into her, bottoming out. They aware they both breathed hard and uneven. His eyes found hers and the feral need and passion glittering there sent an erotic thrill racing through her.

He might have power over her.

But she had just as much over him.

He wanted her. The ferocity of that sunk into her bones.

She wrapped her arms around his neck, pulling herself closer to him, his arms tight around her waist. Their lips danced in time with the quickening beats of the music. He thrust up into her, and she pushed down. It was sublime. Every time he pushed back in, she moaned from the rightness, from how damn good he felt inside her.

Her muscles gripped his hardness, heightening the tension between them. Together, they moved with renewed urgency towards the peak, each pushing the other for more.

The sex was wild, fast, urgent. It could have been just them in the world or they could have been in a crowd in the middle of the day. Right then, she didn't care. All that mattered was him in her, and the building sweet-edged tension.

She could feel herself reaching her orgasm. Her breath quickened, and then the ecstasy burst through her like a bolt of lightning. A long sound of pleasure came from her lips as she flew, the bliss flooding every part of her as he spilled his seed inside of her, the pulses of his cock drawing out her orgasm as he reached his own.

With a sigh, she paused, savoring the moment as their lips reluctantly completed the kiss, then parted.

She smiled and opened her eyes to meet his, seeing the reflection of the contentment buzzing through her. This was a hell of an afterglow. His eyes were soft and gentle. Then, there was a flicker, and she thought she was looking into the eyes of a dog. Her body chilled as her fear surfaced.

Kodiak reached up and pushed a strand of her

brown hair off her face. The touch of his fingertips sent ripples of delight through her, sending away the bad memories. Somehow, he managed to reassure her with one simple action.

What the fuck was it about him that caused her to lose control? She rested her forehead against his as they both eased down from the bliss they'd created.

As Tamaska floated back down to reality, she began to remember where they were—on a couch, in a darkened room with hundreds of people on the other side of the curtain.

Her entire being vibrated with sexual desire. Despite that, a hint of anxiety welled inside her. What had she done, opening herself like that to Kodiak?

Fuck.

She'd never done that before. She blamed the sips of alcohol and the music. There was something about this club that begged people to lose control. She'd succumbed to the allure, like a hungry fish seeking an easy meal. She'd gotten hooked on the line.

This wasn't like her at all. While it had been fucking fantastic with Kodiak, it was time to let her lustful fantasy go. She had a job to do. She needed to find the Blood Opal, not get fucking laid.

She pushed away and off him, with a groan of desire and regret. She stood, shimmied the hem of her dress down to her thighs, and adjusted the neckline so she wasn't exposing herself any longer.

How could I have done this?

Kodiak buttoned up his designer jeans. Regret whirled inside her mind, but there was way more pleasure and satisfaction. He was fucking hot, totally worth the ride and the risk of doing something reckless like having sex in a club.

Now, it was time to get herself together.

Fuck. What had happened to Tahla?

Tamaska ran her fingers through her hair, worried and guilty. She'd been too busy, too wrapped up in this man to honor the friend code. She'd failed to look out for Tahla. Anything could have happened while she'd been... seeking pleasure.

"I have to go."

"Is that it?" he asked, looking at her with an intensity that caused her skin to prickle. "Just you have to go?"

"It was good," she managed to say, as her cheeks flushed with heat.

"Good?"

"Fine, fucking good." It had been better than good. It had been off the charts phenomenal, and she wanted to do it all again, this time slow.

What was she thinking?

She had to return to reality, find Tahla, and get out of there before anything else happened. The search for the gem would have to wait. Tahla had been right; it had been too dangerous to come to the Blood Moon, but not in the way either of them had thought.

"That's better."

"I'll see you around." She turned to go, but it was more difficult than she thought.

It was just one-off sex. Nothing more, right? Then why was it as if something more had happened, something she couldn't explain?

A heaviness pulled at her, begging to go back to him, to let him wrap his arms around her and forget everything. But she wouldn't allow herself to give in this time.

She forced herself towards the velvet curtain. She had to get the fuck away from him before something else occurred. Her sexual desires seemed to get out of control whenever he was around. He screamed "lone wolf," the type of player to fuck, then run away from. But she didn't want to run from him. She wanted to run to him.

That was why she needed to get the hell as far from him as she could.

Tamaska pulled the velvet curtain out of the way.

Then the curtain moved further, pulled from her hand, and a man stood there with a smile that chilled her. Instead of pushing past him, Tamaska stepped backwards with a gasp of surprise. Fear slid down her back like a snake with evil purpose.

"There you are." He smiled, but it didn't warm her.

It was *him*—the man she'd been talking to before Kodiak interrupted. But why would he want to find her?

A chill seeped into her bones, a warning to get away fast. Who cared why he'd found her?

Whatever the reason, it wasn't good.

Frozen in terror, she willed herself to move, to put one foot in front of the other and get away from the creep, but her body would not obey the command—almost as if someone else had taken control.

odiak

Kodiak growled under his breath as he rushed forward. He pushed her to the side more abruptly than he'd intended and glared at the vampire.

"Hey!" Tamaska yelled, stumbling behind him.

Kodiak didn't look back at her, even though he wanted to, nor did he reach out to help her. It was more important that he stands between her and the vampire. He had to protect her from that monster. Who the fuck knew what he wanted her for? A feeding? That would be the obvious answer.

But he doubted it. Kodiak had told him she was marked for the leader, and what vampire who wanted to live would defy such an order?

Unless...

Unless he'd uncovered Kodiak's lie.

It would be easy enough. A dark shadow in the vampire's eyes suggested more going on.

Maybe it was just Kodiak's wolf instincts, but he wasn't going to let the vampires hurt Tamaska—especially now that he'd had sex with her. His body still vibrated with the bliss she'd elicited, and his drive to protect her was even more intense.

Had it just been lust they'd indulged in? A shiver slid down his back. This wasn't the time to consider if they had inadvertently created something more.

He bared his fangs, a low growl rumbled from his throat as he stared at the vampire.

He loved a challenge, especially a fight with a vampire, but tonight he was grossly outnumbered. He needed to fly under the radar and find information about the Blood Opal, not cause a fucking scene. He was in a vampire stronghold, for crying out loud. This wasn't the time for rash behavior.

But he knew a scene was coming. He was in the way of the vampire and his food source. He could get ripped apart any moment.

"Don't be rough with the lady," the vampire said, stepping forward as if to help Tamaska.

"I warned you. Amdis laid claim."

"Yet here you are," the vampire said, "with her, sampling Admis' goods."

"You disgust me."

The vampire leaned forward. "I can smell the sex. I'm thinking you wanted her for yourself. But I saw her first. Give her to me."

Kodiak shifted to the side, and the vampire bumped into him. Kodiak glared at him, sensing his wolf part gathering strength, readying him to transform and fight the vampire. He willed his wolf to stay calm, puffing up his chest and broadening his stance, ready to fight.

The vampire hissed, baring its fangs in Kodiak's face.

"Showing your real nature." Kodiak smirked, hoping Tamaska hadn't seen the fangs. Although, they would be easy enough to explain away as some kind of quirk for certain people who came to the club.

His inner wolf edged closer to the surface. This vampire needed to be taught a lesson. He was too confident. Maybe Kodiak could take him back to the clubhouse for questioning.

But he couldn't, not with Tamaska there, and certainly not when they were in the club owned by the vampires.

"I'll make you show yours." The vampire came closer and lowered his voice. "Would she like you then, dog?"

"Keep out of this and back off."

This wasn't about like. It was about urges that needed to be scratched and nothing more.

Kodiak paused, then frowned, realizing the vampire

had detected he was a wolf. The pheromones in the air were strong, and not even Martha's potion could mask that.

Things were about to get worse.

"What the hell?" Tamaska said as she pushed between the men with a strength that surprised Kodiak.

He moved for her, and the vampire also stepped out of her way.

"I've had enough of you acting like children. I'll go with whoever I want, and right now that's neither of you idiots." Tamaska glared at Kodiak and the vampire in turn, then pushed through the red velvet curtain back into the night club.

Kodiak went to follow her. She couldn't go out there by herself. Would his wolf scent have marked her? It was too risky. The vampires would be after her even more if he had left his scent on her, with the intent to kill.

She had no idea how much danger she was in. How could he have let this happen, especially with a human? Oddly, though, his sexually charged feeling wasn't as intense anymore. Sex with her had already changed him.

"Not so quick, wolf boy. I'm not finished with you." The vampire's voice chilled Kodiak.

Before Kodiak could head out of the private room, which heaved with the scent of their lustful sex, a heavy weight landed on his back. Sharp nails dug into his skin and the vampire tightened its hold on Kodiak's shirt.

"Fuck you," Kodiak said.

Kodiak dropped down, then turned. Using all his strength, he flung the vampire forward. The vampire landed heavily in front of the lounge and lay still.

Kodiak shifted into his wolf form. He couldn't let the vampire have Tamaska, and the only way to stop him was to fight him.

Fighting the vampire in the club was foolhardy at best and a death wish at worst, but he needed to take the risk. He was strong, strong enough to win, and this room was sequestered enough he might be able to get away with this.

Standing on all four paws, Kodiak looked down at the vampire with his animal vision. The desire to kill was strong.

Let's get this over with.

In wolf form, he leaped forward, aiming to land on the vampire's chest and sink his teeth into its soft neck. Instead, the vampire rolled out of the way at the last second.

Kodiak swung around. The vampire crouched down on the other side of the room, too close to the curtained door. Kodiak couldn't let the vampire go now that he'd transformed.

Kodiak stepped forward, snarling, eyes fixed on his

target. The vampire grinned, as if confident he would win the fight.

Kodiak bared his teeth, saliva thickening in his mouth with the building excitement of a fight. He stepped forward to test which direction the vampire would go. But the vampire stayed still. Their eyes locked, each waiting for the other to make the first move.

Impatience welled inside Kodiak, along with rage towards the vampire that had set eyes on Tamaska. He was glad his wolf side approved of her, even though she was human. Whatever it was between them, it didn't matter. The need to protect her dominated his thoughts.

"Not sure what to do, dog?" the vampire said.

Kodiak snarled deeply, wishing he could talk.

"Doggie is about to get whipped by a vampire. I can't wait to tell the others." The vampire smirked, adjusting his position as if getting ready to move.

Kodiak watched him closely, his instincts on high alert, ready to help him act. His patience waned, even as he held tightly onto it. He wanted that filth dead, now.

"Then I can sink my teeth into her neck and suck out her divine blood," the vampire said. "She'll be mine to use for as long as I want."

Kodiak's resolve broke. How dare the vampire speak like that about Tamaska? There was no way he would get even a drop of her blood.

Kodiak snarled as he leaped towards the vampire, his vision edged with a deep, furious red. The vampire laughed, jumping out of the way. Kodiak followed him, driven by rage, snapping and clawing at the vampire. He lunged forward, swiping his front paw. His claws dragged across the vampire's shoulder.

The success motivated Kodiak to double his efforts. But the vampire scurried around the room, randomly turning back to attack.

Kodiak pushed off the lounge chair, his claws cutting through the fabric as he rushed towards the vampire. The lounge knocked over as he lunged for his prey. The vampire stayed just out of his reach. In his failure to catch his target, Kodiak tore apart the room, driven by rage instead of a clear head.

He paused, panting, tongue hanging out of his jaws as he released the last of his anger and struggled to find his balance. He was a better fighter than this. Was it because Tamaska was involved? How could he feel so protective over a fucking human, even if they did just have great sex? All the wrong things had added up and unhinged him.

He dragged his resolve around him and balanced it with cold determination, blocking out all the other feelings that raged within him.

The vampire stood in the center of the room with an air of confidence that irked Kodiak. "Poor doggie, no bone for you. You can't even protect your girlfriend."

This time, Kodiak didn't react to the torment. Instead, he circled close, measuring potential attacks that could finally bring this fight to an end.

The vampire hissed.

Kodiak lunged at the vampire and clamped down on his leg.

The vampire yelped in pain, which delighted Kodiak as he bit down harder.

Keep away from her.

Blood seeped into his mouth, confirming he'd injured the vampire. It wasn't enough.

She'll never be yours.

He pulled back, dragging the vampire deeper into the room with wolfish strength. The vampire fought back, biting Kodiak's upper shoulder. Kodiak nearly let go, but he held on. Then, with one big pull, he got some momentum and let go. The vampire rushed away. Kodiak turned and clamped down on its neck.

With a deliberate flick of his head, Kodiak snapped the vampire's neck with a loud crack. Then, he let go of his hard-won restraint and went wild, tearing the vampire apart to ensure the kill was complete. There was no way that vampire would ever heal enough to go after Tamaska.

Kodiak stood over the mauled body with the satisfaction of a job well done. He shook as if he'd just had a bath and needed to remove excess water from his fur. Instead, he needed to remove the excess blood.

Satisfied, he changed back to his human form since

there was no way he was going to make it out of the nightclub as a wolf no matter how good a fighter he was. Adrenaline burned through his body as he stood naked in the room, which was now the site of a massacre.

He had to get the fuck out of there before he was caught and attacked by a hundred vampires. But the scent of blood on him would complicate his exit.

It was a mix of some of his and vampire blood, so hopefully he'd be able to get through. But he couldn't take more chances.

He ran his hand through his hair. There was no time to waste. Killing a vampire was more dangerous than fucking Tamaska in a club full of them. How the hell had this happened? Olcan was going to go batshit when he found out. He could probably keep the sex with a human part hidden, but a dead vampire, clearly killed by a wolf, would spark the old war between the two supernatural species.

Kodiak's gut twisted painfully, warning him to get out. First, though, he needed clothes. Walking out of the club naked would only draw even more attention and risk his life.

Plus, he wasn't going to leave without Tamaska.

He carefully peered out between the red velvet curtains. Where could he get clothes, and how could he make a quick escape. Fortunately, the patrons nearby were lost in their own worlds of bliss heightened by drugs, with some couples pushing the boundaries of decency as their sexual desires edged out of control. If it hadn't been for the Blood Opal, there was no way Kodiak would have been caught in such a place.

There were other exits, but they weren't where he was. He had to cross a room full of vampires to get out.

The curtain next to him revealed another empty private space.

But no exit there, either.

Kodiak let the curtain fall back and looked out into the crowd.

He felt like a mouse hiding in a room full of cats, but the only way out was to walk past them. The situation was unusual for him since he was a wolf. He was used to being the highest predator, not the prey.

First, he needed clothes.

Nearby, a guy swayed with the music, drink in hand, eyes glazed.

He'll do.

Kodiak reached out, grabbed the guy by the shirt, and dragged him into the empty room before he'd even realized what was going on.

"Hey..." the man started.

Kodiak punched him hard, knocking him out cleanly. Then he took off the man's trousers, leather jacket, shirt, and shoes before putting them on. He looked decent enough to get out. Satisfied, Kodiak pushed through the curtain back into the night club.

I should get the fuck out of here.

He wanted to get Tamaska, but he couldn't see her.

And she didn't want him around. She'd said as much.

The problem was, he knew Tamaska was still there. If one vampire had already taken a shine to her, then another would surely be after her, too. She seemed to call them. How else had the now-dead vampire found them?

It would have been far easier to take her when they were in the middle of fucking, when Kodiak was most vulnerable. Maybe the guy had been a voyeur, but he didn't think so. The whole situation felt like he'd tracked her in some way.

Is she marked or something? The thought stopped him from hightailing it to the back exit. He had to protect her, even though it went against all his logical instincts.

He needed to find her, no matter how dangerous it was for him to stay.

CHAPTER 19

amaska

When the curtain fell back, covering the entrance to the room as Tamaska left, she paused. Should she go back inside?

Inside that room was Kodiak. The distinct desire to go back to him nearly caused Tamaska to return. But she didn't. She stood on the edges of the dance floor as she looked about the writhing people for Tahla.

Anger still simmered in her blood at the insane testosterone display between the two men fighting over her like a bone.

She didn't like the man who'd followed her, not before and certainly not now.

That was another thing: she'd abandoned her friend.

Her skin prickled. There was something sinister about this place, something dark that went far beyond the debauchery that happened here. The club was so much more dangerous than she'd thought possible, if patrons stalked others like...prey.

Was the strange man going to try to force her into something she didn't want? Or had Kodiak thought she would just go off with the guy?

She shivered, the lingering effects of the sex glow starting to fade.

None of it made sense. She couldn't imagine wanting to be with that creep who'd given her a sip of the drink—and why had she had some?

It was so risky. Who knew what she'd really been consuming. Then again, she'd never imagined herself having sex with Kodiak in a nightclub, either. Was she losing her mind?

To prove she wasn't, she moved further away from the room where Kodiak was. Perhaps the theft and the dog incident had pushed her over the edge.

Would Kodiak come after her? Tamaska stood meters away. She would still be in the line of sight if Kodiak came looking for her.

Her pulse increased at the thought. Was that what she secretly wanted? Fuck, how did she get so messed up over a guy that only cared about himself? A man she didn't care about, did she?

Tamaska glanced back to stare at the curtain, thinking she saw something. But it must have been her imagination. It didn't move.

What the hell was he doing in there? The guy hadn't come out, either. Her guts twisted at what that might mean. She didn't think they were the type to talk things out. But why would they want to fight over her?

Pull it together.

Going to the club had been one hell of a mistake. Tamaska's chest tightened as she remembered she had no idea where Tahla was, and she was no closer to finding the Blood Opal.

I'd best leave those two to blow off some testosterone.

She wanted to get out. That was the safest thing she could do. After all, if one guy had tried to track her down, who could say someone else wouldn't, just because she was a female alone?

But she couldn't leave without finding Tahla. Tears of worry pricked at Tamaska's eyes. What could've happened to Tahla? She would never forgive herself for being such a flaky friend.

Maybe Tahla had gotten lucky with a guy, like Tamaska had? The behavior of the nearby couples, and even the groups of three or four, made it obvious that sex in the club happened openly.

Tamaska's belly roiled. Something intuitively told her that Tahla was in trouble and didn't even realize it. So where was she?

Back in college, Tahla was always in the middle of the dance floor. That was where Tamaska had to go.

Forgetting about the room where she'd fucked Kodiak, Tamaska pushed herself into the sea of intoxicated people on the dance floor.

She struggled to push past the patrons as they danced in close proximity. What had she been thinking, having sex at a nightclub?

Tamaska was in her late twenties. She'd left crazy sexual encounters behind years ago—not that she'd ever done it often. It was too risky, just like it had been with Kodiak. It was as if she'd lost her mind with him.

The music tempted her body to dance, and she fought against the beat. Was that it? The music was like a drug? She didn't think it was possible. It had to be the drink she'd had. With horror, she realized it might've been spiked.

Fuck, that would explain it.

Great, now she was a statistic: a single female targeted at dodgy nightclub.

How could I have been so stupid?

Whatever it had been in her drink, it must have been strong. Thank goodness she'd only had a few sips. She could already think more clearly now.

Was it something about Kodiak that had caused her to lose her sense of propriety and have sex with him?

A man bumped hard into Tamaska, and she stumbled backward.

"Hey." She glared at him, noting his glazed eyes and

the odd marks on his neck. He looked white and ready to pass out.

She moved past him, unable to help, even if he wanted that. She had to find Tahla and get out of there. But where the hell was she? So far it had been too difficult to find her. There were too many people there. Lights flashed from the stage, making it difficult to make out other people.

She's going to kill me for leaving her.

Guilt stabbed Tamaska's gut as she kept moving through the high-density crowd. She pressed up against bodies as she pushed through the crowd, and a few wandering hands on her arse grossed her out.

The longer she was there, the more she wanted to leave, Blood Opal be damned. In fact, she would walk right out the door, if she could. But she didn't want to leave her friend.

Maybe she left?

Tamaska rolled her lips in thought. That would make sense. Sure, the place was busy, but with a bit of concentration she'd always found her friends during her intense clubbing days.

The stench of body odor, mixed with an array of perfumes and aftershave, sex, and a metallic smell she couldn't place flooded her senses as she moved towards the center of the dance floor.

It was hard pushing between the patrons, who were all hot and sweaty from dancing. Most were probably high, too, which was just another reminder that she shouldn't have come to the Blood Moon.

Tamaska looked around in an attempt to find Tahla. She remembered clearly what her friend was wearing. She was confident she could pick her out of the crowd, despite the dull lighting and closely packed patrons.

Was that her friend, only a meter away? She had on a similar dress. Tamaska's breath caught in her throat as the woman pushed her away, but it wasn't Tahla.

Tamaska couldn't explain her building desperate need to get out of there, one that went beyond what was normal, but it was getting harder to resist. She feared what might happen if she stayed, especially if that man came after her again. She couldn't rely on Kodiak to appear out of nowhere and protect her, not after the way she'd left him.

She took a deep, slow breath to settle the fear within her, the fear threatening to make rash decisions for her. Then she spied Tahla's blonde hair and the right dress.

Relief washed over her as she shoved people out of the way to get to her friend.

Thank fuck. Tahla's all right.

"Tahla," Tamaska called as she struggled against the wave of dancers moving in the opposite direction. Tahla didn't respond as she danced close to a strange man. He gave off the same creepy vibe as the man who'd come after Tamaska.

What had she been thinking, getting so angry at

Kodiak for dragging her away from that man? She could see clearly that Tahla wasn't thinking straight, and it sickened Tamaska to know she'd looked like that, too.

Should she be grateful that Kodiak had removed her from that guy? Maybe she'd gotten everything wrong about Kodiak.

Not that it mattered. She'd left him, and with any luck, she wouldn't see him again.

It perplexed her how he always appeared out of the shadows to find her. A guy like that couldn't be relied upon. She'd had some sexy fun with him, and now she needed to move on.

"Tahla!" she yelled, her voice lost in the loud music. She squeezed between two people dancing back-to-back, then another group who couldn't keep their hands off each other's privates. Totally grossed out, she finally managed to get to her friend.

"There you are," Tahla said with a smile, her eyes only slightly glazed.

"I'm glad I found you. It's time to go," Tamaska said firmly.

"No, I want to stay longer."

"What?" Tamaska looked at her friend, wide-eyed. It had taken all her skills of persuasion to convince Tahla to come to the club. She wasn't sure her friend's complete turnaround was a good thing.

"You go if you want to, but I'm staying." Tahla spoke clearly without slurring her words, but Tamaska couldn't help thinking her friend's drink had been spiked.

"We meant to stick together," Tamaska said. "Come on, let's get out of here. I've had enough of this place."

"No, I'm fine. You go. I'm having the best time ever, especially with Athan."

"Who? This guy?" Tamaska pointed at him and tried to pull her friend free. "You don't know him."

Tahla shook her off. "I've been with him for hours since we were separated, and we've only had a good time."

"I've not been gone for hours," Tamaska said. Had it honestly been that long? She didn't think so. It felt like her time with Kodiak had only been minutes. This place was really fucking with her senses. If she'd ended up having sex with Kodiak and losing all self-control inside the Blood Moon, there was no way she could allow her friend to stay there—at least Tamaska knew Kodiak.

"You have." Tahla lifted her chin. "Now, go off and leave me to my fun. I've got other people to meet, and I don't want you to stop that from happening."

"What other people?"

The conversation alarmed Tamaska. Was she going to have to drag Tahla out of there? Something made her think that Tahla wouldn't let her do that, and neither would this Athan. He was dressed smartly in a suit, looking confident, cool, and sexy, but there was an air about him that chilled her. Weirdly, she didn't find him attractive at all, and she should.

"Amdis wants her," Athan said, shifting closer to her friend.

"Yeah, he does, and I want to see him," Tahla said. "He doesn't just ask for anyone, you know."

"Only the special ones," Athan added.

"You're not thinking straight, Tahla," Tamaska said. "And who the fuck is Amdis?"

"Owner of the club," Athan said. He leaned forward, so close to Tamaska that only she could hear. "He would rather see you, but since you've got a doggy friend, he's going to take Tahla... unless you want to come see him instead."

Tamaska's eyes widened with fear. What fucking trouble had she found herself in? And what the hell was Athan talking about? She didn't have any doggy friends. She fucking hated dogs.

Things were getting fucked up way too quickly. If she didn't get out of there pronto, she was going to end up dead—or worse.

"I don't know what the fuck you're talking about."

"You will." His smile chilled her despite the hot, stuffy dance floor.

She hated how Athan's voice was clear despite the loud music, how he looked at her as if undressing her with his eyes, and how he smirked when he gazed at her.

"Hey," called a deep voice she knew now too well. "Get away from her."

"Your dog is right on time," Athan said, bitterness edging his voice. "What a shame. Soon enough, he'll time it wrong, and you'll find your way to us...and the Blood Opal."

Shock shot through her.

"What, you have the Blood Opal? Give it back, you fucker," Tamaska said.

Could she go with Athan and get the Blood Opal back? Could she do that, despite the fact that her entire being was screaming at her to grab her friend and run away from the creep?

Athan laughed at her, putting his arm around Tahla, who let him draw her in towards his slender body. "I'll see you later."

Tahla waved at Tamaska.

Tamaska reached for her friend. "Tahla, you'd better come with me, or I'll bloody wring your neck!"

She took a step towards Tahla.

The patrons dancing on either side of Tamaska pushed in front of her, preventing her from following her friend.

Someone grabbed Tamaska's arm and pulled her backward.

"Tahla," she yelled.

She had to stop her friend from making the worst mistake of her life.

CHAPTER 20

 *odiak*

Kodiak glared at Tamaska. Did she have a fucking death wish? It had taken all his wolf skills to pick up her scent and find her in that stinking place. He shivered at the thought of what might've happened if he'd arrived only seconds later. That was way too close.

The way that vampire had looked at her…

She pulled out of his grip. "How dare you stop me?"

Kodiak ignored her.

His priority was to get himself and Tamaska out of there before the vampires descended on the two of them with revenge in their eyes.

He'd killed one of their kind.

The way Tamaska was glaring at Kodiak, though, he

LILLIANA ROSE

didn't think it was going to be easy to get her out. Could he just pick her up, sling her over his shoulder, and leave? He would, if it came to that. The need to protect Tamaska at all costs consumed him.

He couldn't afford to question why—not when he was surrounded by vampires, smelling like a wolf who had freshly killed its prey. His time in the Blood Moon Nightclub was rapidly diminishing. Standing there in the middle of the dance floor, surrounded by vampires, was too dangerous.

He grabbed her arm again. "We need to get out of here."

"The—"

"I don't care. We have to go. Or you have to go."

"Fuck off," Tamaska said as she attempted to twist her wrist out of his grip.

He countered her twist to stop her from leaving him. While she resisted his help, he realized he felt more complete, now that she was by his side touching her. Almost like they belonged together. A clear connection existed between them, and it couldn't be denied. Just another complication for him to deal with.

"No," he said. "You have no idea what's really going on in this place. You have to get out of here."

"My friend is here."

"That doesn't matter."

"Like hell it doesn't." Tamaska managed free herself from his grip. She squeezed between the dancers to get away.

Kodiak felt the loss as she rushed away from him. "Where are you going?"

The vampires were too interested in her. There was something else going on.

Fuck knew what, though. Tamaska appeared clueless about the situation, and it wasn't like he needed yet another mystery occupying his mind.

"Away from you."

"You can't be alone," he snapped, keeping up as she weaved away from the dance floor through the sea of packed people.

"I can look after myself," she said.

"You can't, not with the guys around here."

"Jealous?"

He snorted and reached for her, but she angled away. "Hardly."

"You were jealous of him."

"Who?" He spoke the word in a dangerous growl.

"Amdis."

"What did you say?" A chill slid down Kodiak's spine. What the fuck did she know about Amdis?

"Amdis. Looks like you have heard of him." Tamaska turned to face Kodiak fully.

Fury and fear for her swamped him.

"You listen to me—you stay away from him." Kodiak pointed at her to emphasize his opinion. "He's dangerous."

She looked a little lost, but defiant as her hands

curled at her sides. "I can't. He's got the Blood Opal, I think."

That information hit him like a ton of bricks. "I know."

"What?" She glared at him as they stood on the edge of the dance floor, where there was a little more room for them to talk.

"And you'll land yourself in trouble if they hear you say the gem's name, so lower your voice." He stepped closer to her, their chests nearly touching. How he wanted to slip his hands around her waist and draw her to him, to let his lips touch hers.

Fuck. He needed to get control of the lustful thoughts dominating his mind.

"Why didn't you tell me?"

"I only worked it out. And even if I hadn't, it's too dangerous for you to find the Blood Opal by yourself." His voice remained firm as he looked into her eyes. His fingers tingled with the need to run them up her arms, to touch her skin as if to tell her that the real reason why she had to stay away from Amdis was that he wouldn't be able to bear it if anything happened to her. But his hands stayed by his sides.

How could he say any of that?

"You need to let me and the police handle this," he said.

He didn't add that the police would be completely out of their depth trying to find the gem in a lair of vampires. That, plus the bribes were a big reason why the club had remained open. The police were easy for the vampires to deal with.

Kodiak, on the other hand, was not.

He was also the only chance she had of the Blood Opal returning to its rightful owners. He would do anything to make that happen.

If he could do that, she'd be safe, no longer some kind of target for the vampires.

"I can help you." Determination reflected in her eyes, which drew him to her even more.

Fuck, she was hot when she got like that.

"It's too dangerous. Just being here is too dangerous." He had to get her out of there, find his pack, then leave. It was only going a matter of time before he was identified as a wolf. The time for talking was over.

They would leave, get a plan underway with the rest of the pack, and return.

First, he needed her safe.

Tamaska opened her mouth as if to say something. Before Kodiak really knew what he was doing, his hands were on her shoulders, drawing her close to him. He pressed his lips on top of hers. He moved his mouth to open hers, sliding his tongue over hers, feeling heat tingling on her skin. She shivered under his touch, which pleased him as he kissed away her words and her stubbornness.

Reluctantly, he broke away from her. They were both breathing hard and uneven.

"Promise me you won't go after the gem," he said.

Tamaska looked into his eyes, and he shivered with delight. She looked woozy with desire after the kiss, but determination still rippled through her.

"Tamaska, this is for your own good. Go home now. Promise me." He used a commanding tone. She had to do what he'd requested. Her life depended on it. If only he could really tell her what was going on.

The vampires inside the club wanted her.

"Promise me," he whispered, resting his forehead against hers, their noses nearly touching.

"I promise," Tamaska said with a sigh.

Relief washed over him. "I'll walk you to the exit."

"You don't need to."

"Humor me." He put his arm around her waist, ready to guide her away, then paused.

There you are. Where have you been?

The pack communication from Ash spoke clearly in Kodiak's mind. He needed to talk to his team, to tell them what was going on and to warn them.

Tamaska wriggled away from him. "I'm fine. I can leave by myself. I'll see you later."

She rushed off before he could stop her. Damn it. He wanted to yell for her to come back, but he didn't like the way a nearby vampire woman was looking at him. She was trying to determine if he belonged in the club. He had to move quickly.

He turned, hoping his wolf scent hadn't been detected. He disappeared back onto the dance floor, following his own path to survival while wishing he could've followed Tamaska.

Have you found anything? Kodiak asked, using the pack connection to communicate as he weaved to the other side of the dance floor. He kept moving, looking for a potential way out.

Nothing, boss, Ash answered.

What the hell have you been up to? Shota asked. *You've been dark on us for ages. We thought they'd caught you.*

Guilt welled inside him along with the recent and X-rated memories, and he strengthened the walls of his mind to stop his pack members from finding out he'd been off having sex. They didn't need to know that detail, especially since they were on a mission. He also needed to keep his kill secret.

Fuck. He'd been more than reckless. He'd been such a dumb arse; it was nothing short of a miracle he was still alive.

Time enough later for self-recriminations. He shoved those thoughts away, too, and concentrated on the issues at hand.

Amdis took the Blood Opal, Kodiak said. *It's here somewhere.*

He kept walking through the club, barely paying attention to where he was going, allowing himself to be swept up in the movement of the people around him. He was so angry at Tamaska for leaving like that.

Well, at least I had a productive time here, Shota said. *But I've seen way too much blood-sucking.*

We need to go soon. Get ready. Kodiak looked around for an exit. There could be one to his left, along the hallway. There were a lot of people—more accurately, vampires—going that way.

Something else came to him and he paused.

Could the gem be down there? He had to go and find out. This could be his one chance to locate the gem, even if that meant putting his life at risk. Surely, someone had found the mutilated vampire corpse and realized there was at least one wolf in the nightclub.

I might be onto something, but be ready to leave. Kodiak severed the communication with his pack so he could concentrate as he followed the small crowd down a set of stairs and into a dark room.

He kept to the back of the group that had gathered in the room. A guard behind Kodiak stopped any more people from entering, saying that they were at maximum capacity. Everyone else would have to wait for the next one.

Kodiak's skin crawled with a warning. He shouldn't be here, a lone wolf surrounded by vampires. He hoped Martha's scent-masking spray still worked. That was the only thing that could save him.

Amdis, the leader of the vampire clan, appeared.

Kodiak's heart plummeted.

It had been years since he had seen the vampire.

Amdis stood confidently, his arms out and head high.

In one hand was the Blood Opal.

"My loyal followers. Welcome." Amis paused. "Are you ready to see the power of this Blood Opal?"

The vampires gathered called out 'yes' and whooped to add to the building tension.

Kodiak realized all the vampires were staring at something in the center of the room.

He leaned up on his toes, hoping to get a better look. His blood ran cold.

A woman lay on an altar, tied up, eyes glazed, barely conscious, with two clear puncture marks on her neck, blood flowing out onto the rock of the table-like altar.

Kodiak's stomach knotted, and he pushed forward, afraid for the woman tied up in chains.

"Hey, stay in line. It's your own fault for not getting here when the call first went out." A vampire pushed back.

Kodiak stepped back to his place. He'd gotten the glimpse he needed.

The bound woman was Tamaska's friend. Did that mean the vampires also had Tamaska, or had she managed to make it outside?

"Then let the blood flow." Amdis held up an ornate knife, its red jewels catching the dim light. In one swift motion, the vampire leader reached down and neatly slit the woman's throat. The crowd cheered.

Kodiak fought against the sickness rising within him and the desire to stop Amdis. But he couldn't act. He would never get out of there alive.

Blood flowed from the woman's neck, pooling into a spiral-patterned crevice of the altar.

Amdis placed the Blood Opal where the blood was pooling. The gem soaked up the blood. The surrounding vampires cheered, their excitement building.

When there was no more blood, Amdis picked up the gem and held it out towards the crowd. "Watch the wonder about to unfold."

There was a marked shift of energy in the room.

Nothing else happened. Was it meant to be a paranormal power boost, or something else?

Kodiak's gaze inadvertently met Amdis' eyes. Did the vampire know Kodiak was there?

He guessed this was a trap. Amdis had used the gem to lure Kodiak deeper into the club. But the vampire leader didn't chase him, no he wanted Kodiak to see whatever power was in the gem.

Kodiak turned and fled, not waiting to see what would happen. He'd overstayed his welcome. As he rushed down the hallway, he sent a warning to his pack members.

Get the fuck out of here, now. They know we're here.

Kodiak sensed panic from his team. They'd heard his message, loud and clear.

He rushed towards an exit, heart pounding hard.

He feared they had all decided to leave too late.

Because of that, his team—and he—might not make it out alive.

CHAPTER 21

amaska

Tamaska's lips still tingled from the kiss, way too long after it was over. What was with his, *See you later* comment? Did she really want to see him again?

The way her body had responded to his kiss, the way the heat from his hands had fanned desire within her, suggested a connection had grown between them. But now that she'd gotten away from him, her resolve to rescue Tahla had returned, along with her urge to find the Blood Opal.

How likely was it that Tamaska would see him again? Based on how much he'd appeared tonight, she didn't think the odds were in her favor of not seeing him.

He'd also made her promise to just leave. But how could she? Her friend was here—and the gem.

So what if she broke her promise to him? It was more important that she find the gem and Tahla.

Besides, Tamaska didn't like how he'd forced her to promise to give up on the Blood Opal. Would he really care if she found it anyway? And he'd said he knew it was in the club. Was that true or a bluff? She didn't know what to make of the latter. Had it been to keep her safe or to get it for himself? She had to contemplate that again, even if she didn't want to.

If he already knew it was there, did that mean he really was behind the theft?

It kept coming back to that.

Tamaska's stomach tightened. How could she have been so weak? She'd given herself over to him, but there was no connection. She couldn't allow that. He'd been using her, hadn't he? That was just him trying to cover up his theft.

But would he?

She squashed that thought.

It didn't matter. Her friend was missing, along with a priceless opal. And it all led back to the club—and Kodiak. Whatever he was up to, she didn't like it. She was even more determined to find the gem now.

As soon as she found Tahla.

Tamaska headed left, skirting around the edge of the dance floor. There was more room to move, but also less light, making it hard to see. Patrons were more intoxicated, and couples were getting more intense with each other.

Not looking where she was going, caught up in her own messy thoughts, she bumped into a couple making out. She stumbled backwards, embarrassed to have disturbed them.

"Sorry," Tamaska stammered as she caught herself.

The couple didn't seem to care. The man kept his mouth on the woman's neck. Her head was tilted back, and her eyes were closed. Her lips opened as she gasped in pleasure.

Then, the man shifted to the side, showing Tamaska the reality of what was happening.

She gasped, covering her mouth as blood dribbled down the woman's neck. Bile rose in her throat, but she couldn't look away.

Then she saw the blood-stained lips of the man and the grin he gave Tamaska as she stared at him in horror. He deliberately sucked on the woman's neck, and she knew for certain he was drinking the woman's blood.

Tamaska couldn't look away, even though she'd been caught watching something that shouldn't have been happening. Simultaneous curiosity and horror seized her.

Oh, God. It was a trick, she tried to tell herself. But she knew it wasn't. There were others, too, and the more she looked, the more she could see what was going on.

These people were drinking blood.

Vampires were a myth, a story, and yet...She wanted to throw up. She wanted to run.

Her skin prickled as someone approached her from behind. The cold breath on the back of her neck warned her to flee, but she remained frozen.

"I could do that to you," said the man behind her, his voice cool in her ear. That coolness spread through her, blanketing the fear and nausea. His words gave her an odd delight, even though part of her mind screamed that this was wrong.

They were—He was—Why couldn't she remember the word?

His hands touched her bare arms, and she shuddered from the coldness of his fingers. This was wrong. No one should be that cold. But she didn't stop him. His hands skimmed up her arms, then he rested one hand on her neck, and she found herself tilting her head to give him access. He touched her stretched neck, fingers pausing on her pulsing vein.

"Right here," he said.

She shivered, watching the couple. The woman wore an expression of out-of-this-world pleasure as she let the man suck her blood.

Would it really be that good?

She offered her neck to him. He stroked her flesh, and she trembled with a strange and hypnotic need. Her whole being shivered as he leaned in closer. His cold breath tickled the vein he'd touched. Tamaska was mesmerized by the couple.

When he caressed her like that, stood so close, breathed on her, she wanted the same. She wanted to lose herself how the woman had.

Then the man stopped sucking, and he swallowed hard. He lifted his head, ecstasy all over his face as the woman went heavy in his arms. Blood dribbled from the edges of his mouth.

Tamaska recoiled in horror. Was she dead? It couldn't be. Yet the light in the woman's expression was gone, and she was pale and completely limp. She must have passed out.

Not even a flicker of a movement came from her.

That was enough to break the evil spell that had taken hold of Tamaska, whatever it was. She stepped away and rushed towards the exit.

"You had to show off, you fucker, and ruin my chance to feed," said the man who had been seducing her.

Tamaska didn't turn back as she made her way through the thinning crowd.

Bile burned her throat as she realized what she'd seen. No one was stopping it. Unsure of the entrance's location, Tamaska began to panic, her mind reeling. Should she call the police? Would they even believe her?

Of course, they wouldn't. How could they? For

fuck's sake, she didn't even believe what she'd seen only seconds ago.

It had to have been a trick of the light. But her stomach curdled. She couldn't brush off what she'd seen as she pushed through the crowd.

She nearly slammed into another couple as she fled. This time, a man wore an expression of ecstasy as a woman sucked blood from his wrist. The image burned into her mind. There was no trick of the light, no misunderstanding, no mistaking what she was seeing. They weren't even trying to hide it.

She turned away, her vision blurring as she swallowed hard against the rising acid in her throat. She had to get out of there.

A door with the mandatory green-and-white fluorescent exit sign above it caught her attention. It was good to know that whoever this Amdis was conformed to the country's legal requirements.

She stumbled to the door and rushed outside. She pushed people out of her way before throwing up in the gutter. They gave her a wide berth as her ancient evening meal spewed onto the concrete, the acidic smell radiating outward.

The cool night air did nothing to ease her confusion. Had she really just seen people willingly allowing others to drink their blood? That place was really fucked-up.

It wasn't worth enduring those horrors just for a feeble attempt to find the Blood Opal. It would be safer for Tamaska to quit her job, let her career take the hit, and move on. At least she would be alive.

Her head spun and her stomach rebelled, and she threw up once more. She stood there, shaking, even as her mind still reeled.

One hand on her belly, she wiped her mouth with the other and stepped away from the mess on the ground. It was time to get the fuck out of there.

That was the exact thing Kodiak had tried to get her to do. Was he really looking out for her? Had she gotten it all wrong? Maybe he wasn't involved in the Blood Opal's theft?

Tamaska put her hand to her throbbing head. Could she trust Kodiak?

At least she'd finally made it outside. In the morning, with a bit of luck, she could wake up, find out Tahla had gone home, and forget this had ever happened.

But what if she was wrong? What if Tahla was still inside the night club? She had to look out for her friend.

Hell, she needed to go back in and— what? Try and locate her friend again and get herself killed? Even though the crowd had thinned, it was darker than before in the club, the beat heavier, more hypnotic. If she stepped foot inside...

No guarantees she'd be able to locate her friend.

None at all.

She needed to get out of there and work out a plan.

With a deep breath that did nothing to settle the mix of confusion and horror and guilt inside her, she looked for a taxi.

Dread pooled in her empty stomach as she realized she hadn't exited through the club's main entrance. Somehow, someway she'd gone out a different door.

She stood on a side street, unsure which direction to take.

She shivered and crossed her arms protectively around her body as she looked up and down the dimly lit street.

She wasn't exactly alone, so she was grateful for that.

A couple stumbled down on the opposite side, leaning into each other.

A few luxury cars were parked in the street, someone to her right was smoking what smelled like the sweet, herby aroma of pot, and a couple was getting hot and heavy to her left, pressed into the wall of the building.

Tamaska looked away, not wanting to watch any more blood sucking. Or anything else, for that matter.

The club's music blared from the inside out, the beat practically calling her to go back and have some fun. She resisted, struggling to get her bearings and wishing she'd never come.

Hoping it was the right direction, she turned away from the couple.

A large shadow leaped in front of her. Her pulse

increased, adrenalin releasing through her bloodstream as she looked directly into the eyes of an oversized dog. Her fear trapped her, her heart racing.

She managed to break free and ran. The dog was on her heels. No one even moved.

She tripped on a crack in the pavement. All she could do was scream as she tumbled down to her knees, her hands hitting the rough cement as she stopped her fall. Behind her, the dog growled and panted. She wanted to run but she couldn't move. Instead, she cowered as she waited for the dog to pounce on her and rip out her throat.

odiak

A chill raced through Kodiak as Tamaska screamed. At first, he thought she was screaming over her friend's death, but she hadn't been there, had she? No way would they have let her go. And he would have sensed her.

He'd let his senses move like a wolf over the crowd, searching for her. He'd tried to find her scent, the feel of her, that awareness that raced like a live wire through him when they were near each other.

But he hadn't sensed her, not until he heard her scream and he rushed to the nearest exit.

Outside, he looked around, trying to locate her.

Ash, transformed, stood in the street, watching as Tamaska cowered on the sidewalk.

Tamaska's fear troubled Kodiak. Did she hate dogs?

Move, Ash, he said through the pack connection.

She's scared out of her wits, Ash said. *I'm here. I can help.*

No! Back off, he said. *I'll go to her.*

I'm right here.

He knew Ash only wanted to help, to protect her from the vampires, but she couldn't see he'd scared Tamaska.

Go, he said.

She fell.

Leave her to me. I'll take care of her. You meet up with the others, he said.

What about you? Ash asked. *I thought you said we needed to get the fuck out of here.*

You do, he said. *But she's important.*

What do you mean—

To the investigation, he said quickly. *Go.*

Kodiak, you can't stay here.

I won't. I'll be quick.

You'd better, otherwise they'll have your hide. For real this time.

Ash leaped away from Tamaska and dashed into the shadows.

Tamaska stopped screaming and collapsed onto the concrete.

Kodiak rushed to her side, her scream echoing in

his ears. Their connection had pulled him towards her, but now it was uncomfortable. They could never have a long-term relationship if she reacted like that to Ash's wolf form.

What the hell did it matter? She was human anyway. This was only a one-night stand, and it was already done.

"Tamaska," he said gently as he squatted down to help her. She trembled as he placed an arm on her shoulder.

"Did you see that?" she stammered, looking up at him, eyes wide.

"That dog?" Kodiak decided to downplay it. It wasn't like they had a future together, just some mind-blowing desires.

"It was *huge*."

"Maybe a touch bigger than usual. Nothing spectacular."

She shoved at him weakly, although her fingers curled on his arm. "You need to get your eyes checked."

Kodiak chuckled. "I'm guessing you don't like dogs?"

The words were hard to say. Did he really want her to confirm his suspicions and remind him that nothing more could develop between them, even if it was allowed?

"I *hate* dogs."

She spat out that venomous response, and any hope Kodiak might have had fell.

"That one will never hurt you," he said, keeping his tone gentle.

She gulped in air. "You don't know that."

"I know dogs." He stroked her back. "Let me help you up and get you out of here."

Tamaska nodded, to his relief. He didn't want another argument with her. They'd had enough fighting for one night.

He helped Tamaska to her feet, holding her tight as she found her balance. She was rattled to the core. He couldn't believe she'd reacted like that, just from seeing what she thought was a dog. That didn't bode well for him in any scenario.

He directed her across the road to a taxi that a couple had hailed. While they stumbled towards the vehicle, he opened the street-side door and helped Tamaska inside, ignoring the insults from the couple who'd had their taxi stolen.

"Where to?" the driver asked.

Kodiak paused. Fuck. There was no way he could bring her back to the clubhouse.

Before he could come up with somewhere, Tamaska piped up and told the driver her address.

She shivered, not from the temperature, but from fear. He eased his arms about her and held her close to him in the backseat. There was no future for them, but he enjoyed the way she snuggled close to him. Using his wolf senses, he felt her fear settle and dissolve.

"I can't believe that club," she murmured.

"What do you mean?" he asked carefully.

"I saw people sucking blood." The words tumbled out of Tamaska, her pulse increasing.

That's because they're vampires, and that's why you shouldn't have gone there. That was what he really wanted to say to her, but he didn't. He couldn't.

"That's crazy," he answered, his mind whirling.

What excuse could he give to alleviate her distress? If only he'd marched her out of there himself—or, better still, never allowed her into the club in the first place.

Allowed? That was laughable. Did anyone allow this woman to do anything? She seemed to do what she wanted, and her determination and stubbornness went bone deep.

It had gotten her into trouble.

But that all seemed like ages ago, not hours. After having had sex with her, the need to protect her and keep her close and safe had grown.

"I can't believe it myself." Tamaska shuddered.

He could tell her the truth, but where would that get him except into a pot boiling over with more questions? Right now, she tried to work it all out herself and that might be the best option.

If he had to tell her, if it came down to it, he would. Otherwise, did she need the added insanity of how the truth might sound?

"Maybe it was some sort of stunt." He met her gaze. "Clubs put on a show to create an atmosphere."

"By pretending to…drink blood?"

"Horrific and thought-provoking?" He shrugged, then pulled her in closer.

"Disgusting. Looked so real." She shook her head. "Then Tahla went off with some guy who gave me the creeps. I just hope she makes it home okay."

"You can forget about the club now," Kodiak said.

There was no way he was going to tell her what he'd seen happen to her friend. To do that would be too much for Tamaska to comprehend. If only he'd managed to find Tahla sooner and saved her life.

He liked how she rested her head against his body, as if taking comfort from him. He squeezed her tight. That was something that he could get used to—if she wasn't a human and didn't hate dogs.

He'd enjoy their connection, but he wasn't going to see her again. It was too risky, and she was always stumbling into trouble. He couldn't imagine what she'd felt like, seeing vampires drinking from humans.

At least she hadn't realized this place was full of vampires. There was that. Small a comfort as it might be.

Either way, though, it would've been horrific and confusing. How the hell she'd managed to get out without losing any blood was a miracle.

That last thought sent piercing, hot fear through him.

He had to see.

He pushed her up, gently but firmly, placing his

hand on her jaw. He didn't give her a chance to protest or to stop him.

"What the fuck are you doing?" She tried to push him away.

"Checking." He looked closely at her neck. There were no puncture marks. He picked up her wrists, but they weren't marked either. He ran his thumb over the pulse in her wrist, her pale skin showing her blue veins.

Fuck. She was so lucky to have gotten out of the club alive.

He lifted one of her wrists and placed a kiss against the soft, delicate unmarked skin. The warmth of her, the beat of her blood against his lips from her pulse point soothed him.

"Kodiak, you're acting weird." She pulled her hand away from his mouth.

The way she said his name sent a shiver through his body. Fuck, how could he want her again?

He did what he usually did when he didn't want to speak to a woman he desired: he kissed her.

Tamaska went stiff, like she was going to pull away, but she didn't. She gave a soft little sigh and relaxed into his advance, letting him open her mouth to deepen the kiss.

She was hot and alive, and their tongues met. It was clear she wanted this as much as he did.

Maybe they could somehow make this work, find a way to—

He remembered her fear of dogs. There was no

way anything could happen between them. He broke the kiss. He hated the look of disappointment in her eyes, because that same feeling tumbled through him, too.

He turned away, looking out the window at the darkness, wishing he was anywhere but there.

For a long moment, they didn't speak. Then she shifted next to him, her gaze burning into him.

"Why are you wearing different clothes?"

Kodiak's mouth dried. What excuse could he come up with for that?

"Slight mishap," he said.

"Like what? What on earth could've happened for you to end up in different clothes? Ones that don't fit you very well, I might add."

Kodiak's breath caught. Tamaska was a smart woman, attentive to detail. He needed to be extra careful around her. There were too many secrets he had to keep from her, which was nearly impossible since her personality stirred his emotions so deeply.

"And do you somehow carry extra clothes around with you?"

How the hell did someone get out of this logistical nightmare line of questioning? "I borrowed—"

Fortunately, the taxi stopped at the apartment block in Tamaska's suburb, giving Kodiak a convenient out.

"You going to pay or what?" the driver asked.

Kodiak went to take out his credit card, then paused. It wasn't there. Of course it wasn't. He usually didn't keep money or cards on him since he would lose them if he changed forms.

"Shit."

"Don't tell me. You lost your wallet?" Tamaska asked, her voice dry.

"Yes." He squirmed uncomfortably.

He didn't like putting her in a position to pay. He didn't like being caught short.

"Not your job." She was direct, and he liked that in a woman.

"I wanted to make up for the evening."

"By following me into the cab? This night just keeps getting better," she said as she took out her credit card from the discreet bag hanging over her shoulder.

Kodiak swallowed hard, then got out of the taxi.

She stepped out and raked her gaze over him. "You're not coming in."

"I want to make sure you're safe. You've seen some disturbing things tonight." He softened his voice, hoping his usual pushy self wouldn't cause a scene. He wanted to check out her apartment to ensure there were no vampires lurking there and to see if he could add any secret security measures to keep her safe.

"Fine. But, just to be clear, nothing is happening, and you are going to leave after you see me to my apartment," Tamaska said.

He almost laughed. What was that saying about bolting the barn door after the horse ran?

He kept his comments to himself. She wouldn't see

the funny side.

"I understand," he said.

Too much had happened between them already, anyway. He had to get back to the pack. They would want answers about what the hell had gone on tonight, why he killed a vampire, and that he hadn't come any closer to finding the Blood Opal. He would have some uncomfortable explaining to do in front of Olcan.

"Good. I mean it." She glared at Kodiak as if to prove her point, then turned and punched her code into the panel on the building's front door.

Kodiak couldn't help himself. He saw the code and memorized it. It was all part of the training he'd gone through for Shadow Security. Sometimes, he needed to bend the rules to do his job.

He followed Tamaska to the elevator, where she punched in the same code before pressing the number 8. The elevator arrived and they got in. The elevator jerked, moving up to the eighth level.

"Nice place," he said as they stood side by side in the small square space.

He really wanted to put his arm around her, but he resisted. She was giving off a distinct *don't touch me* vibe, and he needed to maintain his resolve since he couldn't share the rest of his life with her. It was best to start practicing now.

"You're still not staying," she said. "Besides, this is only the elevator."

Kodiak shrugged off her comment. He took in the

details of her nice place, like the security system he was sure Ash could hack. Plus, Kodiak had the code, which would make things easier, if necessary.

The elevator stopped gracefully, and the doors opened without a sound. Tamaska stepped out, turned right, and hurried along the corridor.

He easily caught up to her, scanning the area for anything suspicious. The floor was carpeted, the walls clean and freshly painted, and all ceiling lights worked. It was quiet, though Kodiak picked up the sound of TVs playing at a respectable volume from inside the apartments they passed.

She stopped in front of a door on the left halfway down the corridor. Kodiak couldn't help noticing everything. Her lock appeared intact. It hadn't been tampered with.

She took a keychain out of her bag and unlocked the door.

His inexplicable, uncontrollable protectiveness made him push her out of the way and enter the room. He needed to check it out and make sure it was safe.

"Hey," she called as he entered. "Get out of my apartment."

Kodiak ignored her as he walked into the living space. It was sparse but neat, decked out with expensive furniture and decorated like a feature from a house magazine.

A cream-colored leather lounge faced the window. A large flat screen TV on a wooden cabinet was set off to the side so as not to hamper the view, which was mesmerizing with its sea of lights in the darkness. A glass sliding door opened onto a modest balcony, just big enough for a few potted plants, a cream-colored French wrought-iron table, and two chairs.

He only sensed Tamaska's presence in the apartment. Her fresh honeyed wax flower feminine scent made him confident that no one else had been there. Still, he systematically moved through her home, checking every inch of it, just to be sure.

If he'd brought some tech with him, he could install a few discreet cameras to keep an eye on Tamaska without her knowing.

She wouldn't like that, though, if she ever found out. No one would. But he would have put them in suitable places, to respect her privacy. He wasn't a peeping Tom. His intentions were honest, and he needed to help her.

But it was a moot point. He didn't have any tech.

The kitchen to the right had been positioned to look through the windows over the city. A small bench was topped with marble beside a stove top, with an oven built into the cupboards. The entire kitchen was sparkly and clean. Did she even use it? A wooden knife block, with all its knives accounted for, stood in its place beside the sink in a corner workspace.

Kodiak turned to face her. "Tamaska, I need you to keep the knife block out of sight, in case there were any intruders."

Then again, it wasn't like vampires needed knives to kill their prey.

"I said, get out." She folded her arms over her chest as she stood in the center of the living room.

"Just one more second," Kodiak said, still in security-guard mode as he walked to the doors on the left.

"Don't you dare go in there."

Too late.

He strode into her bedroom. Desire spiked through him, but he pushed it away. He was here to keep her safe, so he kept hold of that inner security guard.

Large windows stood to the right of the bed, their curtains pulled back to show off the night lights of Sydney.

The king-sized bed sat neatly made with a soft blue cover and lots of pillows, all deliberately arranged. At the end of the bed stood a white, floor-to-ceiling wardrobe. The neat room made it easy for Kodiak to scan for any signs of intruders.

"I really don't think this is necessary," Tamaska said.

Kodiak didn't want to remind her what she'd seen.

For someone in their late twenties, she'd done incredibly well for herself, living in a decent apartment decked out with designer furniture. The furniture and setup was timeless and modern.

Tamaska was incredibly well put together.

He could see a future with a woman like her. See all the small and shining details. The ones that went beyond mere lust and that protectiveness she roused in him. He could see something that sang with possibilities.

If he wasn't a shifter. And she wasn't human.

"But it is, Tamaska, and I'm nearly finished," he called back.

Finally, he checked out the bathroom next door. It was tiny, with only a shower, toilet, and basin. Nothing more was necessary. The room was so clean. There wasn't the tiniest spot of mold anywhere.

"Quite finished, now?" Tamaska asked as he strode into the living room.

She stood there, glowering, and it hit him in the solar plexus. Everything about her said hands off. Her eye shone with hunger, though.

It didn't matter they shouldn't be together. The pull was too strong to ignore.

He should keep his hands to himself, but he didn't think he could. Not when she gave off those warring vibes, those things that were so base, so carnal that they were all he could hear, all he and his wolf wanted.

She was a fighter.

In bed. Out of it.

And he loved it.

No matter how wrong.

He crossed her, cupped her face, and kissed her. When she moaned, the soft kiss morphed into more.

Passion flared high and the kiss deepened, her body melting into him, need clawing at him to take it further.

Instead, he raised his head and took in a ragged breath.

"I'm going to go now," he said softly. "Like I told you I would. Will you be all right?"

Their noses were nearly touching, their mouths close enough to slip into another kiss. The sexual tension between them sparked, electrifying the air.

There was a cloud of doubt in Tamaska's eyes. Although they couldn't be together, Kodiak held his breath, half hoping she would change her mind and ask him to stay. He would do that, even though it would cause huge trouble for his pack.

Something about Tamaska made him irrational.

"I'll be fine," she finally answered.

Kodiak bit his bottom lip to stop himself responding with, *Are you sure?* Her place was secure. No one had been there, and Kodiak had done his part. There were more pressing matters to address if he wanted to keep his place in the pack, and he'd already toed the line by being here with her.

"You won't go after the Blood Opal, will you?" He needed to hear her say it.

"No, I won't."

"Please, for your own sanity, don't."

"That gem has brought me nothing but trouble, and I've had enough. I want it to end."

He nodded, relieved. His lips met hers once more.

"Make sure you don't." Reluctantly, he ended the

kiss, pulling away from her. "I'll see you around. Call me if you need anything."

Tamaska nodded, averting her gaze.

It was hard leaving her alone, but at least he knew she was safe for now. When he got back to the club-house, he would take a few more measures to keep an eye on her place. It wouldn't be easy to pick up the vampires on CCTV, but Kodiak hoped Ash's techniques would be enough. He planned to stay close to Tamaska in his spare time, anyway.

He took the elevator back to the ground level and stepped into the night, the cool air sharpening his senses. He took a quick walk around the building to check it, but nothing was out of sorts.

It was time to get back to his pack and debrief. He headed down the road to the park, which would provide a short enough path back to the clubhouse.

The vampires were certainly showing interest in her. His gut twisted as he realized what that really meant. They weren't going to forget about her anytime soon. He needed to stop seeing her, but that wasn't going to happen.

It couldn't.

Not until she was safe, and the vampires were stopped.

He shuddered. The thought of the vampires getting to Tamaska curdled his stomach. He would have to keep a close watch over her and keep her safe, all without her knowing.

CHAPTER 23

 odiak

As Kodiak continued down the street, anxiety churned harder in his gut. It didn't feel right to leave Tamaska, but he had to. Where would he take her, anyway? The clubhouse?

He hated conflicting emotions.

She is all right. He kept repeating the mantra to himself.

He crossed the street, heading towards the grassy park adjacent to the bush behind their clubhouse.

His wolf side edged closer to the surface, demanding to be let out. Kodiak easily kept his animal side in check as he walked. A run in his wolf form might have been just what he needed to clear his head before facing Olcan, who would expect a briefing on the night's event, but he couldn't. Kodiak wasn't one to back down and hide, no matter how much he would rather forget it all.

Back with us again? Shota's thought broke through Kodiak's musings. *You really have a way of disappearing when we're supposed to work together.*

Kodiak sensed Shota's annoyance. Kodiak didn't need to hear it now, but Shota was right. He hadn't been there for them, and it was only luck that the team had made it out safely.

Do you even know if we all got out of the club alive? Shota asked.

Kodiak's mind filled with worry and fear. Had they? He was sure he'd checked in, but then he'd gotten so absorbed in helping Tamaska that he'd strengthened the barriers in his mind to keep the team out.

The last time he'd connected with them was when he told Ash to get away from Tamaska, because she was scared of Ash's wolf form. Why the fuck had Ash been in her wolf form, anyway?

He took control of the sudden burst of anger and frustration in him. He knew why. Ash had been trying to protect Tamaska. She knew Tamaska had hired them, and she knew her job.

Just like the rest of his team did.

He would never have sent anyone in if he thought for even a split second they couldn't take care of themselves.

I know you all got out safely, Kodiak responded. It wasn't a complete lie. He would've felt it if they'd been in trouble. *Besides, I trust you all to handle yourselves properly.*

No thanks to you. Shota's thoughts were getting stronger.

What the fuck is that supposed to mean? Kodiak's hackles rose. His wolf side was close to the surface, begging to be let loose. He wasn't quite at the bush yet, the place where Tamaska had gone running before, so he couldn't transform.

She better not go running again.

So that woman...was she the human you've marked?

Kodiak's breath caught. Had he really marked her?

That wasn't possible. He might have been attracted to her and developed an unexplainable connection to her, but he was repulsed by her humanity.

I've marked no one. Especially not a human, Kodiak answered. His wolf form pushed to get out, and he quickened his pace. *Don't you go around starting rumors about it, either.*

He didn't need Shota or anyone else to think he was weak and challenge him as Beta.

They needed to find the Blood Opal, now more than ever.

It wouldn't be at the club, not now, but the Blood Moon had strongholds and surely it would be at one of those. Or maybe they wanted him to think that.

One thing he was sure of, the situation with the vampires was about to get ugly.

He'd seen first-hand the opal was more than a priceless gem and he wondered if Olcan knew that, too.

He also had to make sure the pack stayed cohesive.

The shifters didn't need the added distraction of an in-house fight for Beta.

They're not rumors if they're true, Shota said.

They're not true. Kodiak growled. Where the fuck was Shota? He wanted to correct Shota's mistakes immediately.

Kodiak stood at the edge of the bushland, spying the spot where he'd watched Tamaska after he'd stopped the vampire from taking her. His skin prickled as he realized he'd rescued her twice already. He turned, ready to run back to Tamaska.

If they'd come for her two times already, there would be a third. He had to be by her side protecting her. He would never forgive himself if she ended up sacrificed, like her friend.

Whatever strange powers the opal had, it needed blood. And if the vampires wanted Tamaska, then there might be something about hers that was special.

If so, he couldn't leave her alone. He couldn't—

A nearby growl made Kodiak stop. He snapped his head in the direction where the sound had come from. It was Shota, lurking in wolf form. It seemed they all had a lot of steam to blow off after the nightclub incidents.

So be it, then.

Kodiak shifted into his wolf form, letting it take control. His human side remained close by, ready to intervene if things got out of hand.

His fight with Shota couldn't be a fight to the death, but Kodiak's wolf was keen to taste blood again. It had been too long since he'd roamed the hunting grounds to satisfy his animal instincts. And all the vampire kill had done was ramp up the urge. If he wasn't careful, his oversight could have serious consequences.

He hunched down. A sniff confirmed Shota's wolf, with his earthy scent. Kodiak's muscles contracted and he sprung towards the bush where Shota prowled.

Shota bared his teeth, snarling. He snapped at Kodiak's front leg. Kodiak changed direction mid-leap to avoid a broken leg. The thrill of the fight flowed through him as did so.

He landed and rolled on the dry leaves, which clung to his fur with clumps of damp soil. All his senses were on high alert, noticing every detail around him. He was determined to win the fight. Determined to put his friend back in his place. There was no way he was going to lose his position as Beta.

Shota rushed towards Kodiak, heavy paws pounding the ground. Kodiak pounced as Shota leaped. Their teeth bared, they snapped at each other, both failing to get a grip on each other's flesh.

Shota's salty saliva tingled in Kodiak's mouth as he turned in the air, their bodies moving in opposite directions. Kodiak only got mouthfuls of fur. Anger pulsed through him, spurring him on.

After landing gracefully, Kodiak turned and rushed Shota. Kodiak swiped, claws extended. He sliced into Shota's muscles and pushed him off-balance.

The metallic smell confirmed that Kodiak had drawn blood. He stood over Shota, who snapped as he struggled to get back to his paws. Shota bit at Kodiak's shoulder a few times but left no injury.

Kodiak snapped his jaws, telling Shota off as if he were a pup, then swiped a paw across Shota's face, smacking him to the ground. He pressed his weight onto Shota to prevent him from moving. Shota fought back, but Kodiak had the upper hand. Kodiak pressed his advantage by towering over Shota, refusing to let him get up.

He swiped again, connecting with Shota's head. Shota whimpered, and confidence surged through Kodiak.

Shota yielded, laying his head on the ground.

Don't you ever do that again, Kodiak said through their pack connection. *You accuse me of anything again, and I'll tear you apart.*

Shota whimpered. *Yes, I understand.*

Good. Kodiak growled, pushed his weight against Shota until he whimpered again, then sprung off him.

Shota continued to lay there, breathing hard.

You'll do well to remember this, Kodiak said.

His wolf form wanted to run hard, to burn off the excess adrenaline thrumming through his body.

I'll see you back at the clubhouse for a briefing. Kodiak turned and let his wolf run, weaving between bushes and eucalyptus trees, paws padding quietly on the dry leaves. His breath quickened from the exertion, the breeze in his fur.

Kodiak enjoyed his freedom, his speed, his strength, his prowess, the complete package that earned him his Beta status. He'd fought for it and wasn't about to let anyone take it away.

Just like he wasn't about to let his time to challenge for Alpha slip through his fingers. A time and a place for everything. And when he did take the top spot, Shota would make a fine Beta.

Kodiak's mind raced as fast as his legs. He needed to put his thoughts in order.

It wasn't enough for him to come up with reasonable excuses for the end of the night at the club. Everyone had known it was a possibility the situation with the vampires could go south.

But there was what they couldn't control and what they could. Olcan was looking for a reason, it seemed, to push Kodiak either into a corner, or away from the Alpha position.

If his team said the wrong thing, or if he did, then they would end up spending more time infighting than banding together against the vampires.

But again, that wasn't the fight right now. He needed to do this right and avoid facing Olcan's temper and strength.

Better that energy spent on the conflict with the vampires.

Kodiak also needed to get his team back in line. The argument with Shota was good for letting off steam, but if it led anywhere else. Kodiak needed to be at his best when he walked into the clubhouse.

Yet there was one point he struggled to clear from his mind, what Shota had said, it could could threaten Kodiak's position in the pack.

But there was no way it was true.

Kodiak hated humans too much. It tormented him to think there might be even a sliver of truth in what Shota had said.

And yet he couldn't ignore it. His mind kept returning to it, over and over again.

Had Kodiak bonded with Tamaska?

 odiak

Kodiak strode naked through the back door of the clubhouse and let it slam shut behind him. His skin shone with sweat.

What he wanted was to take a shower, eat, and get back to Tamaska. After running for as long as he'd dared, he'd convinced himself that his desire to protect her didn't mean he'd bonded with her on any level.

Sex had a way of getting in deep. Nothing more. Protecting others was part of a shifter's DNA.

Wanting to keep her safe had nothing to do with bonding. At all.

Only the gem's theft had put him in this position, primed to protect, and he'd promised to find and retrieve the Blood Opal. If that meant keeping an eye on Tamaska, keeping her safe, he would do that, but it was all part of the job.

But he couldn't do that right now.

First, he had to get his team together and they needed to get on the same page, and discuss what they'd seen and found. He'd killed a vampire, and they were all going to have to be a cohesive unit and be right at the top of their game if they wanted to survive.

Get down here now, Kodiak said as he entered the changing room on the right. He grabbed a pair of folded jeans and a white shirt from the stack, then put them on.

When he came back into the meeting room, glad to be dressed, his team had already begun to assemble. Only Ash and Shota weren't wearing their original clubbing outfits, but obviously none of his team had been back long. Their scents were still heavy with smoke, drugs, and with Shota and Ash, the scent of wolf since no one had had time to shower.

That was good. It told him people had been doing their jobs, and hopefully hadn't had time to report to Olcan.

He glared hard at Shota, who averted his eyes. Shota had a darkening bruise on his cheek from the fight. *Good.* At least Shota wouldn't cause any more issues for now.

He didn't normally, but these weren't normal times.

"Anyone see anything?" Kodiak asked.

Others shrugged and shook their heads and a few snarls of frustration echoed in the room.

"Get yourselves under control. We can go out for a training session to blow off whatever's eating at you, then you can do some rounds with me in the ring to make sure you're all in line. We're all on the same team, right?"

Shota nodded and the others mumbled in agreement.

"Good. Remember that, or we're not going to stand a chance against whatever the vampires are planning."

"You think they're going to cause trouble for us?" Shota asked, but it really wasn't a question.

They all knew trouble was coming.

It hung in the air.

Kodiak sat on the edge of a small table and looked at his team. "I saw the Blood Opal tonight."

"What?" Ash's eyes widened. She'd positioned herself on the arm of the lounge chair, as close to Shota as possible. Those two had to be in the process of becoming mates.

"So, the night wasn't a complete waste of time, then," Shota said.

"I'd say it was oddly successful." Kodiak narrowed his eyes at Shota. After running in his wolf form, Kodiak's thoughts were clearer, and he'd reframed the events of the evening.

Well, most of them. Tamaska still haunted his mind,

but he could put that aside for now while he dealt with his team.

"We didn't hear from you for ages at the club." That was Ash.

Kodiak leaned back on the table, giving off an over-confident vibe he wasn't sure he felt as he glanced between his teammates.

They were all at the club. They knew what it had been like.

"You kept in close contact with every team member tonight, didn't you, Ash?" Kodiak sat tall, forcing her to look up at him. He needed to drive home his point for reasons he wasn't sure he entirely understood. "Not just Shota?"

"There were a lot of people, vampires, and fuck knows what else, plus the music."

He nodded slowly. "You're saying you didn't maintain your pack connection, then?"

Ash cast her eyes down and shook her head, waves of misery rolling off her.

"Yet, you all heard from me when you needed to get out. I'd say I maintained our connection just fine while I looked for intel." He raised an eyebrow. "And what did you find that will help us find the Blood Opal and keep us in the pack?"

The room went silent as everyone avoided eye contact with Kodiak. He didn't enjoy their discomfort, but he needed it to really bring home the complexities of it all. He liked to lead. He was good at it, and good leading meant hard choices, pushing certain buttons, and making sure things happened in the right way.

Right now, he needed to get that fucking opal, crush whatever the vampires might be up to, and keep both his people and Tamaska safe.

Not just her, but the rest of the humans.

A knife twisted deep inside him at the thought of something happening to her.

The team looked at him, and he realized he needed to do something, to push how intricate complexities were, and how they were sometimes beyond control. Some of his teammates needed an extra reminder to listen to him, no matter what.

"You know what I think?" he asked, keeping his voice soft. "I think Shota and Ash are too focused on each other, and this team is going to be weaker for it."

Ash swallowed hard, looking at Kodiak with surprise. "That's not true."

"Didn't you spend the entire night together at the club?"

She nodded, twisting her fingers in her lap. "But that didn't stop us from searching for the gem."

"We get more done together, Kodiak. You know that," Shota said. "We started on the dance floor, but that was nothing but a drug festival, so we spent time upstairs on the balcony."

"Your wolf scents could have been identified together," Kodiak said. "It was too risky. Even with Martha's spray."

He ignored the fact he'd changed into wolf form at the club.

"But that didn't happen. We were close to finding out how to get to Amdis' business room." Ash met his gaze. "And Martha's spray is designed for that."

"Just pointing out the added risk."

Skoll made a sound but didn't say anything, and Kodiak ignored him. Shota and Ash might have located the business room, but there was no guarantee that was where the opal was kept, or if it had, would it be kept there still. Even if it was, there was absolutely no way any of them were going back to the club.

If they did, they would all lose their lives for sure.

By now, the vampires would have found the body, and Admis had made eye contact with him.

He looked at Shota. "Did you find out how to get in, or not?"

"Yes, but it's not easy. There are vampires guarding it, of course." Shota inhaled slowly. "Then we got your warning."

"Finding the room is not enough to outweigh the risk we took in going to the club," Kodiak said. He thumped the table with his fist, hard and loud.

Shota jumped. It pleased Kodiak to see Shota uncomfortable.

"Well, then, what did you find?" Ash asked.

The edges of Kodiak's vision turned red. It was a reasonable question, but it didn't stop the wild anger and guilt bubbling. He wanted to break something.

Instead, he pushed off the table and stepped towards Ash. She cowered, realizing her mistake.

"You were in wolf form, scaring humans. Why did you transform?"

"Shota and I split up to leave the club. A vampire followed me, and I needed to move quicker." She looked at her hands.

Almost like he needed a reason for himself that had nothing to do with the woman with the magnetic eyes and long hair.

Fuck. He pushed that away and back to the issue at hand.

"Transforming was your only option? Surely you could've lost the vampire, with your training. There were plenty of people in the club. You could've gotten lost in the crowd." Kodiak loved a good interrogation and enjoyed making Ash squirm.

"I didn't realize I was being followed until I got outside." Ash looked at her lap, biting her bottom lip. "And they went for her."

"I see." Kodiak paused, drawing out Ash's discomfort. She'd made a huge mistake, not realizing she'd been followed, and it had drawn unwanted attention to their pack. "You know that resulted in a human seeing us."

"She has a name, which you know well," Ash said. "*Tamaska*. Don't turn this on me when I was helping. And speaking of her...why the fuck was she there?"

He shrugged.

"Humans. Who knows with them?" Channing said. "But she's probably looking for the same thing as us, right, Kodiak?"

He swung his gaze to the pup. "She did organize the event."

"We shouldn't be fighting," Fern said. "We need to work together, and this opal seems to be important."

Onai nodded. "More than monetarily."

They were coming together, but he kept the triumph to himself.

Skoll looked about. "So she was there for the opal? Working with the vampires? But that doesn't make sense..."

He thought about the right response, but everything that came to him led to so many difficult questions he didn't know if he had an answer for. "For whatever reason, her path seems to follow the Blood Opal. The vampires are after her, and she's in need of protection."

"Who needs protecting?" Olcan asked, storming into the room. "It's about time you lot were back. You better have something good to tell me."

Kodiak swallowed hard, feeling Olcan's Alpha presence as the man tried to dominate the room. He pulled back his energy to give Olcan space.

"It depends on what you call good."

"The opal in your hands." Olcan pinned his gaze on Kodiak. "And who needs protecting?"

"The human who employed us for the Blood Opal job," he answered, his voice cool.

"Why the hell would that be the case?" Olcan stood where everyone could see him, and Kodiak let him take control of the room.

"She was at the club tonight," Ash said.

"Did you know that, Kodiak?" Olcan frowned, crossing his arms across his chest.

Kodiak left his own loose. "Why would I?"

"Not what I asked."

"I didn't know she was going to be at the club. She's intent on finding the Blood Opal and found her way there."

"That's concerning."

"I agree." Kodiak had to play this right. "In her desperation to keep her job, she wants to find it and return it to the company. It's a human thing."

Olcan pressed his lips into a thin line. "How much does she know?"

"Not much. Luck got her there, more than anything else, but the vampires gave her a little too much attention. I'm worried they're going to pursue her." Kodiak hoped against hope Tamaska wouldn't look for the gem anymore, not after what she'd seen at the club.

"That's not our problem," Olcan said.

"I disagree," Kodiak said.

"Really?"

"Yes, I do," he said, ignoring the sarcasm in the Alpha's voice. "They'll kill her, just like they did to her friend."

Olcan looked sharply at Kodiak. "What do you mean?"

Kodiak drew in a breath. "Tamaska took a friend. They got separated and her friend got killed."

"Should I care about the friend?"

He wanted to say, *she might have been human, but we're meant to keep them safe from vampires*. Instead, he simply said, "Yes, because I found something that forced us out of there."

"You were detected, you mean," Olcan corrected.

"If that was the case, if we bungled things, we wouldn't be here." Kodiak inhaled slowly, gathering his thoughts. "It was a trap. Amdis wanted me to see what he was doing with the Blood Opal, but it didn't work."

"Now, you have my attention," Olcan said. "Why weren't you discussing this instead of squabbling over all the wrong details? We have to be on the ball if we want to get ahead of the vampires and their plans."

"I agree. Which is what we were doing."

"Again, why weren't you discussing this?"

Kodiak ignored the question and continued his story. "They sacrificed a human and let the gem soak up the blood."

"Gems don't absorb blood," Ash said, her gaze wide.

"This one did." Kodiak narrowed his eyes at her, wishing she would shut up. "Weren't you supposed to find out details about the Blood Opal? Surely you would have known about its powers already if you were halfway competent."

Ash pouted. "It hasn't been easy to find information."

"Look harder," Kodiak snapped.

Olcan growled. "Enough!"

The Alpha was right. Giving into fears and frustrations didn't help at all.

Kodiak shifted back to the important issue. "The blood flowed through an elaborate design in the floor and pooled around the gem and then it soaked up the blood."

"That was it?"

Kodiak nodded. "Then Amdis looked straight at me, and I got the fuck out of there. That's when I raised the alarm. I think it was a trap. They wanted me to see the power of the Blood Opal, or whatever power they believe it holds. But it didn't work."

Kodiak didn't want to think why that was.

"Thank goodness for us it didn't," Olcan said. "Can you draw the design they used for the blood?"

"I can. It was a spiral pattern, with a few extra spirals coming out as if it were a tree."

"Good. Give it to Ash." Olcan looked at her. "Look for the meaning of the symbol."

Kodiak wanted to kick himself for not thinking of this earlier. If the opal was meant to be a way to gain power or something, then perhaps that design would get them on the right track.

"And fast," Olcan added. "We need a lot of information, and quick."

"I will."

"Does Tamaska know what happened to her friend?" Olcan asked, turning his attention back to Kodiak.

"No." Kodiak paused, careful with what he said. They were getting somewhere, and he didn't want to upset progress by eliciting more questions about Tamaska and his interest.

"Out with it."

"She witnessed some of the vampires feeding on the dance floor."

"Fucking vampires. Feeding? Out in the open? I know a lot of perverted things go on in their club, but they usually don't do that."

"My thoughts," he said to Olcan. "The vampires tend to use clubs and sex dungeons as places to recruit and to stake out future prey. They're not entirely above the law, and too many deaths in one spot—"

"Or too many people going missing—"

"It would bring down attention and shut them down. They're arrogant but not exactly that stupid."

"Which begs the question, what are they up to?" Olcan clenched his fists. "We must find out."

"Good." Kodiak rolled his shoulders. "I want to keep an eye on Tamaska. She—"

"Like I said, she's not our problem, and right now our hands are full. We're staring into the dark with no direction" Olcan snapped the words. "Fuck, I hate it when the vampires have the upper hand."

"We can't just feed her to the lions," Kodiak said, unwilling to leave Tamaska unprotected.

What would he do if Olcan wouldn't budge? Disobey? No one disobeyed the Alpha. Not unless they were going to challenge.

"It's unfortunate that she saw what she did, but that's all the more reason to stay away from her. She can't find out about our kind. It's too risky to be around her. Let the vampires have her." Olcan's gaze barely flickered Kodiak's way as he poured himself a drink.

Kodiak clenched his hands. "What if she's important to them?"

"Let them have her." Olcan took a sip of the dark liquid in his glass, bourbon by the smell.

"That's not who we are. We're better than that."

"You have a problem?" Olcan raised a brow.

Kodiak nodded. "I do. The blood of her friend didn't work, but if you look at how they've been interested in Tamaska since the start, then maybe there's something about her blood. Something in it they need."

Olcan took another sip and set down the drink. "A nice fairy tale, but we have no proof of that. We'll be better off focusing our attention on stopping the vampires. We need to act now if we want a chance of defeating them."

"But—"

"This is what I want to happen. Kodiak, get the design drawn for Ash." Olcan waved a hand at him to shut him up, even as he turned to Ash. "As soon as you get it, Ash, don't leave your computer until you find out what it is. Kodiak, you're to set up a double watch. Two of us will visit the vampires' usual hangouts and see what we can learn. I want you to lean on the lesser vampires in the clan to see what you can uncover, but no killings."

"And what you said earlier? About our role in the pack's future? You won't be kicking anyone out, will you?" Kodiak's chest tightened painfully.

If that did happen, it would be on him. He hadn't been truthful about what had gone on in the club. One vampire was already dead, thanks to his protective instincts over Tamaska—just what Olcan wanted to avoid.

But Kodiak couldn't tell the truth. That would mean admitting that he had sex with Tamaska, the most dangerous thing he could have possibly done in the club.

Olcan would have Kodiak's hide, and what had happened was private anyway.

Besides, the Alpha would take it out on the pack if he knew.

If Kodiak played it right, he might be able to find some useful information. The shifters could get ahead of the vampires without Olcan learning about any of Kodiak's indiscretions.

"Only if you keep making progress with the Blood

Opal. Get it back from the vampires." Olcan squared his shoulders.

"But—"

"Don't you dare spend any more time with your human. Focus on the vampires, not the gem." He pointed at Kodiak.

Kodiak opened his mouth to argue, but Olcan glared at him.

Kodiak's inner wolf filled with fury. He knew he couldn't change his pack leader's decision.

Kodiak made up his mind not to obey the Alpha's instructions.

He would break the pack rules.

All because of a human woman he couldn't get out of his mind.

amaska

The theft of the Blood Opal had rattled Tamaska's team, and they were struggling to get on with marketing the Cupcake Lady's small account. Wall partitions allowed Tamaska's team separate office spaces but also allowed her to easily keep an eye on them.

They were all fighting to keep their jobs, thanks to her, or maybe they were scrolling the Internet to find a new job and leave her. She wouldn't blame them if they were doing the latter. If they stayed loyal to her, they could very well be on a sinking ship.

Carlene had already been in to give her another dressing-down in front of her team.

Nothing seemed to please Carlene more—with the exception of making money—than putting someone in their place. If humiliation was a part of it, so much the better.

A week ago, that hard-assery would have been another spur to set up her own business, and she would have taken the humiliation, knowing leaving on the best terms helped her future.

But now her future looked to be headed straight to the toilet.

There had been a huge setback in her plans, anyway, but it didn't make her feel better.

Nothing made her feel better.

The Monday morning blues plagued Tamaska. She found it hard to focus at her small desk.

Her office space had glass walls that looked over the city behind her. The view usually lifted a dark mood.

Not today.

Her right-hand man, Cory, had been busy on the phone all morning, so they hadn't held their usual Monday morning weekend gossip debrief before starting the business week.

Tamaska was glad about that since she wasn't sure how to admit that she'd gone to the Blood Moon, fucked the security guard, *and* lost her friend.

She had always trusted Cory. He'd been a good friend and he had great instincts, both in the personal and professional arena. Normally, she would have told him everything. But not after Friday night's nightmare, and not after the club.

Besides, there was no time for any kind of debriefing. Not when they had a shitstorm to deal with.

Professionally, having someone like him to help her organize events had helped her gain notoriety and popularity. That was all on the rocks now, and they were working hard to keep what clients they still had from leaving.

She blundered through phone calls and emails, convincing clients not to cancel while trying to lay low and prevent any negative attention.

Apart from the dressing down, at least she didn't have a meeting with her boss today. Or the with the Blood Opal clients, OzOpals.

Extra makeup hid the dark shadows under her eyes. Her tailored skirt, ruffled white shirt, and red heels suggested a confident edge, even though she felt like shit inside. If she didn't keep it together, her façade would crash. That would cause difficulties within her team and raise questions she didn't want to answer.

Her desk phone flashed with an incoming call. Glad she'd thought to silence the phone, she ignored it, letting the call go to voicemail. She could deal with it later.

She leaned forward on her swivel chair, put her elbows on the desk beside her keyboard, and placed her face in her hands, willing the pounding in her head to cease. It hadn't stopped since she'd woken up late Sunday afternoon.

She had to have been drugged, but she wasn't sure how. She remembered everything about the evening— the sex with Kodiak, people drinking blood, which she'd decided was a trick, and her missing friend.

Bile rose to her mouth, and she swallowed quickly.

Tahla, where the fuck are you?

The nausea still rocked her, but she kept it down. But fear for her friend bit deep into her and it was hard not to think the worst. Tahla always called back.

She wasn't exactly a big partier.

So where the hell was she? Of course, Tamaska had rung the police as soon as she'd tried to contact Tahla yesterday and didn't get an answer. Then she'd rushed to Tahla's apartment, but she wasn't there.

Maybe she'd gone home with that guy and was so wrapped up in him she hadn't looked at her phone. But she didn't think so. Even if she was caught up in the guy, that scared her, too. There'd been something off about him.

And after everything she'd seen at the club...

Her fear had spiked as she'd cursed the police for not taking her friend's disappearance seriously. Apparently, she hadn't been gone long enough for Tamaska to file a missing person's report.

In desperation, she had even contacted Tahla's parents. They sided with the police thinking that she would turn up soon.

Tamaska just knew something horrible had happened to her friend, and it sickened her.

Every time she thought about it, she sent out a prayer for Tahla to be found safe and sound. She looked at her cell one more time to see if there was a message from her friend, but there were no notifications.

Inhaling slowly, she tried to settle the nausea in her stomach after her weekend from hell. Even her occasional thoughts of Kodiak had changed a little since they'd had sex. She kept wondering when she would see him again, her dislike towards him wearing away.

That was a lie, wasn't it? Somewhere between when she'd met him and the club, she'd stopped blaming him, stopped hating him for reasons she couldn't comprehend.

She didn't know what to make of him.

The pull between them was now stronger than ever.

Exhaling, she lifted her head from her hands and reached for the black drip coffee she'd made. It was her second coffee of the hour, but the caffeine was doing little to help her focus on work.

She sipped the hot black liquid, and the bitterness hit the back of her throat. For a second, her mind cleared before the thoughts tumbled back into a tangled mess. Her stomach lurched. She clenched her jaw, breathed, then forced herself to take another mouthful of coffee.

Earlier that morning, she'd considered taking the

day off, but she needed a distraction. Something to help her get it together.

She put the mug down, stretched her neck, and then reread the email on her computer screen. Another client had voiced their concern over her ability to prevent priceless items from being stolen.

With a heavy sigh, she began typing a response to reassure them. They didn't have to worry, she typed. She would employ a different security business in the future, she told them, squashing guilt as she did so.

Somehow, she managed to get into the rhythm of responding to emails. Time slipped away as she did the job she loved. She'd once hoped to be completely in charge of her career by the time she was thirty, but there was a lot of damage control to deal with now. Knowing it would make a difference, she managed to get on with the work that needed to be done.

"Good to see you working your fingers to the bone," Cory said as he strode into her office.

Tamaska glanced up from the computer, her fingers still moving over the keys as she typed the last of her response. "As I hope you are."

"Of course." He gave her a cheeky grin, holding a small stack of folders against his chest. "Which means it has to be time for our Monday morning debriefing. Otherwise, at this rate, it will be Tuesday, and we can't just do it then."

She loved Cory's odd sense of humor. He had a way

of lightening the mood, which she desperately needed. But today, his timing was completely off.

"I'm a bit behind, so it might need to be later."

He faked a shocked gasp, holding his free hand to his chest. "No hot goss? No!"

She laughed. "Yes. Now, what have you got there? Anything for me? Otherwise, I'll have to kick you out."

"Just some contracts for you to look over."

Her eyes widened with hope. "You convinced clients to stay with us?"

"Fingers crossed." He set the small pile of folders, which were bulging with paper, down on the smoky glass desk.

"I'll look at them straight away, then."

"Good." He paused. "You sure you don't want to have a quick debrief?"

She looked up at him, wanting a distraction so she could forget how bad she felt. "What, you had a juicy weekend you just have to tell me about?"

"Something like that." He raised an eyebrow. "Do you want to find out now, or are you going to put me through the pain and make me wait to tell you?"

Tamaska was ready to give in when she noticed something on his neck. He'd been wearing his collar high, but it had lowered, revealing two small puncture marks.

A memory flooded into her mind, of the man biting the woman. Blood had dribbled from the corners of the man's mouth. The moment came back with horrifying clarity.

He'd had fangs.

He'd bit the woman and then he'd pressed his mouth into the woman's neck, sucking hard.

Her blood drained from her face, leaving her light-headed as the memory replayed in her mind. What she'd seen had to be real, despite what Kodiak had told her and despite her own disbelief.

"Are you all right?" Cory's voice sounded distant, even though he was right beside her.

Her eyes blurred as she turned to him, then she blinked hard, clearing her vision as she put her hand to her head. The two puncture marks on his neck came back into focus. The fangs in the man's mouth flashed in her mind. It was too much for her to process. She didn't want to face what she was seeing.

"Tamaska?" Cory asked.

"I'm fine."

"You're not."

She couldn't stop looking at the marks on Cory's neck. Had he been at the club? Why was she reacting like this? She was making too many assumptions; this couldn't be true. But the way the memory flooded into her mind when she looked at the marks on Cory's neck rattled her.

"I'll get some water." She tried to stand, but the movement made her dizzy.

Cory grabbed her arm to steady her. "Hey, careful there."

"Let me go." Panic rose inside of her. The way he looked at her and the memory of blood tangled inside of her.

Did he have fangs, too?

Was he going to drink from her?

"Hey, Tamaska, sit back down."

"No, I need some fresh air. I...shouldn't have come in this morning." She put a hand to her stomach. "I feel a little ill."

"I'll walk with you." He frowned and reached for her again.

"No, it was just a moment. I'm fine." She veered back, then slammed her laptop shut, shoved it into her bag, and grabbed her purse. "If you need me, I'll be working from home."

"I think I should walk you home."

"No!" Tamaska realized how odd she must sound. "I'll text you when I get there so you know I'm okay."

Cory frowned at her, shaking his head. Tamaska didn't wait for him to say something more.

She rushed out of her office, glancing back as he rearranged his collar, his eyes wide.

Then he looked at her and smiled in the same way the man with the blood on his mouth had. She shivered and hurried away.

She had to get away from Cory, or whatever he was.

Realization finally sunk in.

Maybe Cory, one of her closest friends, wasn't human.

amaska

Tamaska stepped out of the office building onto one of the busy inner-city streets of Sydney's central business district, right near Pitt Street, her breaths painful. Why the fuck would Cory let people drink his blood, like she'd seen in the nightclub? Was he the one who'd dropped the business card during the auction? Was he the one who'd stolen the Blood Opal?

But Cory? Stealing?

The idea was laughable, ridiculous.

Besides, Cory hadn't been near the opal. He'd been at the door, like always.

Unless…

Unless he'd planned the robbery with someone.

He wouldn't.

Ice cold fear lanced her, and she found it difficult to breathe. Each of her thoughts were like a knife in her neurons. A wave of dizziness washed over her. She turned onto Pitt Street and stopped, leaning against the wall of a building to steady herself.

If he had planned the theft with someone, the huge question squatting in the room was whom?

A rival who wanted to buy the gem? The person who'd bitten him?

That last thought made her head spin. She forced herself to relax as much as she could.

Each breath she took was slow and careful. She was trying to calm, get the hard, brutal race of her pulse down to a casual walk.

In her bag, the ring of her phone came through, but when she pulled it out, the call was from one of her work colleagues. They could wait. She slipped the phone back into place and continued to calm.

What the hell had happened to her life in the last few days? Friday morning had been normal, the regular stress of a high-level job, but that was something she thrived on.

She'd been full of nerves, but happy, because she'd believed everything would work out. It would be chaos and then things would click because she'd worked so damned hard. Then the security arrived late. She'd met the dark gaze of Kodiak and her entire world went haywire.

Try as she might, she couldn't pin this on him. They'd been late, but according to what she knew from the police, the opal's theft had taken time and orchestration.

So…Cory?

She couldn't quite make herself believe that either. But he'd been there from the beginning. He knew the way everything operated.

If he had taken it, why?

And why execute the theft in public?

The police didn't suspect him.

All she had was nothing at all and horrible, debilitating guilt over her missing friend.

Breathe, she told herself. *Calm down and fucking breathe.*

People rushed up and down the pavement as cars blasted their horns. The typical city sounds made her head pound more. Being outside didn't make her feel any better. She needed somewhere safe, somewhere she knew.

She needed to get home.

She stumbled away from the building and, more importantly, away from Cory, in the direction of her place.

He still creeped her out, which he'd never done before. That smile when she'd left, along with the bite marks, made her beyond uneasy.

She needed to trust that instinct.

Clutching the bag with her laptop gave Tamaska an

odd sense of comfort. It was difficult to walk in the high heels she'd picked out this morning. Or maybe it was the shock of seeing the bite marks on Cory's neck that made her steps wobble as she walked. She didn't care right then. She wanted to get home. She pushed herself forward.

Her vision blurred, focused, then blurred again. She paused, leaning against the concrete building on her left.

A wave of nausea passed through her, along with another vision of what she'd seen at the club: the man with fangs biting that poor woman.

Why was she reacting so strongly to her memories from the club? The memory had surfaced in her mind, so intense and clear.

And it made her feel sick.

It must be because I was drugged or something, she tried to reason. But that didn't make sense.

Her reaction was irrational. Yet, her body shook as she pushed away from the building and began walking again. She went slow and steady, ignoring the people moving past her. Every step put space between her and her office.

Acid churned in her stomach. If only she could forget about the puncture marks on Cory's neck and the blood drinking she'd witnessed. The way her mind had rapidly connected the two sights haunted her.

What was it about the Blood Opal? She'd already decided to give up on finding it, just like Kodiak had suggested...well, ordered. But after seeing Cory's neck, Tamaska felt as if he were somehow connected to the gem. The thought made no sense, but she couldn't shake it.

With every step the connection seemed to get stronger, seemed to make more sense.

Another memory surfaced as she tried to hurry home.

It had been Cory who'd suggested using a different security business at the last minute, something she would never have done, ordinarily.

Tamaska hadn't been overly happy with their security and had grumbled to Cory, so it seemed reasonable that he'd suggested the change. She'd heard the name Shadow Protection before, and it was a good choice. Then Tahla had confirmed they had a good reputation. At least, it had felt so at the time. But now she was seeing things in a new light.

New security, missing gem, Cory's suggestion for the last-minute change. It connected.

How could she have missed that?

Cory first suggested they use Shadow Protection because they could handle the work and were brilliant at last-minute jobs seemed the height of good fortune. Now, it seemed more a Trojan horse.

Or she was leaping to conclusions.

But what was she meant to do here? Not explore every avenue?

It wasn't just the gem missing. It was Tahla. It was the bite marks. The fangs.

If Cory had chosen Shadow Protection for an ulterior motive, did that mean Kodiak was in on it, too? Was he working with Cory? Could Tahla also be in on this too? She had spoken up for them as well.

But she couldn't see Cory as a mastermind. And she couldn't quite paint Kodiak the villain. And she definitely couldn't picture her friend Tahla wanting to steal a gem.

Cory could, however, be a cog. Perhaps Kodiak hadn't realized what was going on.

That didn't seem right, either.

Even if Cory was involved, he hadn't recognized Kodiak when he'd turned up. And if she wanted to believe Kodiak was involved, then it didn't make sense that he hadn't recognized her assistant. Something told her she would have seen that recognition.

Then again, so what? Shadow Protection was an agency. Cory wouldn't know them all, and Kodiak was cocky enough that he would walk in not even announcing who he was.

Everyone had been flustered that night.

Still, something didn't add up at all.

Kodiak wasn't exactly Mr. Open Book. He might be hot, and he might be overbearing and protective outside of his job title but there was something else there. Something he hadn't told her.

She tried to look at the situation in another way,

but she still came back to feeling Kodiak was hiding something from her.

She didn't know if she could trust Cory, especially with the bite marks she'd never seen before. As for the security guy she'd stupidly had sex with, at least he was the safer bet here.

The only way out of her mess was to corner Kodiak and get some answers.

Her heart beat fast at the thought of seeing him again. She hated that.

But only because she didn't know what he would say.

That was, if she could get in contact with him.

Had she kept his business card? She wasn't sure. She swore under her breath as she waited to cross the road.

She began to feel more settled as she approached her apartment. The thought of contacting Kodiak gave her something productive to focus on other than forgetting about the memory of that blood drinking.

Fuck. Kodiak had turned her life upside down in the moment he'd strode into the ballroom the night the Blood Opal was stolen. It didn't feel real that her feelings for him had completely flipped after she'd fucked him. Or that she'd done that, there.

Had he drugged her? The moment she thought that, she dismissed it. A man like that wouldn't need to drug a woman. He could just look at her and crook his finger, and no matter how flat out irritating he was, she would come running.

She knew that first-hand.

Besides, he didn't seem the type to drug people. He wasn't a creep. When he'd left her at her place, he'd kissed her, and she'd loved it. It wouldn't have taken him more than one more kiss to get her into bed, but he'd stopped and walked out the door. He'd also gone over her place to make sure she was safe.

Everything he'd done had been to protect her.

She needed to grow up, not think of sex, and contact him. Even if she didn't have his card, she could reach him through his employer.

And if he didn't want to talk to her?

Too fucking bad.

She would make him.

She would speak to him and get some answers, and she wouldn't leave him alone until she did.

Tamaska lifted her chin and took a deep breath. When she got into her apartment, she would plan out what to ask Kodiak. Then, she would find him and demand answers. If things didn't add up, she would work out what to say to the police to make his life difficult.

Feeling better now she had a plan, her body felt more settled.

The smell of the coffee cart near her home made Tamaska stop and order a latte to-go. She held the cup in her hand, its warmth soothing her after the shock she'd had. Her body trembled a little as the last of its adrenaline swam in her blood.

At least now she knew she would be all right. She had coffee. She had her home in sight. She had a plan.

Then, she almost dropped her latte.

There, right ahead, stood the last person she expected to see. Her stomach spun and her heart squeezed tight.

She wasn't prepared for him, not yet.

Kodiak came down the street, straight towards her.

It disturbed her that he was coming from the direction of her apartment. Had he been looking for her? They way he'd intently searched her apartment when he'd dropped her off no longer made her feel secure. Instead, it made her suspicious. Or was that just uneasy? She didn't know anything except Kodiak made her completely unbalanced.

Tamaska looked to either side, as if to find an escape, but the road to her right was busy and to her left were code-protected apartments.

He was so beautiful. He moved with a masculine grace and power that took her breath away.

He was also a man on a mission, and it looked like that mission was her.

Tamaska couldn't move.

There was no choice. She had to confront him now.

CHAPTER 27

 amaska

Gathering all her strength and wits about her like a shield, Tamaska glared at Kodiak as he strode up to her. He came to a stop.

"What are you doing here?" She lifted her head to meet his dark gaze that lived and breathed with so many secrets she couldn't begin to untangle them.

Kodiak's mouth was in a grim line as he stood close enough to touch if he wanted to close that gap but he didn't. The energy in him vibrated.

He ran his gaze over her, lingering at her neck, down to her wrists and back again, taking his sweet time.

When their gazes met once more, his had softened.

Within a strange urgency she saw there, lay something else, something soft and appealing that she wanted to climb into, wanted to wrap around herself and never let go.

"Checking on you," he said. "Based on how pale you are, I made a good decision."

She frowned. "Did my work tell you where I was?"

"No. I didn't go there. I came here."

"But—"

"I got worried, Tamaska," he said gently, "so I came right here, to your place."

His response unnerved her. Did he have an extra sense?

His expression got to her, and she let it. He was here, and with him, she could just let go. Her entire body shook.

He rushed forward, wrapping his arms around her, careful to avoid bumping her coffee or her bag that contained her laptop. "Hey, you're safe with me."

She melted into him and gripped his shirt, closing her eyes for a blessed moment.

She'd been all set to give him what for, but now she was falling apart. More than that, he let her, and it felt good. She dragged air into her lungs as she tried to gather herself back into one coherent, strong woman.

Pull it together.

"I'm fine."

How did he manage to show up every time she really needed him? It was like he was finely tuned to her. Part of her wanted to ask if he was following her, only she didn't think so. Embarrassingly, if he was, he would be doing it to keep her safe and that appealed to her.

But she gave him a small shove, anyway.

"Yeah, like hell you are. What happened?" Kodiak stepped back a little but kept his hands around her body as he stood by her side. His strength kept her from tumbling to the concrete.

"I…" She breathed out heavily, unable to find the right words.

Kodiak had told her the blood drinking had been a trick. Why would he believe any differently now?

Something told her he would. She wasn't sure why. But him believing or not believing her wasn't the problem. No, she wasn't sure she wanted to say the words out loud.

Like saying them would make somehow make them real.

They are real, she found herself thinking.

Kodiak squeezed her. He leaned in, like he could take all her fears and worries by osmosis. She breathed him in, that earthy, fresh scent of his. Something deep in her stomach coiled, sending shards of sweet desire flying through her.

"You can tell me anything," he whispered.

He caressed her cheek, and she shivered again.

This time it had nothing to do with fear or weakness.

It had everything to do with him.

You can tell me anything...

Tamaska swallowed her rising emotions as she recalled what she'd seen. For whatever reason, despite her uncertainty over whether she could trust Kodiak in other aspects, she sensed herself doing just that. Everything else melted away.

"My assistant has two puncture marks on his neck."

Kodiak didn't say anything. When she looked at him, he gave nothing away, just that air of invitation to say whatever it was, with no judgment. It was like a gift.

"When I saw them, the memory from the club, of the blood drinking came back. I remembered..." Tamaska couldn't finish her sentence. Instead, she rested her head on his chest, closed her eyes, and wished for it all to be forgotten as if it were simply a bad dream.

"What did you remember?"

"I thought I saw fangs."

He didn't say a word.

Tamaska raised her head. "I sound insane. I left work. I need to go back. I—"

"You can't go back to work," Kodiak said. "It's not safe for you."

She frowned. "What do you mean? I ran off, and that was stupid. I need to go back."

He tightened his hand around her, even though she hadn't tried to move off. "You can't."

"Why?" A burst of panic rose up in her. "I have to. My job is everything to me."

"I know that, but you need to listen to me, okay?" He frowned but didn't move away. "It's not safe for you."

"What do you know that I don't?" Tamaska bit her lip and took a step back from him. The panic had wings and sharp claws now. "You need to tell me, Kodiak. What are you keeping from me?"

He breathed out slowly. "There's a sort of underbelly living here in Sydney, and I don't want you caught up with them."

"What kind of underbelly? Some organized crime syndicate? Or something more...fantastical?"

"Something you need to keep away from," he said. "Far away. Getting caught up with them is deadly."

"But I already am, aren't I?" Tamaska's gut knotted painfully.

The word was there in her head, but she couldn't let it out. Vampire. That was what she thought she saw. A vampire at the club. The fangs, drinking blood, the bite marks on Cory. Vampire, or dangerous people playing at it.

And Kodiak knew.

"You are."

"So, what am I meant to do?" she asked. "Leave town? Get a new identity?"

"Tamaska," he said, "if I thought that would make a

difference, then I'd do everything in my power to make you do that."

Nausea rose up in her, but she pushed it down. "And you know what they are, don't you?"

This was like something straight out of a movie, a bad B-rated movie, and she'd never agreed to play the lead.

Kodiak nodded. "That is why I'm going to look out for you and put a stop to this."

"Tell me."

"You already know, I think. I shouldn't even be saying any of this to you, except I'll keep you safe and end all this. It's my oath to you."

His tone soothed her fears. But she had to be sure she could trust him, so she asked. "Did you take the Blood Opal?"

"Of course, I didn't." He frowned at her.

A couple of days ago, they would have argued in an explosion of words, but now he only sounded tired. That made her believe him more than bitter or angry words ever could.

Still, she needed to push a little further, take the small opening he'd given her. "But you knew about the club, and you were there."

"So were you," he countered.

"Because I found a business card on the floor next to the cabinet where the gem was stolen."

He chuckled. "Your basic detective skills got you there."

"And you?" Laughing was the last thing she felt like doing.

"I know about the underbelly full of criminals."

"The ones who bite people with fangs and suck blood. Those criminals?"

He ignored her words. "This is something they'd do."

"But you didn't stop them from taking the gem."

Regret darkened his eyes. "No, I didn't. Everything about the night said run of the mill job."

"Run—"

"In protection terms. I know what you put into it." He shrugged. "It's been a long time since that…faction made any kind of real move, so I'm taking the blame for it."

She frowned. "No, that's not what I meant."

"I was too confident they wouldn't be there. I dropped the ball in my cockiness, and I'm sorry. I didn't take it. My team didn't take it, and it would be so much better if that had happened, if I was nothing more than a common criminal. But that's not what occurred. I blame myself," he said. "I'm making amends now. I will get it back for you, and I will make sure they won't harm you."

"Why…" Tamaska didn't like the idea that they could harm her.

"I don't know why they're interested in you. But whatever they have planned, I'm going to stop it. I promise you."

"Kodiak," she whispered, aching for a break from this horrible reality she'd been dropped into.

He stepped closer to her, slipping his arm around her slender waist. "Come on, let's get you somewhere safe."

She nodded. "I want to go to my place."

"I don't know if that's a good idea."

"I don't care," she said.

She didn't like the idea that criminals had taken an interest in her. The idea made her skin crawl. Her home was her space, her one safe haven.

"You're a pain in the ass."

"I just want to be home. Is that too much to ask?"

She turned to continue along the street, even more shaken than before. She stumbled, and her hand went up to prevent the coffee from dropping. Kodiak caught her.

"This is becoming a habit." She tried to laugh, but it came out sounding strained. "You just helped save a damn good cup of coffee."

"I'll do anything to save damn good coffee."

"But not me?" She winked at him. It was her poor attempt to lighten the mood.

His mouth lifted in a small smile. "You? No. I'm here for the coffee."

She took in a shaking breath. "Thanks, I can get home from here."

"I'm coming with you." He frowned. "No arguments."

"You don't have to." She steadied herself with his help. Despite her words, she did want him to come with her. His answers had seemed genuine, and while the memory of the club haunted her, she could do with some company.

"I want to."

That was the answer she'd been hoping for.

"I want to come with you," he said softly. "And not just to keep you safe. I want to be with you today."

The ground shifted beneath her feet.

"Fine, then." She tried to sound casual.

She allowed him to help her back to her apartment. Inside, she dumped her laptop bag and handbag on the dining table and sipped her coffee.

Her mind buzzed from the caffeine. Safe in her home, she already felt better, especially with Kodiak by her side.

Kodiak went through her apartment like he had the other night, checking everything.

It unnerved Tamaska even more, now that she was in real trouble.

She'd been in trouble then, too, she supposed. But this time it seemed real. She couldn't brush it away.

She kicked off her heels and flopped down on the lounge to drink her coffee, which was finished by the time Kodiak got back to her. She put the empty cup on the side table next to the couch.

"Am I safe?" she asked, trying not to sound scared.

"For now." He sat down next to her, his thigh touching hers like a brand.

She didn't move. Her body tingled, and she sank into the heat and wild possibilities, some of which she'd tasted.

His gaze was on her, hot and sparking with the same desires that danced in her.

A little escapism wouldn't hurt. Would it?

"Does that mean you have to stay here with me, and I can't be left alone?" she asked, giving him a suggestive look.

A slow smile, one full of sexual promise, spread on his beautiful mouth. "That all depends."

"On what?" Her breath caught in her throat as the world shifted down to just her and him. Need beat hot and hard between them.

Their connection drew her to him. What was this thing between them? It was big, way bigger than she'd ever thought. It threatened to consume her, and she wanted to be.

She hardly knew Kodiak. She'd accused him of stealing the Blood Opal. She wasn't sure whether to trust him. Now, she gazed at him, wishing he was naked so she could explore his body. She wanted to do it properly this time, not swept up in the club's atmosphere.

She wanted him more than she'd ever wanted anything before in her life.

Her lower abdomen clenched with need. She'd

convinced herself that Kodiak was a fling, that the attraction would go away if she just had sex with him.

But it hadn't.

Now that she was alone with him in the comfort of her home, her feelings skyrocketed. Was there something more going on between them?

There was only one way to find out.

CHAPTER 28

amaska

The desire surging through Tamaska was too hard to ignore, and she didn't want to.

She leaned forward and kissed Kodiak. His dark, moreish taste burst into her mouth, and she sighed, shivering as moisture pooled between her legs.

Fuck, she wanted him now. The need was hot and heavy in her veins as she moved to straddle him.

He ran his hands along her thighs and then gripped her hips as she pushed down into his groin, feeling him harden at the junction of her thighs. He wanted her, too.

As she rocked against him, he slid his hands under

her shirt. They were delightfully hot on her skin as they slipped up her back.

Their mouths met in a searing kiss as the passion burned brighter.

She pushed her hips harder into him, the feel of his hard cock sending shivers of need up her spine. She didn't want clothes between them. A fresh wave of moisture dampened her panties as her need grew.

He slid his hands over her skin, leaving a trail of tingling heat over her ribs. She could sense the urgency in his touch, his desire to explore her. She wanted that, too. Wanted nothing more than to sink into him and the pleasure she knew he could give her.

From his erection pressing against her, the harsh sounds of his breath, and his urgent movements, he wanted exactly the same things, too.

They kissed hard and deep and then soft, their bodies rocking and coming together in a simulation of the act that was more erotic, more sexually charged than almost all sex she'd ever had before.

Except with him.

Fucking him had been mind blowing. It had been life changing. A drug of its own.

She rested her hands on his shoulders, eyes closed as they kept kissing. She allowed her body to be swept up with the rhythm they'd set.

He fumbled with her shirt buttons, which were hidden under the ruffle of material cascading down her front. She broke the kiss, smiling cheekily at him as he struggled with the small buttons.

"You're not going to help me?" he asked, frowning as he managed to slide one button through a hole at the bottom of her shirt.

She shook her head with a small laugh and cupped her breasts. "Trying to get to these?"

She wiggled a little on him, eliciting a low-throated groan.

"I can rip them off."

"Or you can unbutton them." She leaned in and brushed a kiss over his mouth, light and free.

The feel of his hard cock at the juncture of her thighs spurred her on, pushing her further into the fantasy of the moment.

"Tease." He got another button. "These are ridiculous."

She licked a small path along the shape of his ear and was rewarded by his fists closing hard on the material of her shirt. "Surely a big, strong, smart man like you can manage a few buttons."

He growled, the sound prickling her skin as he continued to tug at the buttons, slowly working his way up. "My way is more fun. And easier."

He tugged hard and she gasped, his fingers grazing the under sides of her breasts.

"I like this shirt."

"I think I'm going to prefer you naked."

She held onto his shoulders, leaning back to give

him access, giggling, enjoying the anticipation of what was to come.

Finally, the last button popped through the hole, and he pulled the material over her shoulders. His fingers brushed over her collarbone, then he traced the pattern of her lacy bra. Her nipples hardened from his gentle touch. He pinched them, sending a bolt of desire through her. She gasped sharply.

"You like?"

"Oh, fuck yes. I want more, Kodiak."

He scooped one hand behind her back, drawing her to him, then clamped his mouth over one of her breasts, sucking hard through the bra's lace material.

She tilted her head back, arching her chest into his mouth while squeezing her legs tight around him. His sounds of pleasure added to hers, filling the room.

This time, the building tension unfolded more slowly but it was even better for it.

"You are so fucking beautiful," he said, raising his head as he released her breast.

He pushed the delicate material to the side, exposing her softness. He breathed out deliberately on her nipple, the air hardening it further. Then he kissed her breast, his tongue finding its hard bud and playing with it.

A small shudder rattled through her as she gasped, trying to slow herself from reaching her peak. He knew just what to do to draw out her pleasure, to bring her back up to the brink yet again.

She dug her fingers into his thick hair and dragged him up and away from her breasts. They stared at each other, the passion raw and primal. It sent an excited thrill spinning through her blood, spiking her heart rate.

She returned her mouth to his, enjoying how his tongue danced with hers. She reached down between them, wriggling backward a little to give herself access. She easily undid his jeans, his cock hot and hard in her hand as she worked its length. A drop of liquid eased from his tip, and she massaged it around his head as he groaned and sucked on her throat.

Fuck, she wanted to feel him inside her. She went to adjust her weight, to slip his cock between her legs. He moved his arms around her, holding her tight as he stood from the couch in one swift movement. She held onto his neck, legs wrapped around his waist, kissing his skin as he walked towards her bedroom.

He playfully threw her onto the bed. She screamed with delight as she bounced up and down, then laughed as he tugged at her shirt. She helped him remove the layer of clothing.

He reached behind her, hands on her bra.

"You think you can undo it?" she asked. "I mean, I'm not sure that you can, based on how hard it was for you to undo the buttons on my shirt."

He raised an eyebrow. "You think so, do you?"

"Prove me wrong."

Kodiak slid down over her, mouth so close to hers. "I just might."

She rose up for that kiss he teased. The tension of her bra released, and it fell forward.

"Oh," she said. "You can."

"Of course, I fucking can."

"More practice with that, then?" she teased.

He growled softly at her, as if warning her to not talk about past conquests. "Give me a chance and an outfit without so many stupid tiny buttons, and I'll get your top off so quick, your head will spin, and you won't know which way is up."

She trailed her hand up under his T-shirt, over his naked chest, the hot silk of his skin over those hard, broad muscles shiver-inducing. She could get used to this. And if sex with him was even half as good as last time, she would want it all the time.

Something told her it was going to be even better.

When she was with him, it seemed like there would never be enough time.

Crazy thoughts, borne of fear and the lightness of feeling safe for the first time in days.

If she let herself think beyond that, she was nothing more than a fool.

But what a fool she'd be. At least for now.

She wriggled the bra off her shoulders, plucked it from the bed, then tossed it on the ground. He grabbed her skirt, searching for a way to take it off.

"Looks like you need more practice with skirts, too."

"As I said, I prefer naked, and these clothes are like some kind of chastity belt."

She shimmied away, reaching for the zip. "Or you lack certain skills."

"Come here," he said, his deep voice sending shivers through her. He stepped off the side of the bed, grabbed her legs, and pulled her towards him. She yelped in surprise, then laughed, enjoying his frustration as he tried to get her clothes off.

He lightly smacked her hands away and tugged at the top of her skirt.

"Don't fucking rip it off." She pushed his hands away. "This is M.A. Dainty, and it isn't cheap."

"It looks good on you, but I want it off," he said. "You're wearing too many damn clothes."

"Luckily, I agree."

She slipped off the bed, then undid the small zipper on the side of the skirt, letting it fall and pool at her feet. Hooking her thumbs into the top of her panties, she slid them off, shaking her hips deliberately to arouse him. He soaked up her body, and she smiled at the pleased expression on his face.

She stepped forward and lifted his T-shirt, kissing his toned chest muscles as he pulled the material over his head. His salty, male taste tingled on her tongue.

Her hands went down to his jeans, which were

already undone, and she pushed them down. He moved to help her take them off. Then she ran her hands over his lean hips, squeezing his tight, muscular buttocks as she pressed her body into his, her breasts crushing into him. She pushed down his jocks, releasing his hardness fully.

He was beautiful. Powerful. Big. Hers.

And she wanted him. Now.

She knelt and took him into her mouth, letting his length slide over her lips. His soft moan encouraged her to drag her mouth up and down his length, sucking hard, flicking her tongue into his tip. This was something she could get more than used to, she realized. His hands tangled in her hair before he pushed her away with a guttural groan.

"No?"

"Yes," he said. "God, yes."

She reached for him again, but he shook his head.

"Too close." He helped her up from the ground, nudged her away from him, and looked at her. "I want to be inside you."

"Kodiak…"

He kissed her softly and stepped back a little, his erection brushing hot against her.

"You're fucking beautiful," he murmured, looking up and down her naked body.

"You're pretty damn hot yourself." She grinned, enjoying the pleasant sight of him naked, cock erect.

She shimmied back farther onto the bed, opening her legs a little to tease him. Then he was there, his hot body on hers, his cock poised at her entrance. She gazed into his eyes, losing herself in the gaze that sent a shiver of desire through her body.

He teased her with his cock, sliding it against her as he took her mouth in a deep, hard kiss. Then, he eased into her, sending her muscles into wild contractions.

He stilled as the wave passed over her and then he started to thrust, long, slow, deep. She groaned heavily, her body moving once more towards her peak as he continued to thrust inside of her, setting a rhythm.

She met him thrust for thrust, kiss for kiss. Her nails scraped over his back as he started to push into her harder, deeper. She raised her hips to meet him, driving him hard. They both panted as the beat of lust took over and she was swept up, wanting that savage heat, the hard thrusts that seemed to bottom out in her.

It was like she couldn't get enough of him. She bit his shoulder, her body hitting a peak. Instead of coming, the movement pushed her higher, into more pleasure and her entire being screamed for more as they worked together.

Then she came, so hard she couldn't see. Pure pleasure flowed everywhere, and her muscles contracted on him even as his filling her felt so good.

He groaned and quickened his pace, coming inside of her as she held onto him.

He pumped her again, sending her once more over the edge with bliss, which clouded her mind.

As she floated back down, he collapsed down on

her, holding her, laying small kisses over her face. She wrapped around him. This man could make her forget how shit her life had become because of the Blood Opal.

He gave her something sacred: hope.

CHAPTER 29

odiak

The afternoon sun shone hot through the windows of the bedroom, pulling Kodiak from the doze he'd enjoyed in Tamaska's arms.

He'd done it again. He'd slept with her, and he shouldn't have.

He would say he fucked her, but it had felt like so much more, nothing like the fling he'd thought she was.

At this rate, he was going to be out of the pack for breaking the rules. They weren't just any rules, either. They were the ones about a human.

He needed to concentrate on the damned opal.

He moved his arm out from under her, not wanting

331

to wake her. She was the picture of beauty next to him. Even with a sheet draped over her, she was far from modest, her breasts exposed, a sheen on her olive skin from their session.

He should fix the sheet, cover her up, but he didn't want to; he liked the view. And it wasn't like he hadn't just spent the last however long touching and enjoying that view.

He brushed her arm with his fingers, the touch reminding him that they'd connected, whether he wanted it or not.

He got up from the bed, dressed, and looked out the window, his wolf eyes searching for anything suspicious outside. So far, he hadn't detected anything, but it would only be a matter of time before he did.

It was also daytime, so he didn't expect to see anything. Yet.

Then again, it didn't pay to not be careful.

Kodiak didn't like that her colleague, Cory, was associated with vampires—or worse, he might be one himself.

Though he had been at work during the day, hadn't he? Then again, a vampire had attacked her Saturday morning, and the opal had drunk up blood. Who knew what had changed?

Or perhaps her colleague hadn't yet been completely turned.

The possibilities were endless, and Kodiak didn't like any of them.

Everything continued to come back to one point: Tamaska. Somehow, someway, she was important to them.

He didn't think it was mere coincidence they'd taken and sacrificed her friend. Kodiak could be wrong, of course, but acting like he wasn't seemed the smarter path here.

The vampires would keep trying to get Tamaska, and there was no way he could let her end up like her friend.

Kodiak had to be here for her, despite Olcan's orders.

He ran a hand through his hair, standing at the window. How the fuck was he going to protect Tamaska without Olcan finding out? He needed to be in two places at once.

This wasn't going to end well.

"Hey."

He turned at the sound of her voice. "Hey."

She stirred as she sat up in bed. "Come back here. I miss you."

His heart squeezed at her words. There was a connection between them. He knew that now. No, had known it since they'd first touched gazes.

What would she do when she found out he was a wolf? She was scared to death of dogs. Maybe then it would be over, and he would have to do what he normally did when a relationship ended—drown his sorrows in another woman.

So why when he thought that it did not sit right? Why did it feel like he wouldn't be able to forget this one so easily? Or quickly?

"I have to go."

He hated to admit it, but if he stayed there any longer without doing his pack duties, he would raise suspicion. He couldn't answer his team's questions honestly, so it would be best to fly under the radar for as long as possible.

Because questions would come.

He had to do everything he could to get to the bottom of the missing opal and what it meant, not to mention what she had to do with it.

When he looked back, it seemed obvious: the vampire talking to her and drugging her, the card for the club, the vampires wanting her once she was there and taking her friend instead. Not to mention the attack in the park and now her work friend, Cory.

Somehow, she fit in. He just didn't know how.

"You do?"

He looked back out the window, scanning the area beyond once more. "Yeah."

"Oh." The disappointment in her voice was clear.

It scraped against something in his chest.

He turned back to face her, his gaze dropping to her lovely breasts. She covered herself with the sheet, and he wished she hadn't. He sighed.

He wanted to go to her, to join her in bed again, but

he couldn't. And he couldn't honestly tell her why he had to leave.

Fuck, he wanted to tell her everything.

"It's work," he said. "But I'll be back later, of course."

She shrugged, like she didn't care, but he caught the fear rising in her eyes. Just like he saw her pulse that throbbed in her throat had increased its beat a little.

Kodiak couldn't help noticing her subtleties, like he'd tuned into her on some kind of microscopic level. Ash had been bloody right. If she'd figured out the truth, then the others would, too. And Kodiak had just spent more time with his mind blocked, so the pack didn't know what he was up to or how to contact him.

"I'll be fine," she said. "I'm sure I've imagined all of this. I mean, it's not as bad as I think, is it?

"Tamaska..." He wasn't sure how to finish his sentence.

She swallowed. "You were only trying to scare me into staying safe earlier, weren't you?"

He wanted to tell her she hadn't, that the danger was real. But it would be best if she thought it wasn't. "Something like that."

"You said that there was danger."

"And I'll take care of it and keep you safe."

"And the rest, the fangs, the blood drinking?" She looked at him. "Did I imagine that?"

"A bad dream, all from Blood Opal stress." The name of the gem she'd accused him of stealing sat in his mouth, bitter and ugly like poison.

Did she still think that, despite the connection between them? He didn't see an accusation on her face.

"You're lying," she said. "It is that bad, isn't it? And I didn't imagine it, did I?"

"It's...bad, Tamaska. I'm not going to lie about that."

"Fucking nightmare, that's what it sounds like," she said. "It's not over yet, is it?"

Fuck. He blew out a breath. "No, and I can't be here all the time with you."

She nodded, pulling the sheet tighter around her. She looked like she was going to say she didn't expect him to, or something else that would be her first move to a barrier between them. A barrier, if he had any sense, he would seek.

But she didn't do that. "Why?"

"Why can't I be here all the time?"

"You said you'd protect me and I'm not saying I need it, but now you're running off and telling me I'm in horrible danger, so why?"

It was the closest she'd come to probing him for information. He sensed her rising frustration at being kept in the dark.

"I have a job." It was sort of true. He did have a job, but that wasn't why he had to get out of there. Telling her the full reason would mean explaining who and what he was.

He met her gaze. "But I'm not about to abandon you."

"You said you were going to leave."

"I have to, but that doesn't mean I'm abandoning you," he said again. "I'll be keeping an eye on your building, and I need to get some security to set up in here."

"I don't want cameras in my home." She frowned.

"I'll respect your privacy." He wasn't about to let her refuse. If he couldn't be there to watch her, he would have to rely on technology to help him. It was the only option.

"No."

"You really want me here all the time? You'd get sick of me," he said, trying to hold onto his resolve and stay away from her. She sat naked on the bed, the sheet covering her as she looked at him with big eyes, her long hair brushing against the skin below her shoulders.

She smiled at him, which eased the tension in his heart. "That might be a little much, although…"

He raised a brow. "Although?"

A blush stained her cheeks. "You're right. You can't be here all the time. Anyway, I'd get annoyed with you. It'd be best if you had some time away from me. Plus, I suppose I need to go in to work myself."

His stomach twisted. Work? Where her colleague he didn't trust, the one who'd been bitten, would be hanging around? No fucking way.

"Can you work from home?" he asked, voice even.

She rubbed a hand over her forehead. "For a bit, but my boss isn't keen on it."

"Call in sick?" He looked at her. "Can you do that, please?"

"I can, but why? My boss is already unhappy with me, and I need this job. Besides, I have to face Cory at some point. I ran out of there like a maniac."

Kodiak made a mental note to find Cory and figure out if he was on his way to becoming a vampire. Until then, there was no way he wanted her anywhere near her assistant.

"Does Cory know where you live?" His years in security had prepared him well. He knew all the small details that could protect her while he was gone.

She paused. "Not the exact address. He knows I live close to work as he offered to walk me home, but I said no."

Kodiak frowned. "I'll go get some cameras. I'll set one up in the living room, and a few facing the balcony with a special alarm system."

"I'm on the eighth level. No one's coming in that way." She held the sheet tighter against her body as if to comfort herself.

"Just a precaution." He tried to downplay his worry as he sorted his thoughts.

Once he had her safe and protected when he wasn't there, he could focus on the pack, find the damn opal, and bring down the vampires and whatever nasty plan they had.

Easy. He would laugh if it was funny.

"And how is this alarm special?" She raised her face to him, the challenge there bright.

"It will inform me directly," he said. "That's why it's special."

Tamaska smiled weakly. "And you're all-powerful, ready to rush to my side?"

"I am." Kodiak looked at her, as if making a promise to her.

"I don't know about all of this." She shrugged, looking down at her hands. "I'll be okay without any of that."

Kodiak couldn't resist anymore. He sat next to her on the bed and put an arm around her. "I've got contacts. I'll do some investigating, and I'll have this sorted out soon, so don't go worrying about it."

"Hard not to." She leaned into him, and he squeezed her tight.

A grumble came from her belly, and she laughed. "Timing. I need to go out and get food. I've got nothing here."

He didn't want her alone and he didn't want to let her go. Not yet.

"How about we go get some fresh air? We can grab something to eat at the park, and then I'll escort you back here before leaving?"

"Sounds good to me." She kissed him on the cheek. Warmth radiated from her lips, soothing him. "Just give me a moment to get dressed, and then we can go."

Tamaska stood up, letting the sheet fall, and he

soaked in the sight of her body. She had no idea how much he wanted to get this whole thing over and done with so he could hurry back and be with her.

If only Olcan hadn't forbidden him from helping her, the situation would be much easier. But a stupid decree wouldn't stop him.

Kodiak was going against the Alpha's wishes, and it would land him in hot water. He needed to keep up appearances at the club. He'd made a schedule to watch the vampires, and his time slot was coming up soon.

But he would be back at Tamaska's apartment soon, not only to help, but to indulge in her again. He didn't need to drink in her naked form that was so delightfully on display in front of him to know that.

She was in his blood.

"A bit of privacy." She threw her shirt at him, and it hit him in the face.

"You're worth watching." He winked, getting off the bed, then walked back to the window for another security check. Redundant, considering it was light outside, but he was nervous. The vampires might use humans to help them.

They'd done it before, and they would do it again.

Kodiak was sure the vampires or their accomplices were out there. To find them, he just needed to sharpen his vision. Come dark, they would appear, and he would make sure he was back with Tamaska.

The afternoon was waning. He would need to hurry through grabbing some food with Tamaska before getting to his pack. Then he'd have to take some security cameras and tech without being noticed.

He inhaled slowly, his stomach roiling.

He was going down a tricky path that could cost him his pack.

CHAPTER 30

amaska

Tamaska walked out of the apartment holding Kodiak's hand. With so much going on in her life, should she really allow herself to connect with him? Yet it seemed like the most natural thing to do.

They'd both agreed the hand holding was helpful in case trouble came along, but when he'd said it and she'd agreed, she knew they'd both lied.

They did it because they wanted to.

It was like a compulsion.

She'd dressed in loose track pants and a short-sleeve top, with white sneakers. Her loose hair was brushed, but still a little tousled from the bedroom with Kodiak.

She placed a quick call to her boss, saying she was sick and wasn't coming in tomorrow to give herself some breathing room. Having Kodiak by her side boosted her confidence as they walked to the park, where a food van was parked.

Goi cuon called to her and she ordered some of those along with cha gio.

He pointed to the Vietnamese food as they found a place to sit on the grass. "What are they?"

"You live in Sydney and haven't had Vietnamese food?"

He shrugged and poked the lettuce that came with the fried pork rolls. "I'm more the steak kinda guy."

"Of course, you are."

She could imagine they were a normal couple, just starting out, learning about each other, and exploring new things.

She rolled up one of goi cuon in the lettuce, herbs, and pickled vegetables, dipped it in the sauce, and held it out to him.

"What's that supposed to mean?"

She grinned. "You're simple. Meat and potatoes."

"I'm a cliché?"

"You said it."

He took the roll from her. "You still didn't tell me what this is."

"That is a Vietnamese-style fried pork roll." She wrapped one for herself and ate it. "And they're delicious. These fresh ones are noodles, vegetables, and shrimp, wrapped in rice paper."

He wrinkled his nose and the sun glinted on his hair, making the dark waves take on a hint of gold. He also needed a shave.

Like that, he was devastating.

"For you, I'll try it." He took a bite. Surprise hit his eyes. "They're good."

"I know.

Together they ate the delicious food while sitting next to each other on the grass. It really was very much a couple's activity, and she liked it.

That was a good sign since they were going to be spending more time together. But how the fuck was that going to work out if she'd accidentally gotten involved with some organized crime group?

An organized crime syndicate stealing the priceless opal made sense, just like such a group owning a club like that horrible one made sense, too. Nightclubs made great covers for all kinds of activities.

She quieted her thoughts, wanting to keep enjoying the time with Kodiak.

There was time enough for dark thoughts later.

"Why did you think I stole the Blood Opal?" he asked. His question changed the tone between them, like dark clouds covering the sun.

But he wasn't angry, at least, she didn't think so. Perhaps disappointed? Or maybe he just wanted to understand.

That was the thing with something new. If that was what this was. If it was something and not just sex and protection.

Or maybe she was seeing things that weren't there. She just didn't want to bring up the accusation again.

She shifted her weight to stretch her legs over the grass in front of her. "Because it happened when you caught me from falling, and you were a last-minute addition, thanks to Cory."

"What?" Kodiak sat upright in alarm. His gaze locked on to hers. "He recommended me?"

"Not you exactly, but Shadow Protection and so did my friend Tahla. He insisted. It was last-minute, not something I would ordinarily do for such a high-profile event, but he convinced me. He said you were the best."

"No one on my team has met him."

His mind raced; she could see that in how he held himself.

"We do have a great reputation. But with everything that happened..." Kodiak shook his head. "That's not good."

"Why?"

"Your opal goes missing on my watch when Shadow Protection was recommended. I knew it was a last-minute job, but it makes us look bad. Beyond you thinking we took it...that I took it. This isn't good."

"Because...?" Tamaska needed answers. "The police cleared you, right?"

"Yeah, but…" He released a breath. "It means the event was more rigged than I thought. I don't like that Cory suggested my security group."

Kodiak danced around something.

"What does that mean?" she asked.

Kodiak shrugged. "I'm not sure, exactly. It could be that he simply wanted to implicate us as thieves, and I guess it worked on you."

"You don't think that."

He sighed. "Partly, yes. But I mean, this criminal underbelly might have their eye on us and wanted to implicate us or send a warning. And that's all I can say. I didn't take the opal."

Tamaska swallowed hard as she gazed at him intently. She believed him. This was looking more like a set-up every minute. But she had to admit he had an uncanny way of turning up just when her life was in danger.

He was being as secretive about the referral as he had been about what had happened at the club.

She shivered.

That damned place. And still not a word from Tahla.

"Why were you at the club?" she asked. "You knew the gem could be there?"

"I suspected," he corrected. "The place is known for all kinds of illegal things. And I know of the group that run it. The man who spoke to you at the event, he is one of the owners. That meant I had my suspects and a place to start, so going to the club—which, I might add, is a place you should never have gone—was the obvious first place to look."

"Well, aren't you smart?"

She tried to make a joke, but the club talk dragged her down like lead.

"So are you."

She glanced at her hands, twisting her fingers together in her lap. "I hope Tahla is all right. I should check on her."

"You can't," he said softly.

A coldness came over her and she met his gaze. "Because…"

He looked away and that leaden feeling settled in the pit of her stomach. There was something he wasn't telling her.

"Kodiak, what do you know?"

"You need to look out for yourself first." He smiled; it was kind and slightly sad.

She glanced down at the grass, blinking hot tears from her eyes. She didn't know why she suddenly wanted to cry. Maybe it was the look on his face, and the fact her friend had simply…disappeared.

"But—"

"Until I get back to you, Tamaska, please stay at home."

She sighed. Could she do that? Stay home and wait for Kodiak, the last person she'd thought would be her knight in shining armor?

It seemed that was exactly what he was turning out to be.

"I've pushed this as far as I can. I really need to get going now," Kodiak said as he finished his last roll and scrunched up the paper until it turned into a tight ball. Then he scooped up the other containers, too.

She nodded.

"It's gonna be okay," he said. "I promise."

Just like that, with those few words, everything seemed better, brighter.

"Okay." Full and still buzzing in the afterglow, she would be fine for a few hours by herself.

She planned to sleep since she still needed some recovery time after her wild weekend. And sleep would help her sort everything out in her head.

"Here, I'll take the rubbish to the bin over there," she said, pointing at the far side of the park.

"I'm going to get another drink. Would you like one?" he asked.

"A soda, thanks." She took the rubbish from him and stood at the same time he did.

He pulled her to him and kissed her. She relaxed in his arms, allowing her lips to move with his. Each time they kissed, it was as if they were becoming closer, creating a path into the future, together.

She sighed into the kiss before he broke away and stroked the side of his face, the slight stubble prickling against her fingers.

"Come on," he said. "Otherwise, I'll never leave you."

She grinned. Who would've thought they could become so comfortable together? She fully believed Kodiak hadn't taken the Blood Opal.

"I'll race you." She ran over to the bin, laughing while he hurried over to the food van. The vendor was just beginning to pack up, now that most people were heading home in the late afternoon. The evenings were becoming darker earlier now that it was autumn, but the lingering heat made it pleasant to stay out.

She threw the rubbish in the bin, then spun around, ready to run towards Kodiak and surprise him. Something caught her eye on the other side of the bin. Was there something there, at the start of the trees and bush?

The branches rustled, but not in time with the wind. Her stomach fluttered a warning. Maybe she'd imagined the movement.

It came again, this time to the left. A squirrel, maybe? She held her breath as a soft growl undercut the noise of the city. Her heart hammered.

A dog? Was there a stray? The growl came again. Fear rooted her to the spot, even as every part of her screamed run.

Running would be worse. If she ran, it would attack. Gulping in air, trying to calm herself, she watched and listened, but the growl didn't come again. Nor did the bush move.

It had to have been a dog.

She stepped backward, the grass soft underfoot. Her mouth dried and her pulse increased erratically. The last thing she wanted to see was another dog. She'd had too many encounters in the last week already.

She still couldn't bring herself to run, just in case the dog was still there watching. She didn't want it to chase her.

The bush moved again. She almost screamed as a man appeared. He stepped out from the bushes, sticking close to the lengthening shadow.

He gazed at her, like he'd been waiting, like he knew who she was.

She took another step back. "Wait."

He smiled at her. A chill raced through her.

He wore smart attire, like the men at the club, with pale skin, dark hair, and...her gaze zeroed in on his throat.

Like Cory, there were puncture marks on his neck.

Her blood turned ice cold.

"What do you want from me?" she managed to ask.

"Amdis wants to see you."

She froze at the name.

Amdis.

Tahla had mentioned him. She'd said she had planned to see Amdis, and then that *vampire*—because that was what they were, vampires—had whispered in Tamaska's ear.

Her skin prickled.

Why would this Amdis want to see her?

"Where's Tahla?" Her voice was barely audible.

The man looked at her, expression cold. "She was no replacement. We need someone like you."

"Where is she?" Tamaska's voice strengthened. He knew something. "I've called the police, you know."

He laughed, and anger rolled through her. She stepped forward, hands clenched by her sides.

"What have you done with her?" Tamaska's voice trembled as her body overloaded with adrenaline.

"Come with me and find out." He stretched his hand towards her. She could feel him in her mind, pulling at her.

Anger and fear for her friend pushed back and oddly gave her strength to ignore that hand.

"Like fuck I will." She narrowed her eyes.

"Fine, have it your way." He stepped forward. "I'll force you, then."

A different fear overtook Tamaska's body, and she froze. The pull was stronger now and it started to fog her mind. It would be easy to take his hand.

Easy, and so very dangerous.

But she couldn't move.

Something collided with the man, pushing him to the ground.

She slapped a hand to her mouth, muffling her scream.

A large dog rolled the man into the bushes. It was

probably coming for her next, but her feet felt as if they were made of concrete, too heavy to lift.

The sounds of the fight chilled and sickened Tamaska, the growling and grunting and hitting. Then the bushes stilled, and the noises stopped.

Tamaska stared, unable to move. The large dog came into sight, its yellow eyes looking directly at her. It was the same dog she'd seen there last week when she was jogging. Had it come to finish her off?

Where was Kodiak, and why wasn't he coming to help her? He knew she feared dogs. She tried to scream, but her throat constricted.

The oversized dog, with its strong body and well-kept fur, clean and free of knots, wasn't a stray. The dog clearly had a family looking after it.

The dog lowered its head, keeping its eyes on her as it stepped forward.

"Go away," she whispered.

It kept coming for her. Its head remained lowered as if it was giving her the upper hand, letting her know she was its mistress.

Her old dog attack scars started to hurt. Her vision blurred. All she could see was the dog coming for her, the pain from all those years ago burning through her body.

"Please don't hurt me." She trembled. She could almost reach out and touch the dog.

She didn't.

"Please," she whispered again, "please, go away."

Then the unexpected happened. It turned and fled into the bushes.

And Tamaska did something she never thought she would be brave enough to do: she followed it.

amaska

What the fuck am I doing?

Tamaska ran hard, trying to keep up with the large dog, not sure what she had to gain by chasing it. But she'd seen the same dog twice, plus a third outside the nightclub, and there had to be a connection. Since Kodiak wasn't coming to help her, she needed to take the matter into her own hands.

The dog hadn't attacked. Even though it had frightened her, the creature had seemed to understand her when she asked it to go away.

What kind of dog would do that?

A part of her, a small part, knew it wouldn't hurt

her. It had protected her. It had fought the man, the vampire, that had tried to take her using...whatever strange mind powers he had.

She pushed a low-lying branch out of her way and continued, breathing hard as her lungs burned. She wouldn't be able to run for much longer. She didn't know why she needed to reach the dog, a creature that scared her, but she did. And this one...it no longer seemed to scare her. Not if she was running after it.

She stumbled on a branch, screamed, and fell hard on the ground. Her wrist took the impact, sending shooting pain up her arm, and her knee banged hard on a rock.

Sobbing, she rolled over. Something hard hit her head. She came to a stop on the damp soil covered in dry, crunchy leaves.

This is the most fucking stupid thing you've ever done. She shook her head. *After going to the club.*

She tried to get up, but pain shot through her body. Her vision blurred. Christ, why had she been stupid enough to chase a dog, to think it was fine, that the dog would understand her? Had she lost her mind?

She looked up and gasped at the dog standing nearby.

This is it. He's got me now.

But even as she thought that, she knew she was wrong. There was nothing to be scared of with this dog. It looked at her like it knew her. She started to reach out to touch it before she took her hand away.

The dog lowered its head and turned to the side.

She didn't think; she just did it this time. She reached out and let her fingers tangle in the dog's fur. It was silky and warm and...familiar.

The dog turned back to face her and she locked eyes with it.

The dog's form began to change. Tamaska lay still, barely breathing. Within seconds, the dog had transformed into a naked Kodiak.

Her eyes widened.

Everything in her swirled with conflicting emotions. Fear and shock, and also unbridled lust because that man was perfection.

Had he just been a damned dog?

Tamaska tried to make sense of it all. She didn't even believe in vampires, but she'd seen them.

"Don't worry, I won't hurt you." He stepped forward, unashamed of his nakedness.

She scrambled back a little, staring up at him.

"What the fuck are you? Some kind of strange vampire? Or—?" She stopped, unable to finish that thought. "I mean, there are fucking vampires. I know that now. You know it. But what are you?"

Tamaska struggled to sit up, her vision blurring then clearing, a wave of queasiness washing over her. Here she'd been worried about what trouble she was in and who was after her when she'd been hoodwinked all along by a hot man who was also a dog.

No, not a dog. A wolf? She'd thought that once

before and it somehow fit. A hot man who was also a wolf.

Oh, hell.

This wasn't real. None of this was real. She was in bed, dreaming. This was Sydney, not some vampire-werewolf filled city of Oz, and she certainly wasn't Dorothy. Where was the yellow brick road?

She almost laughed, but she didn't let herself. If she did, that hysteria building in her would never stop.

I haven't been thinking straight. She touched her temple as her head throbbed. *I hit my head and now I'm hallucinating.*

"Careful," he said softly, stroking her skin on her arm, "you've got a huge bump forming. You fell hard."

"You're telling me, Kodiak." She sighed. "I'm not even sure you should touch me. I don't know what you are. Are you even real?"

"Of course, I'm real," he said. He picked up her hand and placed it on his chest so she could feel the steady beat of his heart. "See?"

"Okay, you're real." She wanted to snatch back her hand. "But I don't know if it's you and not some imposter."

"It is me."

"An imposter would say that."

He half-laughed. "You're a stubborn woman and a pain in my ass. And we fucked in the club and half the day at your place."

Heat streaked through her. "Okay, it's you. But…"

"If you're asking, can you trust me, then yes, you can. I promise I won't hurt you."

She shook her head, everything crashing down over her. "Please, I don't think you should touch me. I don't know who or what you are."

"You do. It's me."

She shook her head again. She pushed through the dirt, away from him, as he stepped closer. "Don't come near me."

"Earlier, you were scared and told me to go away," he said, keeping that gentle voice, "so I did. And then you followed me. I think you know you can trust me."

"I hate dogs."

He closed his eyes a long time. Finally, he looked at her. "I know you were hurt by one. You told me. And I get it. It's hard to get past something traumatic like that. But you don't hate dogs."

"I do—"

"No, I know you're afraid of dogs, and that's different than hate. It can just feel the same. But that's not what I am. I'm not a dog."

"Could've fucking fooled me," she said. Her body shook with the overload of adrenaline from the fall. From all of this. The vampire. The fact that Kodiak clearly wasn't human. "You're trying to trick me. This is all a trick."

"How? When? We've sort of been busy, and not just in the bedroom."

Confusion swarmed her mind like a hundred bees

unable to find a flower. "I don't know. But I also don't know what you are. This has to be a trick."

"No trick, Tamaska."

"Why didn't you tell me you're...whatever the fuck you are before?" She stared at him, still trying to wrap her mind around it all.

"You wouldn't have believed me, anyway."

"Really?"

He sighed. "Yeah, really. Look at you now. You saw it and you're trying to come up with excuses. I only transformed in front of you now, because otherwise I would've lost you to that man. I don't want to lose you."

"You don't want to lose me?" She stared at him. "You don't play fair."

"I'm not playing."

Tamaska felt the connection between them. It was still there, strong and compelling, despite his transformation. But she wasn't about to admit that, let alone give into it.

Not until he told her the truth.

"Tell me what you are," she said, even though there was no answer that could make the situation better. The man she'd fallen for wasn't human.

She closed her eyes. Fallen for? Oh hell, she had, hadn't she? In such a short time.

It was why she'd fought him every step of the way. Now she'd found out he had a world of secrets, and he was only sharing because he had to.

"You're not human."

"I am and I'm not. I'm living, breathing. I feel. I'm more than human, I suppose. I should have told you all this earlier, but it's not really something a person goes around announcing or printing on business cards."

She opened her eyes and met his.

The man looking at her was Kodiak. He smelled like him, that earthy, male scent.

She understood now what he was, but she needed to hear it from him. Needed him to just be damned honest.

"Tell me what you are."

"I'm a shifter."

Even though she knew, she sucked in a sharp breath. "A werewolf? But it's not a full moon."

It wasn't even what she wanted to say. She wanted to say they didn't exist. Yet she now knew that was wrong. She'd seen him transform.

Why it didn't scare her was beyond her. It only made her mad he didn't tell her, because when it came down to it, she wanted to mean enough to him that he would tell her what he was. And not like this.

"Not quite. I'm a wolf shifter, which means I can shift into the form of a wolf. I don't have to wait for the full moon."

"Okay. Next, you're going to tell me vampires are real."

She knew they were real, but she wanted him to tell

her that he knew. She wanted him not to leave comments open for her to come to those conclusions or pretend it was something else. She needed him to say it. To show she wasn't crazy like she felt.

"There are vampires. Is that what you want me to say?"

"Not particularly," she muttered, "but yes, I want you to actually come out and tell me the truth."

"I am. Shifters are real. So are vampires. But Tamaska, those vampires? They're coming after you."

The seriousness in his eyes sent a chill through her. It was what that vampire who'd tried to put some kind of vampire spell on her had meant. They wanted her.

She didn't know why.

"Fuck." What world had she landed in? How had all this happened?

A few days ago, she'd thought the world a different place with its usual and mundane dangers and threats. Now, she knew creatures from horror movies were real and they wanted her.

And the man she'd fallen for was a wolf shifter.

It was like she'd ended up in another universe and she didn't know how she'd gotten here.

Still, it made some weird, scary sense. Everything that had happened—except maybe the disappearance of the opal—clicked into place.

Kodiak went to help her up, his hand catching hers. "I can protect you. Let me take you to my pack."

"There's more of you?" She ripped her hand from his.

Maybe, just maybe, she could trust him. There was no way she could be surrounded by more dogs, or wolves, though. Her fear wouldn't allow it.

"We won't hurt you. But men like the one who just came for you will."

Her mouth twisted. "Let me guess, a vampire."

"Yes. They already killed Tahla."

Tamaska's eyes widened. Everything inside her turned into ice.

Tahla was…dead? Oh, God. Tears pushed against her eyes as her throat grew hot and tight.

Wild grief swept her, threatening to drown her. Along with it came a terrible hot fury.

Kodiak had lied. He'd kept information until he could use it to manipulate her, like now.

Otherwise, why tell her this now? To try and get her to his pack? Who was to say these shifters weren't as bad as the vampires? He still hadn't told her why both sides seemed to want her.

He raked a hand through his hair.

"Sorry. I shouldn't have said it like that." He dropped his hand and pinned her with a hard stare. "You need to come with me."

"Is that a threat?"

"If it needs to be."

"So I'm some kind of pawn?"

He frowned. "No. I'm the one who's going to keep you safe. It's clear the vampires are amping up their attempts to get to you. They killed your friend, for fuck's sake. Who knows what they want with you. So you need to come with me."

"I'll make my own way." She forced herself to stand, ignoring the pain.

"Good—"

"Not with you," she said with as much venom as she could muster. "I don't want anything to do with you."

"Please, Tamaska. If you run off alone now, I won't be able to help you as easily."

"I can't be with you." She'd always sensed he'd been keeping something from her. She supposed this was it. It still didn't seem real, but she couldn't be with him. Ever. He was a liar and up to something. She wanted to be as far from him and the other supernatural creatures as she could.

"You don't have to be with me. Just come with me so I can keep you safe."

"I'll take my chances with the vampires." She turned, driven by fury, fear, and loss, and limped away from the only person who'd helped her. The one person who seemed intent on lying to her to get his own way for whatever reasons.

"Tamaska, you're being an idiot."

She turned to face him. "No matter how hot you are, you're a wolf. I could never in a million years want to touch you again. I'm going now before you bite me or turn me into a wolf. Or kill me. I don't know. I just don't trust you or like what you are. You disgust me."

He didn't, and that was the problem. She was scared and hurting, and she didn't know who or what to trust. She couldn't trust anyone she thought.

She could definitely never trust Kodiak again.

It was up to her to find the Blood Opal. No matter how scared she was of those blood drinkers, the vampires, Tamaska would put an end to her nightmare.

Even if she had to do it alone.

The End ~ for now!

Continue the journey with Tamaska and Kodiak in Marked Wolf

Protector Wolf Series:
Bk1: Shadow Wolf
Bk2: Marked Wolf
Bk3: Rogue Wolf
Bk4: Cursed Wolf
BK5: Mated Wolf
Bk6: Dark Wolf

Keep up with Lilliana Rose's new releases by joining
her newsletter.
https://landing.mailerlite.com/webforms/landing/
g9l7p6

ABOUT THE AUTHOR

Lilliana Rose is a bestselling author who writes romance in the subgenres of contemporary, paranormal, urban, and fantasy. She enjoys helping characters overcome problems or issues and the misunderstandings that often plague relationships to help them fall in love. Whether it's city heels being replaced with country work boots, or some magic beyond this world, each story shows how love can prevail. She has over fifteen years of experience in various education systems as a teacher, a skip, and a jump from starting out in genetics research. It is all helpful for inspiring her writing. She has poetry, middle grade, picture book, novellas, and novels published under various pen names.

http://www.lillianarose.com/

Sign up to my Newsletter:

https://landing.mailerlite.com/webforms/landing/g9l7p6

Keep up to date with Lilliana on social media
Facebook, Twitter, Pinterest, Goodreads, Instagram

ACKNOWLEDGMENTS

Big thanks to Rebecca for helping bring Shadow Wolf into the world. You've been super patient and been there to kick me along the way when needed.

Thanks to Nicole and Rainy for your careful editing. You're stuck with me now.

Thanks to my creative friend Marianne, who is always there to boost me up during the journey.

Thank you to Susan who patiently reads through my work and encourages me to keep writing.

Of course, thanks to my dogs, Kimba and Sprinkles, who are always at my feet being the quiet support I need.